UNDEAD REBIRTH

SHORT STORIES

UNDEAD REBIRTH

THE ENGEN UNIVERSE

Published in Canada by Engen Books, St. John's, NL.

A CIP catalogue record for this book is available from Library and Archives Canada.

ISBN: 978-1-77478-061-9

Copyright © 2021 Engen Books

This book is a work of fiction. Names, characters, places and incidents are products of the author's imagination or are used fictitiously. Any resemblance to actual events or locales or persons living or dead is entirely coincidental.

Distributed by:
Engen Books
www.engenbooks.com
submissions@engenbooks.com

First mass market paperback printing: November 2021

Cover Image: Ellen Curtis

CONTENTS

A NOTE FROM
THE PUBLISHER

A note to you, dear reader.

This is a collection of short fiction from within the fictional setting known as the Engen Universe, a world much like our own where strange and wonderful things can happen. The setting is currently explored over twenty novels and short stories, in genres ranging from science-fiction, fantasy, and horror.

The stories included in this anthology exist in that shared universe but are intended to be able to be read on their own. The title 'Undead | Rebirth' comes from the fact that through line that connected the stories together. Although this collection is predominantly horror, like the universe they were inspired by, it encompasses a broad range of tones and themes.

We hope you enjoy.

TIMELINE I

I can recall with perfect clarity the day my wife died.

It was early in the fall of my thirty sixth year. I remember that the summer's crops were not looking promising this year. I suspected that the ground was becoming fallow. The water basin along the eastern ridge of town had started to go dry, and the seasons... well, the seasons have been slowly becoming one long season since I was a small boy. Without a change in season, it becomes harder to make a change in crop, and without a change in crop the group become fallow and unsustainable.

I'd managed to keep this fact from Jennifer by eating considerably less than her... she was eating for two, after all.

Actually, I'm fairly certain she noticed that I had only been eating a third as much as she was. We'd been living together for the better part of fifteen years, had been married for the last two — she probably knew more about me than I knew about myself.

In any event, on this day I woke up in my bed alone. I remember my eyes opening on their own on or about 7 am staring straight up at the ceiling. The sun was bright, brighter than it was in my boyhood at seven... time moved differently now. The children of town thought that that was a myth, but any of us lucky enough to have survived to near forty would tell you: the world was slowing down.

The ceiling was low in its middle, a reminder that I'd have to reinforce the roof sooner rather than later.

I sat up and dangled my legs over the edge of the bed. After a moment, a smile I couldn't fight came to my lips: I could hear her, just down over the stairs. Nothing specific or significant, just the regular sounds of her going about her day.

The first thing I noticed was the sizzle of bacon on the frying pan: that constant hiss and occasional pop of several thick, fatty strips as they became crisp and hard. There were almost assuredly eggs next to it, although I couldn't really hear those. I could smell them though, thick with the smell of savory and garlic. It made my mouth water.

Every few minutes there would be a fresh slosh of water as she gave the hand pump another push, along with the whine of the copper handle as it arose again. That was another thing to fix, that one sooner rather than later. The last thing I needed was for Jennifer to strain herself because of a rusty joint. I wasn't sure why she was filling the basin, but it's either to wash dishes or wash clothes... and given the time of morning, I'd lay wager on clothes.

There were vultures outside doing their morning greeting, harping at the rising sun and scraping their feet along my roof. I could hear them pecking at the beehive far in the back, trying to coax out a yellow-and-black meal. They're out of luck; the hive went dry several seasons ago.

Everything dies here.

Some mornings the birds were unbearable and gave me a headache from the get-go, but today they were almost peaceful. Like all the parts of the morning were coming together to make a song just for me.

And singing to the tune of that song was my wife.

She was humming along to no particular tune or beat I could recognize, intermittently switching to "da da da's" and "la la la's". She must have been in a great mood, and that put me in one, too.

I got up and checked myself in the mirror quickly, then headed down the stairs.

Our house was small, even by this town's standards. Two floors and only about nine hundred square feet, we opted for having several small rooms rather than big, unnecessarily large ones. Small rooms were easier to heat, and we wanted children. Lots of children.

Our bedroom was on the eastern face of the house and was barely big enough to fit our bed into lengthwise. The dresser and mirror were next to it and served as out night table as well, but other than that there was barely enough room for two people to stand. Especially me, with the ceiling on the top floor so low that I felt certain I'd have a hunch by the time I was forty. The room was blue... that wonderful sky blue that blended in with the view outside of truly nice days.

The hall outside was equally narrow. The carpet was a rusty colour that had been on sale at Sal's. Neither of us really liked it. It was knobby and rough but kept our feet warm in the colder months. Our bookshelf was out here, the top shelf mine, the bottom hers. Mine were mostly historical texts, hers fiction. Any kind of fiction, really. All the books were lined up carefully except for whichever one Jennifer was reading at the time, which always lay perched on the corner nearest our room.

There were three more small rooms (each a different colour: yellow, white and a kind of dusty rose) and a small washroom very close to mine. There was also a closet at the far end where we kept all out clothes, not having any in the rooms themselves. I headed there now and grabbed myself an asparagus green tee shirt and jeans that were suddenly too loose for me. I grabbed a belt and hoped Jennifer doesn't notice.

The stairs were narrow, and the carpet made them slippery. There's a small writing desk at the foot of it that I hated, kept meaning to move but don't.

The downstairs was largely dominated by the kitchen, which despite my protests Jennifer insisted be tile. The tile for that one room cost almost as much as the lumber for the rest; and there wasn't enough of any one pattern so we ended up with a patchwork looking floor... but tile she wanted, so tile she got.

The kitchen itself was the largest of anyone we knew and gave Jennifer the room to do the things she really loved. Only a small section to the left of the stove was actually used for cooking, the rest was much more functional. The table was meant to be for a big family and hopefully would be yet.

There was an easel not far from the bay window that looked out onto the rest of Long Bay, along with two stools: one for her to sit on, one for the mixed paints to rest on. Sometimes she painted what she saw out the window, sometimes she'd just look out until she got a gleam in her eye and then paint something completely different. Either way, it was almost always beautiful.

There were chairs, so many chairs. More chairs than we ever had need for. There was a wine rack in the corner, and I always bragged about making the rack and its contents the best. She usually chimed in at that point and commented that she wasn't sure which smelled woodier.

There was a small sitting room off of the kitchen and a porch, but that was all. There was a sink in the porch that I put there while I was building the house to clean my hands and still hadn't bothered to get rid of, but beyond that it was simple. It was humble. But it was ours and it was wonderful.

Jennifer was next to the stove, moving the frying pan from the fire to a cool one as the bacon and eggs started to crisp.

"Good morning," I said, smiling. My voice was hoarse. I didn't notice how sore it was until I tried to use it.

"Morning," she said, turning to me and smiling. There was nothing wrong with her voice, still as smooth and silky and perfect as ever.

That smile was the first thing I ever fell in love with. Long before I ever loved the girl as a whole (which happened fairly fast I'll admit, but not at first sight), I loved that smile. It was cheeky and wide with thin lips and perfect teeth and more than anything it was real. Jennifer never faked a smile in all the years I'd known her. She would pretend not to be angry, pretend not to be annoyed, even pretend to be enjoying herself... but she would never fake a smile. And nothing made me feel better in life than when she smiled at me, in knowing I caused this one small miracle to happen.

She turned back to her work without another word, humming her little tune. She'd been humming more the last few months... but then, so had I. Her brunette hair was pulled back in a ponytail to keep it out of her eyes and our food, but a few strands still escaped the elastic defiantly, falling into her forehead. Her eyes were a wonderful shade of green, like freshly picked limes. Her skin was pale and clear... even more so lately, but always had been as far as I was concerned. Beyond all that, she was tiny. I was convinced we must have looked comical when we walked to The Market together, me a great deal over six feet and she just shy of five. Every part of her was tiny and sweet, with one exception:

Her stomach bulged, barely contained by the loose white blouse she wore. It looked like she'd stuffed a watermelon underneath it.

I stepped up behind her and kissed her on her neck, then rested my chin on her. I knew she hated the wiry scruff of my beard, but she didn't complain. Hell, she smiled again. I brought my hand up her shirt and felt her stomach and couldn't stop myself from smiling like an idiot. "How'd you sleep?"

"Wonderfully," she hummed, her speech still musical and warm.

"Did she kick any?"

"A little earlier, while I was singing... I think she was trying to tell me not to quit my day job."

"She was probably just keeping time." I laughed and

wrapped my other hand around and giving her as tight a squeeze as I dare.

There was really no way for us to know the sex of the baby. That type of technology existed of course, but it wasn't easily accessible. The nearest medical center with that type of technology was in Parse, and the danger of a trip across the Badlands to Parse wasn't worth something so trivial as being certain what colour nighty to knit.

Besides all that, we were certain it was a girl. All the signs were against us. She was carrying low, craved lemon juice like it was air, and had gained weight in her face. Despite all that, we were sure that we were having a little girl. So sure we hadn't even talked about any boys names. It was a girl, and we were naming her Gwen. Gwendolen Jennifer Hunt.

"Can I help with anything?" I asked, sliding my arms out from around her.

She stifled her laugh, almost spitting up the orange juice she'd been drinking and bringing her hand up to her nose just in case she did. She swallowed, then turned to me to laugh until she saw that I was serious. She still laughed a little, in her eyes.

"Here," she smiled, handing me two plates and a handful of cutlery. "You can set the table."

"Why don't you ever let me help with any of the cooking?" I asked as I took the dishes and brought them to the table.

"Because, Mik, I'd like to be able to actually eat it afterwards."

I gave her my hurt face.

She laughed. I loved that laugh. Devilish, really. She

was the sweetest girl in the world, but she had a demon's sense of humour. Could be a real bitch when she wanted to be... but thankfully, she very rarely wanted to be. Even when she was in one of her moods, she was heads above any other woman I'd ever met.

I set the table and poured us each a fresh glass of juice before sitting at my place. A minute or so later she brought the pan over, its contents still sizzling as she scooped them onto the spatula and then onto our plates.

I remember that meal better than any other in my entire life. The bacon was perfect... each strip was thick and crispy on the outside, just a little wriggly in the middle. The eggs were underdone, but I didn't mind... actually kind of liked them that way. When we'd first been married, I wouldn't have been able to eat sunny side up eggs and keep it down, but if you live with someone long enough their habits become your own.

She sat across from me the whole while and talked about our plans for the today and the dreams she had the night before. The last seven months she'd had some of the weirdest, most lucid dreams of her life, and she attached great meaning to each and every one of them. I don't particularly buy into that myself, but I listened intently. I didn't have to agree with her to be interested in what she was saying. We talked about our plans for the baby's room and whether or not we were going to christen her, and if so, in what faith (our faiths differed). We didn't talk about anything terribly important or meaningful... we just talked and enjoyed our meal and, most important of all, enjoyed each other.

I think it was the best meal of my life.

If only the rest of the day had gone so well.

My farm lay of the far northern edge of York, and had ever since my father had completed his erection of it when I was a boy of nine. The truth was that it was by some distance removed from York, but nobody from York (Jennifer included) liked to admit that we were alone. In fact, the only men who enjoyed the solitude that the distance from town brought us had been myself and my father.

York was the largest of what remained of the colony towns, those that had been erected originally as a baseline to keep the Reps from getting too far East and to man the border with the salt water. They'd been built where work could be found, around mining and forestry and the needs of food and water and shelter: hundreds, sometimes thousands of huts and houses built almost on top of each other, like Tanagers huddling together for warmth. Each home had a small plot of land to till, and sustenance was built on the notion of shared coexistence. If Mr. Dumpling grew tomatoes this season, then Mr Creed next door would grow green onion, and the two would trade one for the other so that neither diet went without. It was a system built of checks and balances that worked very well and yet I, and my father before me, could not get behind. Were we loners from the start? I had never thought so, but I wonder now what part that played in what would come.

York and Signet and Goin were the three communities I'd known well enough to say I knew them in my thirty-six years. They dotted the inland of the coast like the stars in Orin's Belt. York, with its largest market, was the furthest north of the three and my farm was the furthest north structure in it. Beyond the ground of my farm — ploughed and tilled to fertility despite the fallow that the constant summer had wrought — lay the No Man's Land of the desert, and beyond that was 300 miles of Reps territory. I had ventured out there twice, once on my twenty-third birthday and a second time when Jennifer had come down with a pox, and both times shook me to think of.

Beyond the Reps territory was the central wall and beyond that was Parse, the last of the civilized free cities. Things in Parse were close to as they'd been in the days of old, if you believed the way people spoke: water that ran without a pump, food that didn't have to be bartered, and light that didn't have to be burned from oil. The latter at least I could vouch for, but as for the rest, I hadn't stayed long enough to find out on my one trip there. Parse had the best hospital in the land, and Jennifer had had a pox that had lasted ten nights. Signet had a clinic that serviced York and Goin sure, but what she'd needed had been in Parse.

Beyond Parse were the Green Lands and the Snow Caps — but honestly, the thought of my life taking me any farther than Parse in one direction or any farther than Goin in the other seemed ludicrous.

Everything we could ever need was here.

After breakfast we went into York for The Market. Once we left our Jeep, it was hard walking with Jennifer, as her added weight slowed us considerably. Seven months ago, she would have moved from table to table as swiftly and deftly as a hummingbird moving from one flower to the next. It was amusing to watch the change in her, but not in a mocking way. Any change in her theses last few months brought a satisfied smile to my face: her changes in diet, in how she walked, in the weight of her next to me on our bed... all these things were tangible signs that Gwendolyn was in the world. Watching their signs was like watching the leaves rustle on the trees in Goin, a small sign that let you know the wind was there even though you couldn't see it.

The York Market was something to behold. It arrived at noon out of a cloud of dust and humidity and remained for just three hours, cluttering the scant alleys between homes and making the entire town pulse with life. For most, the home was their storefront: a canopy extended on three poles from over the owner's front door and a table was laid beneath it, and voila! You could start selling.

As I said, each home produced their own foodstuff or product. While one member of the household, typically the patriarch, minded the family booth another member (matriarch, often with children in tow) ventured forth for the items they need. Everyone sold and everyone bought. Almost everything was done on the barter system. Credits were as rare as owl's teeth and treated accordingly. Credits typically only came from Parse, either by way of a Yorker who had returned from selling his wares there or via a Parser who had come into town, looking for the artisan crafted originals. These credits, once given, were rarely spent but handed down from generation to generation, in the unlikely event that some future descendant would one day accumulate enough to live and be educated in

Parse itself.

I had under my arm a baker's dozen of beets to barter with. Before she became of child Jennifer would carry
some too, but there was no point. We could not barter for
more than we could carry back.

Cultivating the beets was difficult, as they took hard-
ship on the soil they fed from. My father and his father's
father had developed a method by which beats were
planted along only one edge of the farmland, and that
edge changed each season: first east, then south, then
west, then back to east again (the northern wall shared the
house). This made for small but steady crops and a Hunt
family secret and kept our crops producing when others
had failed. As a result, the Hunt beets could be bartered
for more than their objective worth: that baker's dozen
would feed us for the week in what we could get for it.

Jennifer stopped at Zelda Goodkind's booth. She was
an old woman, whose husband had passed some five seasons ago when he struck ill and Parse could not be reached
in time. Now she knit shawls and made small children's
trinkets with balls and dried stalks and twine: cheap toys
that she could produce on her own and be bartered for the
necessities of life.

Jennifer was eyeing a small woolen one-piece, the size
of a newborn. It was the light blue of undyed wool, and
Zelda had made a small design on the left breast... a duck
I thought, though it was hard to tell as it was not coloured,
and I had in truth never seen a duck.

Without turning back to see me, she reached her hand
back and placed it into the basket under my arm and
withdrew a beet. She handed it to Zelda who took it and

nodded once. With anyone else she might have inspected the egg, but we had dealt with her many times before and she knew we only brought good beets: any slightly irregular eggs were kept and cooked, and several generations of growing had made their appearance slight.

Jennifer picked up the one-piece and held it up by pinched shoulders for a moment, as though presenting it to anyone around to see. Then she folded it over her arm and nodded once more at Zelda.

That one beet could have bought us corn or wheat or beans enough for the week, but I said nothing. Jennifer had lived her entire life acting as though she were in want whether she was or she wasn't: this time was hers. She had sown the seeds of life and now it grew within her, and she intended to live.

At The Market were all things. There were swords fashioned from fine metals and bone and stone, crafted by those who had honed their forges for ten generations. There were fruits and vegetables and small quantities of dried meat, though that had become rarer as the seasons had come together more and more. There were arrows that flew straight and true and arrows that bent in their middle. There was black powder and oil and petrol that came in from Parse. There was medicine, but not of the sort you would want. Real medicine was in Parse or, failing that, in the Signet clinic: the medicine sold at The Market was the sort of serpent oil that only helped the buyer's delusions and the seller's wallet.

Children ran in tattered earth-toned clothes with the knees scraped out, unwatched by parents who bickered and haggled whether two tomatoes were truly and equal swap for two limes or not. In an alley between two houses, four girls of about nine were playing skip-rope and chanting to keep the time.

Red eyes bad
Green eyes worse
Beware the demon pain has cursed.
He tries to trick
He tries to sway
Don't be the fool don't be his prey.

I remembered the jingle — and others like it — from my youth. My friends and I would recite it while playing jacks, timing the bouncing of the ball to the beat of the song until the words themselves lost all meaning.

The memory made me smile. Jennifer must have seen it, because she squeezed my arm and elevated herself onto her toes to give me a kiss on the cheek. It was a motion she had performed many times before, but this time was somehow... ephemeral.

We bought a small basket of tomatoes, some dried fish, a sliver of pork and some black powder. We sat on a large flat stone and ate the two remaining baysrif eggs with the sun warm on our backs before heading back to the jeep.

It was a simple day without incident, like many others that had come before it.

By the time we got home, we were tired. We portioned the meat and stored the tomatoes. Then as evening fell, we sat together in our chair. I read Odysseus to her by lamplight with her head resting gently on my shoulder and our daughter kicking mildly at my side.

I also recall the day I met my wife.

I was twenty-one and my father was still alive. Those two things had one cumulative effect: making the young fool I was believe he was indestructible.

I was in Goin to barter for a rather large supply of comfrey and myrrh seeds. I was going to have to buy enough to fill up the Jeep — which at that time was new — but the upshot was that until the sale at end-of-day Lastday I had it to myself. If it seems an odd thing to remember, the specific sort of plant and seed I was in Goin to pick up, it's because it's linked directly to my first memory of seeing Jennifer.

She was standing near the counter at Oz's Emporium, bent slightly over the counter. Her dress was new and was red and had yellow flowers printed on it, with straps that went over her shoulders and a matching red ribbon keeping her hair up. She was surrounded by flowering dandelions that caught the light and cast a golden glow all around her, and the air was so thick with aloe and mint that it made the hair on the back of my neck tingle.

I had fully intended to haggle with Oz on the price of myrrh before catching a show at the theatre and possibly checking at the recruitment office to see if any Remer hiring stations were active. But something about seeing Jennifer changed my priorities all at once: suddenly, the only thing that mattered was speaking to this woman.

She turned and caught me in her gaze. She was seventeen and her lashes were long in a way I did not understand then and do not understand now. Her nose was perfect, her chin angular, her mouth small even when she smiled. She stepped away from Oz's counter, her business apparently complete and she had since been making small talk.

"Good 'morn," she said, with a voice like fine sugar.

I attempted to reply, and do not recall what I said, only that it was unintelligible. The disuse of my tongue took me off guard: it had never happened to me before. It was too big for my mouth and would not form words, any more than my mind would form coherent thought.

After a moment's pause, she smiled and nodded at me, either understanding or suspecting me a patient, and then said goodbye to Oz and walked from the Emporium and into the bright sun of the street.

Oz watched me with a knowing smile, then took out a box of myrrh seed and placed it on the counter in front of him to begin our business.

I left the shop without a word and went out into the street.

If you've never experienced it, there's something about meeting the love of your life that focuses your priorities. Until that moment my future had been like the trunk of a kraken: diverging out into multiple arms with multiple outcomes. Would I take the farm? Enlist with the Remers? Move to Parse and try to make a life there? There were countless possibilities all narrowed down to one by a small smile and a flowery dress: whichever one allowed me to meet her.

I stayed some distance behind her as she visited several shops, always occupying myself outside until she came back out of them. I didn't intend on following, I was only biding my time and keeping her within eyesight for when I thought of something to say. What could I say? What do you say to someone you don't know who doesn't know you?

I watched as she stopped to talk to some children that were playing pick-up with lines drawn in the gravel road. She gently took a stick and helped one draw a cleaner circle for his base, and the child smiled reassuringly. She went to a deli and ate, she walked by the theatre but did not go in. Then finally she stopped by the range and leaned against the fence to watch the archery match happening at the time.

I found out many years later — when I was recounting this same story to another couple — that she had known I was there the entire time and had been waiting for me to gather the courage to say something.

Though I had spent the majority of my life in a desert climate, my mouth had never been so dry. Though I had faced danger and the fear of death every day, I had never been so scared. I was standing five feet behind her for what seemed an eternity, as her nimble fingers danced along the wire mesh of the fence and her head twitched minutely from side to side, watching as the archers set their arrows to flight, followed the arrow, then turned her attention back again.

I couldn't think of what to say. Anything I thought of sounded like a line or a lame attempt to get her into the back of my Jeep. Nothing sounded genuine, nothing could: I barely knew her. That was the truth of the matter, and it slowly dawned upon me: I did not know this girl and had no idea what to say to her. Aside from a few scant words, I had no real proof she even spoke English.

I was turning to walk away when a chilled breeze came over the sand, the sort of Chinook wind that used to be commonplace in the Northlands. She bristled against the cold, her hands rubbing the opposing arm and she clutched into herself.

"Here."

That was the first word I said to the woman who would become my wife as I placed my coat gently around her shoulders. She turned to me and smiled, then we both watched the archery.

Had it not been for that breeze, I know not what I ever would have said.

It's amazing how small things can affect larger things.

We were exhausted by the time early evening hit, her from hauling our child around all day, me from hauling the extra weight she no longer could because of said child.

I had horrible dreams. I dreamed the Reps got past the blockades and into the township and were running amuck everywhere. Jennifer was atop a high hill across a long wheat field, the sort I hadn't ever seen outside of books. It stretched on forever, and no matter how far or how fast I ran, it only seemed to get farther and farther away. Eventually I came across a trap door in the wheat, the sort that look like cellar doors flat to the ground. It had a heavy iron handle but when I pulled at it, I woke up with Jennifer screaming next to me.

Jennifer was screaming next to me.

It took a moment to register as not a part of the dream, but when it did, I was on my feet immediately. She was curled and lurched into the fetal position, her face a taut mask of pain in such a way as I had never seen it. Had someone shown me a picture of that face and that face alone, I would never have recognized it as my wife. Her hair was soaked with sweat and pasted to her scalp and forehead, the rest of it tumbling around her like a pool of blood in the low light.

I was as helpless and useless and speechless as the day we met, standing by her with my tongue at my feet. "Jenny?" I managed finally.

She screamed, clutching at her midsection. She'd wet the bed with urine and tears and sweat and who knew what else, but there wasn't the wet of water breaking. The baby was coming, but what was wrong? I had seen birth before and had been preparing for it for months, but not like this, and not this early.

"Mik!" she screamed between gasped breathes and screams, and I realized stupidly that her eyes were clasped shut: she didn't know where I was. I jumped over the bed and over her to crouch next to her on her side of the bed. I clutched her hand and pushed her hair back from her forehead and kissed it; she tasted like fried chicken. My God, how long had she been suffering while I slept? By the moon it was only half-passed nine.

She opened her eyes at my touch and found mine. She was full of fear, crazed with it. There is a point of pain where the brain shut off sanity, it shuts off the cultural norms and etiquette and leave you only with base instinct.

The lobes of our brain don't know how to deal with that and become confused. Jennifer was like that now, and again I didn't recognize her. Such was her pain that one pupil was a pinprick and the other so wide it was like she'd had milk of the poppy.

She grabbed my face in both her hands and tried to focus on me, as though I were spinning in her vision and she were trying to stop it. "Guh," she said, and I still don't know what that was supposed to be. Saliva came out of her mouth, as though she were choking on it.

"I'll ready the Jeep," I said, standing quickly. "I'll ready the Jeep!" My voice was cracking and panicked. I wasn't even sure where I was bringing her, but I knew I couldn't help here.

I was at the door to our bedroom when her water finally broke, although that's not quite the right term. The red that came from her could not be called water by anyone who had ever seen it. She let out a loud, long scream and I ran back to her as more and more red came, soaking through the mattress into the feathers beneath.

Every time I stepped away from her, she screamed, and I ran back.

She never uttered another word I could decipher.

She was dead within the hour.

Preeclampsia, complicated by acute anemia, complicated by something else I had zoned out for.

I can recall with perfect clarity the day my wife died.

LIVING LIGHT

The moon was high over Turkey, its pale light the only thing visible in the night sky. Aysenur ran, her dirty blonde hair bobbing with every stride. Her chest heaved with every breath as a stitch grew in her side. Her footsteps echoed off the abandoned buildings that hemmed her in, their darkened windows offering no sanctuary. As she desperately searched for an open door or window, somewhere to get out of the open, a helicopter crested the hill.

The harsh yellow light from its searchlight brought her slight frame into sharp relief. She stopped and turned to face the helicopter, her hair pushed into her eyes from its downdraft.

She brushed her hair out of her eyes, and began to count.

One.

Her hair began to billow around her, changing to a platinum blonde. She closed her eyes.

Two.

Her skin seemed to glow, the thin hospital gown she was wearing seeming to become translucent.

Three.

She opened her eyes, and the world exploded.

One week, twelve hours earlier, roughly fifteen kilometers away.

Aysenur stared at the bowl of so-called 'food' placed in front of her. It was grey and lumpy, but she knew it didn't have any texture whatsoever. Sighing, she picked up her spoon and dipped it into the soupy mixture. It filled the cup of the spoon lazily, the grey puddle slowly growing. She lifted the spoon to her mouth, and ate the grey slop. It was disgusting. As she slowly ate from the seemingly bottomless bowl, the cafeteria doors opened, three men striding into the room, previously empty except for her and two guards.

"W-we weren't told about this surprise visit, sir." That would be Dr. L, an old, balding man who did Aysenur's weekly "training" with her. He was stumbling behind two other men.

The much older of the two turned and answered with a deep Central African accent. "Well then, Dr. L, if the directors told you that Mr. K and I were coming, it wouldn't be a surprise, would it?"

"Y-yes, but usually we are told to get a presentation ready. This is highly unusual."

The African man turned to face the doctor, stopping a mere five feet from Aysenur.

"These are unusual times, Dr. L. With the recent issues in Russia and East Germany, there is need for more security, to avoid more... Escapees."

"I assure you, sir, our security is top notch, and we

only have one current liability. Nothing like Siberia III, you understand."

The African man smoothed his suit, and calmly asked, "And where is the liability now?"

Dr. L looked shamefaced at the floor, and muttered his reply: "Sitting next to you, sir."

The African man nodded, and sat down across from Aysenur. "Take your security personnel and leave, Dr. L. I need to assess how dangerous this liability is."

After Dr. L had ushered the two guards and himself from the room, the African man turned to Aysenur and smiled.

"Now, what's your name?"

Aysenur didn't look up as she responded: "Aysenur."

"Aysenur. That's a pretty name, much better than Mazi or Thomas." He pointed to himself as he said this, and then to his companion. Aysenur giggled in spite of herself. "Now, Aysenur, if I were you, I'd want to escape, right?" Aysenur nodded. "Here's how I would do it." Aysenur looked up, startled.

"Missy, don't worry, we're the good guys." The African man's companion had spoken for the first time, revealing his British accent. "Just trust us. We want to help." Aysenur then noticed that the British man, who she guessed was Thomas, only had one eye. Mazi continued.

"Now, Aysenur, if there were to be a blackout in, let's say, a week, would you be able to find your way out?"

Aysenur nodded.

"Then, what would be the problems facing you?"

Aysenur took a deep look into the aged brown eyes, seeing the smile lines against the darkness of his skin.

"The doors lock if the power goes out." Mazi nodded, and Aysenur continued, rushing out the words as fast as her tongue could manage. "And they have helicopters to find me if I escape." Mazi sat back, lacing his fingers behind his head. Grinning, he replied.

"Me and Tom here can deal with a helicopter or two, easy. Now, about the doors…"

One week later.

Aysenur had butterflies in her stomach, tickling her esophagus as the plan tumbled in her head. She was waiting in her room, the cool air of the vents giving her goosebumps. She nervously chewed her hair, waiting for that alarm that would signal her chance to escape. She had no watch, and the walls of her cell were a blank white, so hours could have passed without her knowing.

But she waited.

And waited.

And waited.

And… What if they weren't going to help her after all?

Then the lights cut out.

And Aysenur ran as the devil himself was at her heels.

She ran through white hallways past shouting guards and then through the shattered doors then onto the gritty sand and sharp rocks and her bare feet hurt from the pounding of her legs, but she ran past the baying dogs past the chain link fence and into the cold moonlight night. She had no time to marvel at the stars she had never seen. She had no time to see the delicate yet hardy plants the desert fostered. She only had time to run and breathe. Run and breathe. No time for pain, no time for doubt as she ran towards the moon. Only time to run and breathe. She ran and breathed for what felt like hours, as long as she could manage.

And that was long enough.

Roughly two hours later and two kilometers away.

Mazi gasped when he saw the flash of light in the distance.

"Dammit. We should have been more careful, Tom. That delay might just have cost Aysenur her life."

Thomas looked at him from the passenger seat of the car. "Yeah, but we weren't more careful." He drew his handgun. "And judging from the fact she got this far, I think she'll be fine. The girl's got skill." Mazi nodded, his throat dry but his hands covered in sweat.

Two minutes later.

The helicopter lay in flames, the two pilots long dead. The walls of the abandoned village were blackened in a circle centered on the lone, facedown girl. Mazi rushed to her side and checked for a pulse.

"She's alive." Mazi started to pick her up to move her somewhere safe. Thomas held his handgun in front of him, staring west towards the compound the helicopter had come from.

"Good." Thomas glanced back, making sure Mazi could move the girl without help. Seeing that he could,

Thomas turned back to watch the horizon. "Do you hear that?" Mazi looked up.

"The helicopter? Yeah, I hear it." He began to make his way towards one of the buildings, Aysenur in his arms. "I trust an old war dog like yourself can handle one measly helicopter?"

Thomas chuckled darkly.

"Of course."

Thirty seconds later.

After a short burst of gunfire and a loud crash, Thomas strode in from outside.

"How's the girl?" Thomas sat down, picking at his shirt.

"*Aysenur's* doing fine." Mazi relaxed and moved away from the sleeping figure. "Why don't you use her name? Just 'cause she was probably born in a test tube doesn't make her any less human."

Thomas leaned back and began to clean his gun. "I can't pronounce it. It always comes out wrong."

"Try."

So Thomas did.

And for the first time, Aysenur awoke to laughter.

THE IRONY OF GLASS

Thatcher Verra drank from the limeade bottle in the cup holder attached to his office chair and waited for the other players of *Civilization VI* to make their moves. He had an assortment of online work, mostly freelance and various levels of legal, and was enjoying the break.

Crumb was winning.

There was a flicker from the window. Without bothering to stand, he simply wheeled his chair to the side of his robust entertainment setup. The computer was so large it was practically diesel-powered, with a plain black CPU tower and three monitors placed in a floor-to-ceiling shelf.

His window was at ground level. There was nothing immediately next to it, but there was a second flicker as something passed through the sunlight. As he approached, he saw that it was a rock dove. He liked to picture them with guitars, rocking out in studded leather jackets.

The rock dove half-flew and half-walked about the gravel at the base of the window, doing nothing intelligible. It flitted about three more times. Leaving the overweight Hispanic man with his computer, it took flight.

At first, it stayed above the street. There was not a single person. Two dogs were wandering about, and a cat lounged atop the hood of a Buick. The pigeon saw what it thought was a metal bird. It fled to one of its favourite feeding grounds: the town's hotel.

First it decided to perch on a branch. Before the tree was a large set of windows looking in on the reception desk. Standing at that desk was a pimply young man wearing a face mask. He'd just set aside his cleaning cloths and was talking to the woman before him.

"Hello and welcome to Towerton," the young man said. His nametag read Isaac. The woman made note of this, out of habit.

She smiled awkwardly, trying to hide the anxiety she couldn't place. "Er, hi. Thank you. Why are you wearing a mask?"

"Germs."

She frowned. "Is there something going around?"

"It's the time of year," he said. It was well into Spring at this point, but she didn't bother to pursue the question further. He followed with, "Can I help you?"

His voice was thin and strained, which was odd because of the muffling of the mask. The new arrival replied, "Yes, I had a reservation?"

As he turned to the computer at his station, the young man started nodding. It seemed to be subconscious, like a pensive person sticking out their tongue. "What was the name?"

"Meredith Heaney," she replied. She pronounced it with slightly more volume and distinction than her everyday speech, as though the name should hit home.

Isaac was nodding. "Room 57," he said, though she couldn't tell if he was talking to her or to himself. As he returned from the key boxes with the appropriate key, he handed her a cleaning cloth and moved the key towards the surface of the counter. Stopping, he blinked and flushed. "Here you go, ma'am," he said, correcting his configuration.

She smiled and brushed off the error. "Thank you," she said as she took it and he pointed in the direction she needed to go. "Oh," she added, and he stopped from picking up a spray bottle. "I would appreciate some help bringing in my personal effects. Would you...?"

His heart sank, but then he remembered. "Let me just page the assistant manager," he said. When she blinked in surprise, he added, "We have a new service she's been wanting to show off." Isaac seemed to brighten as he spoke, and Meredith detected relief in his tone, though she couldn't put a finger on why.

"I...uh...okay," she said.

It didn't take long for the assistant manager, a middle-aged Aboriginal woman, to show up. "Hello, hello," she chirped. "I'm Chantelle Naranja, delighted to meet you. I hear you'd like to see our new drone carriage service?"

Meredith made herself grin. "Why, yes." She hadn't mentioned her corporate background when she made the call. Had her name gotten ahead of her? Did one of her colleagues head her off?

Chantelle led Meredith to a sparsely furnished side room. A young man sat before a control terminal. "Stewart," the assistant manager began, "Please demonstrate for our guest how the new system works."

"Sure thing!" he said. Meredith cast a perfunctory glance over the control board, which included a display from a camera in flight.

"Now," Chantelle resumed, "Let's meet up with it!"

Feeling a little breathless, and unable to explain the prickling at the back of her neck, Meredith followed. After a brief stroll down a hallway, during which time they exchanged small talk, they arrived at a scene that made Meredith beam. Before her was a wall-height window, modified with something like an oversized mail slot.

"Meet Hummingbird," Chantelle grinned. Holding a stable flight on the other side of the window was, in fact, a drone. It had limbs added to the base model, so that it looked like a metal insect pretending to be a bird. The logo it sported featured an android head out of the eighties, shaped like a flying saucer with a white space for the visor. In that visor space was a font designed to look like music notes. It read: Humdroid.

Meredith tilted her head. "Did it come with those?" She pointed at one of the limbs.

Chantelle opened the slot as she answered. It swung down like an oven door. "We had to have them added as a special order. That's why we only have this one drone. It's expensive, you see." The assistant manager offered an apologetic smile. "We're hoping for something a little prettier if this project goes well. We'd like to have a slot in every guest room."

Meredith blinked theatrically. "Oh, my. That would be something. But I'm sorry, I didn't answer your question." She handed the drone her car keys while she spoke. It had a hand that appeared to be built specifically for keys. "I'll let the drone tell you how I feel," and she smiled coyly.

"What do you mean?" asked Chantelle.

Meredith only replied, "You'll see." Chantelle gasped as the hotel's drone returned carrying a version of itself that only had two basic forearms, and that could have fit snugly into a medium-sized suitcase.

Meredith smiled at Chantelle's hanging mouth. "I do apologize for not giving you warning," she said, presenting a business card with the Humdroid logo. "I didn't want your fine establishment up in arms about a personal visit."

Chantelle closed her mouth. Her expression was carefully blank.

"I'm not here for an inspection or anything," Meredith assured her, holding one hand palm-out. "The company's been getting a lot of orders here in Towerton, and I wanted to see for myself what the commotion was about."

Chantelle frowned. "But we arranged the entire project with the company and the town. Have you seen the local papers? A boy in town played a big part in it. No one's sure how old he is, but we think he's young. Calls himself Incenio."

"I've heard of some of those details, but I haven't actually read the paper. I'll look into that," she said with a professionally warmed smile. "And your arrangement with Humdroid was just one product. A hefty one, granted, but just one. I'm talking about the rest of the town. Just coming in, I could see them. From afar, Towerton looks like it's...got a flock of birds." She had to stop herself from comparing them to flies.

"Then why bring one of your own? I mean, if I might

ask? Just curious," the assistant manager added.

After they took her car keys, her drone, and her suit-case and closed the wall slot, Meredith noticed that a handful of guests had come to see the hotel drone in use. "It pays to be prepared," she answered.

The assistant manager was already grabbing a flatbed cart to help her. "I suppose it does," the other woman re-plied, smiling at the onlookers.

They proceeded toward Meredith's room. The guests dispersed, though one of them went off with Chantelle be-cause of concerns he had with his room. "End of the hall," Chantelle reminded Meredith. "Left side."

As she thanked the assistant manager and proceeded to her room, a little black girl followed her. She found her room and looked down at the girl. "Why, hello."

"My mommy's sad," said the girl.

"I'm sorry to hear that," Meredith replied, taken aback yet again. There was something at the back of her mind, or maybe the tip of her tongue, that was bothering her. *What am I so worried about?* "Where is she?"

Before the girl could respond, a dark man in a bright dress shirt rounded the corner at the end of the hall. "There you are," he said, looking at the girl. His strides were long, and he caught them up quickly.

"Is there pie?" the girl asked hopefully.

"Not yet, you little rascal, but soon," he answered and scooped her up in his arms. He smiled at Meredith, look-ing somewhere between playful and embarrassed. "Sorry, her brain is in her feet."

"Hey!" she gave the man her best indignant look.

Meredith laughed. "Not a problem."

They bid their farewells and Meredith entered her room, letting a sigh out of her nose. She was a professional now. Being around people shouldn't be awkward anymore. She shook her hair loose and set aside her baggage.

Two mornings later, Abigail Fischer left the roadside motel where she'd spent the night and sat atop the motorcycle Tasha had provided for her. That part was still a little surreal. Abby pulled out her phone. First, she texted Tasha:

I'm okay.

Tasha: The bed didn't kill you?

I was worried about the bike.

Tasha: I'm not. You'll be fine with that. Those motel beds, though…

Abby looked at her phone, and one corner of her lips quirked at that.

Thanks.

Tasha's response was an emoji of an upside-down smile. Not a frown; the head was upside-down. Shaking her head, Abby put the phone away and hit the highway for almost two hours before taking an off-ramp. She felt uncomfortable when the bike was still, when she was on streets, and when she was turning. But when she was on the highways, it was a little easier. Just go straight. Pick up speed. Don't do donuts.

She took a side road after the off-ramp and checked her phone's GPS to make sure she'd gone where she thought she had. There was a new message:

Chad: Near Towerton.

A flash of annoyance.

Thought I was doing this alone?

She waited a moment to see if there was an answer forthcoming. She was just about to put her phone away when she got one:

Chad: And you totally can. It's good to have back-up, though. Why don't we meet at the welcome mat, and take it from there?

I'm just scouting.

Chad: No one's talking about Jaycee. It's driving me nuts. Had to get out of the house, anyway. We'll just say hi, and I'll wait outside of town, if you want.

She didn't know what to say about Jaycee.

Alright. Right by the sign?

Chad: See you there!

It wasn't long before a green sign loomed: *Welcome to Towerton*.

Beneath it, leaning on a rental car, stood Chad. He waved when she drew near. She stopped and set one foot to the ground. Lifting the visor of her helmet, she said, "Hi."

"How's she treating you?" he asked, flicking a glance at the bike.

Abby shrugged. "I'm getting used to it."

"Didn't know you had a licence for motorbikes."

Abby was looking at the town. Chad frowned at her silence and turned around. "I know. Isn't it something?"

There were black dots in the air. It was hard to tell from here what they were. The town itself was standard enough: buildings, a gas station on the way, a water tower in the distance. "Did you race me here?" Abby asked.

"Huh? Oh, no." He put his hands in the pockets of his

shorts. "I thought you'd be here first. Just didn't want to be too far behind."

"They're not moving like birds," Abby said suddenly.

Chad squinted. "You're right. Let's get a closer look."

"I'm just here to snoop around," she reminded him. "Victor said not to actually go into the town."

"Why did he ask you to go?" He'd stepped back a pace.

Abby watched him. "By myself? I don't know. He said he thinks I'm looking for something. Made some weird remark about Xeno."

"Yeah, he does that. Will we just take the car? Seems silly to use two vehicles just to look at the front door and turn around."

She looked around and shook her head. "You stay here, I'll drive around a bit and meet you back here."

He stood up straighter. "Are we cool?"

Abby looked at him like he was daft. "Yeah. We're cool. I'm just supposed to take a quick look around, and that's what I want to do. Something makes me nervous. I Googled the town in my motel room last night."

Chad absorbed all this and rubbed his chin. "…and?"

"Nothing. For months."

"Well, it is a small town."

"That's what I thought. Apparently, it literally started as a place people could go to get off the highway."

Chad laughed. "For real?"

Relieved by the turn away from tension, Abby chuckled a little too. Despite the fact that it was only spring, she was not liking the heat now that there was no highway wind. "Yeah, it's just far enough from everything that it fits kinda snug in the middle of nowhere. They deal in supplies. Rope and camping stuff, car repairs, basic things you need on the road. You know."

Chad nodded. "Doesn't sound like Victor's usual thing. All right, let's get this over with."

"See you in a bit!" Abby said, and started off. As she approached the town, she started feeling a little anxious. She shook her head. She watched the dots grow and looked for a turn so she could go around the outskirts of the town. Then two things registered to her: those dots in the air were machines, and Chad was driving behind her. She pulled over.

Chad went past her, followed suit, and walked back.

"What's up?" he said.

"Why are you following me?"

Chad ran a hand through his hair. "Call it a hunch. Don't you feel a little worried?"

"No," she lied. She lifted her chin and flicked her gaze behind him.

Turning, Chad had to acknowledge she was right. "That must be a few dozen drones."

"At least."

"Hard to tell with all the moving about," he remarked. Then he looked around. It was a slow, almost three-sixty-degree turn.

"What?" Abby asked.

"You see any traffic?"

"Nope."

"In any direction?"

"Should I?" Abby replied. "I mean, it's a small town. Even their advertising practically says, 'Great to see you, please keep moving.'"

Chad laughed. "Yeah. I dunno. Gut feeling, I guess. Let's just drive straight through the town, then we can turn around and go right back."

"But-"

"You got a rabbit's foot in there?" He nodded at the bags behind the bike's seat.

Abby hesitated. "Well, it would be faster…"

"That's the spirit!"

Thatcher, meanwhile, was taking a break from gaming. At the moment, he was frowning at his screen. The tattered remains of a TV dinner lay on the nearest surface he could find: a bookshelf. He'd clean up when he next stepped away from his computer.

He was reading e-mails that included the mayor of the town, local news and communication networks, and several local businesses. Thatcher had never seen circumlocution like the mayor's. Their project with the drones was going well. Apparently, the town even had a visitor from Humdroid.

There was pressure to go public about their progress.

The argument went as follows: get the press in on the events, and there would be investors and other financial backing on the horizon. But get them in too soon, and the town risked looking foolish. The mayor, in essence, wanted a fully successful project before they unveiled it. The appearance of this Humdroid employee, whose role wasn't actually stated, was making both sides of the argument push harder — and therefore listen less.

But the media, according to one of the reporters who was part of the discussion, had already gotten word of the state funding that was going into supplying the municipal service drones. Just a few days ago, Thatcher's proposed unit of experimental service drones had arrived.

"Los Reparadors to the Rescue!" read the headline on the local paper. Thatcher, of course, read the article online. There was a picture of two flying drones handling a garbage bin at the end of someone's driveway. The photo included some of the frame of the window from which it had been taken. When he asked about it by e-mail, Thatcher was told it was supposed to "convey a home-of-the-everyman vibe."

He thought it looked unprofessional.

Pushing back, he spun his chair by pressing against the horizontal bar of the legs with his feet. Spinning back and forth, he mulled over his position. Behind him was a degree he'd hung from the wall. MIT. Computer Science and Course 15-1: Management. He kept it there not as a reminder of the achievement, but as a reminder of the fact that he'd barely passed.

He turned back to his three screens. The centre one displayed his e-mail conversation. Flanking that screen were two screens of porn. Thatcher felt that business and politics were smutty undertakings, despite the fact that he excelled at business. Cracking his fingers, he went to work composing his response:

Esteemed Colleagues,

I agree that we should have a short delay before press releases and public announcements. Towerton should be well-represented when the project bears its fruit. Yet at the end of the day, this is an investment, so we should not delay too long. I recommend that we bring together the entire town for this initiative. Already I've noticed independent agents ordering their drones from suppliers other than the business I began two months ago. The hotel and the hospital, among others, are also running their own initiatives.

Bringing everyone together for this will take time, but I look forward to seeing what our townspeople can do. I must express gratitude for the support many of you have shown, financially and otherwise, in getting my small business up and running. Humdroid has surpassed my sales in dollars but not units sold, because mine are smaller and more accessibly priced. Perhaps we might convene with them? Please advise.

With respect,

Incenio

He clicked Send, then grabbed a portable (but still rather large) control console and set it up at his desk, connecting it to his computer. Two of the cameras were his own additions, and he didn't like the display on the control unit itself. So, he had created software that automatically linked his computer to all three cameras whenever he attached the controls to it. In the left screen was the feed from the camera beneath his drone. In the centre was the front camera. His right screen displayed the view from behind the drone.

He put on a headset that included a microphone and guided his drone into the air.

Abby and Chad pulled into the first parking lot they could find. It belonged to a mom-and-pop diner. So eager were they to get away from their vehicles that they parked at oblong angles, terribly mismatched from the parking spots. Abby tore her helmet off and dropped it in her eagerness to secure it to her bike.

She left it there.

The pair ran to the diner and found it locked and closed.

"Why are they closed!?" demanded Chad through heavy breathing.

Abby gasped a few times, swallowed, and shook her head. They were sweating, and both told themselves it was the sun beating down on them. It wasn't yet noon.

They stayed next to the wall of the building, getting as much shade as they could, and walked around the corner so that they were facing the street; the door had been on the side. Backs to the window, breath restored, they watched as three drones floated down in front of them. They were all equipped with speakers.

A fourth drone came in sidelong. "Hey, it's Incenio!" said a man through the speaker.

Thatcher turned his drone in response, so that he could see the one that was speaking. He recognized the voice. From his drone came his rough voice. Chad thought it sounded too young to be as grizzled and grumbly as it was. "Hi, Shore. Did you bring the newcomer?"

"Nope," came from the first speaker. Then it sounded like a little girl. "Daddy, can I play with the throne?"

"It's a drone, sweetie. And no," said the man's voice. "This is grown-up stuff."

"You never let me play with your toys."

"It's not a toy!"

A woman's voice came from Shore's speaker, though distantly. "Alex…"

"Pew pew!" said the girl's voice.

"Okay, later," said the original voice. "We have company."

Chad and Abby looked at each other. All three of the other drones were facing Shore's. Abby coughed. "...do you guys live here?"

"Yep!" answered Shore.

"I do not," replied one of the larger ones. It could still squeeze into a suitcase, Abby thought. "I'm Meredith. Pleased to meet you all."

There was a chorus of greeting. "I'm Chad," he chimed in to get things rolling, "and this is Abby." He pointed at the one calling itself Shore. "Are you Shore, or Alex, or a bunch of people?"

The little girl laughed. A second voice, apparently a different girl, said, "Mom, we're out of cookies." Abby giggled despite herself. Chad looked at her and grinned awkwardly. Abby's face was tight.

"I'm Shore."

"He's Alex," said the background woman.

"That's my wife. She's trouble. Oof!" There was a whumping sound. The girls giggled.

"Can any of you get that hair off my camera?" said the only drone that hadn't spoken yet. "It's driving me nuts."

Abby stepped forward. Chad looked up and down the street. No one. His rental and Abby's bike looked ridiculous, but they were the only ones on the lot. Abby frowned. "It's not a hair. It's a crack."

On the other end of that drone sat a young petite Hispanic woman. Her control scheme was not as large and sophisticated as Thatcher's, and her computer sat off to the side. On the screen for her controls, the crack occupied just enough space to draw attention.

She cursed.

"That's Crumb," Thatcher's drone said for him.

"So you all have gamertags?" said Meredith's drone.

"Yeah, pretty much," Thatcher answered as Incenio.

"I'll be…uh…Chap Stick!" came Meredith's voice.

"Look out, we're in for some Chap!" said Shore.

"You're the worst," remarked Crumb.

"We'll see about that," replied Shore. "We should keep…droning on and on!"

Meredith groaned.

Thatcher could not position his drone to keep everyone in view at once. He turned decidedly away from Shore. Abby giggled tightly. Thatcher was having a hard time looking at the newcomers. They were strangers. He tugged on one ear. There was a knot in his stomach. He wanted to have his drone leave. Or get them to leave.

"Anywhere indoors we can take this?" Chad asked. His fingers twitched.

"I'm at the hotel, if that helps," Meredith ventured. "Do you two happen to have any drones?"

"Uh, no," Abby stammered. "We're…just passing through."

Meredith adjusted her bathrobe. She'd only meant to go on a test spin, but these were the only two people she'd seen on the streets besides herself since she arrived a couple of days ago. There wasn't even any litter populating the streets. She absently applied her chap stick.

Abby's heart sank at the prospect of going all the way to the hotel. It was down the road. Six or seven minutes' slow walk. Chad licked his lips. "We — I — well, it's just, the heat. Yeah. It's different than out west. There's wind when we need it."

"Why don't we let you folks find more comfortable arrangements?" Thatcher suggested diplomatically.

"If I could," Meredith interjected, "I'd really like to have a word with those of you using drones. Do you have a club, or a place to meet?"

"We have clubs in spades!" Shore said.

"Please stop," said Crumb.

"Aced it!" Shore retorted with a chuckle. There was another whump, and his wife's voice distantly came through with, "Be good, dear."

"Yeah," Abby said, louder than she meant to, "let's be on our way."

"N-nice meeting you!" Chad said and waved as the machines all bade their farewells and flew away together. He was running almost the moment they turned away.

Abby watched only long enough to notice that "Incenio" was flying far more skillfully than the other three pilots. He had more cameras, too. Then she ran after Chad. She was still in her biking gear, and sweating bullets, but couldn't stop to take them off.

They tried two doors before barrelling into a house. As soon as they were in, Abby took off her chaps and her jacket, recklessly tossing her red hair about as though struggling with a spider web. Chad stood farther in, hands on knees, catching his breath.

"Hello," said a Hispanic man.

They both jumped.

"It's all right," he said placidly. "I won't hurt you."

The pair looked at each other. Abby awkwardly gathered up her things. The man leaned against the wall of the hallway, entirely at ease. He had lithe musculature. His eyes were chocolate brown and sharp as nails.

He wore jeans and a Slipknot T-shirt.

"Who…?" started Chad.

"Please, set that down there," the man said, pointing to a two-level bookshelf at the beginning of the hallway. Since she had nothing better to do, Abby obliged. As she and Chad stepped through the doorway out of the porch, the stranger stood properly and turned around. "Join me," he spoke without looking back at them. "I was just brewing tea."

They found themselves in a kitchen/dining room combo. Three piping mugs soon adorned the table. The door to the back yard — little more than a patch of grass between two fences — was just past the table.

Abby sat and started drinking the tea without a word, watching the man curiously. Chad stood with his hands on the back of a chair. The stranger sat and sipped. Chad looked between the two in bewilderment, then turned his attention to the stranger. "You're not in any of the pictures I've seen in the house. And all the people in the pictures are white."

Abby sputtered.

"That's because this isn't my house," the man replied amicably.

Abby put down her mug. "Okay, what's going on here?"

She kept darting uncomfortable glances at Chad. Steam wafted past him, tea untouched, as he sat and levelled his best glare at the stranger.

"My name is Geronimo," said the Hispanic as he took another sip of tea. His calm gaze centred upon Abby.

She absently tossed some of her red hair with her left hand. Her right gripped the handle of the mug. "Why are you here if this isn't your house?"

Gripping his mug with both hands, Geronimo sighed. "Step outside," he said, nodding to the door that was barely four feet from Abby.

"You're being weird," Chad pointed out. "Why should we do anything you say?"

"Just do it," Geronimo replied, looking Chad in the eye.

"Look, clearly something is wrong with this town," Abby joined in before Chad could test his luck. "Why won't you just fill us in?"

"Step outside."

Abby stood suddenly and headed for the door. "Ah, hey," Chad interjected, turning his head but keeping his eyes on Geronimo. "Don't."

She looked out the window. "It's not a big yard."

"Step outside."

"We're gonna leave soon," Chad said, "but you should at least tell us why you're in this house. Did you hurt—"

"Step outside."

Abby inspected the door, looking through its window every which way. "No sign of anything off," she remarked.

"Step outside."

"Dammit," Chad started, but Abby put her hand on the knob.

Silence.

"This is rubbish," Abby said, taking her hand off the knob. "Just answer wo-"

"Step. Out. Side."

Abby looked out the window.

Chad stood and walked around the table on her side, either to be closer to Abby or farther from Geronimo. He opened his mouth, half-lifting a hand toward her, but said nothing as she moved.

As the Hispanic lifted his mug to his lips again, the redhead took a deep breath. She took another. Sweat sheened her brow. Swiftly, she yanked the door open and stood upon the back step of the house. The door could not close behind her before she bolted back in.

"Care to try?" After three heartbeats, Chad realized Geronimo was talking to him. He stared at the door. He wiped his lips.

His tea was untouched.

Glancing at Abby, he turned to face Geronimo head-on. "We're done here. Play your games with someone else."

With that, Chad marched out of the room. He heard footsteps behind him. Turning left in the hallway, he entered the living room with the intention of looking out the large window there.

Geronimo leaned against the entryway, arms folded, and said, "Card fan?"

Chad was surprised by a thin surge of hope and kept his expression flat.

"Care for some poker? I have an open pack in the other room."

"We're not settling in," Abby cut in. She looked at Chad.

He stayed silent. She shifted and sweat made her clothes feel more ragged than they really were. Swallowing, she marched to the window to study the unpeopled world outside.

"I've been here three weeks," Geronimo said suddenly.

The pair faced him.

"Awful lot of drones in the air," Abby remarked.

"What's going on in this town?" Chad finally asked.

"I'm not sure," Geronimo sighed.

Abby repeated her earlier sentiment: "We can't stay."

"You can't leave," answered Geronimo a little too quickly. An edge in his tone recalled fear, but Abby couldn't tell if it was to threaten or implore.

Chad took out his phone and started typing.

Geronimo started, "Who are y—"

"Never mind," said Abby. Then: "We should leave as a group."

Geronimo and Chad looked at each other and then the woman. "I thought we didn't trust him?" Chad pointed out as he returned his phone to his pocket. His text to Victor had been simple: **Something's wrong not sure what with Abby can't leave.**

"If we stick together," Abby reasoned, "we might be able to work through whatever's making us want to stay inside."

Geronimo shook his head. "I can't be seen."

The pair looked at each other. Chad voiced the obvious suspicion: "What happened to the people who lived here?"

Geronimo blinked, then laughed. "The place was empty. Didn't you see my car on the lawn?"

Abby returned to the window. The grass was torn in two swathes of the tires' violence. "I guess we were in such a rush to get in…"

"Well, you weren't the only ones," Geronimo pointed out.

There was a pause. Chad took a deep breath. "Three weeks, huh?"

Geronimo looked away, but then nodded.

Abby marched out of the room, Chad in tow.

Geronimo was slow to follow and spoke as they were putting on shoes. Abby looked at her road gear and wished she'd thought to take it off as soon as she'd gotten off the bike. But the panic…

Geronimo stood squarely in the hallway. "Where are you going?"

They had their shoes on. Abby's chaps and jacket were still on the bookshelf. The pair looked at each other. "Not sure," Chad replied.

"We have to keep moving," Abby added. Suddenly, she picked up her road gear and held it out to the Hispanic. "Gerry," she said, ignoring his twitch at the name, "there's a motorcycle next to a car at the diner's parking lot. We did the same parking job you did." She felt a flush of self-consciousness, but soldiered on: "Please leave my stuff with that bike. I'd like to be able to leave in a hurry, and I'm too warm with them on."

"I can't leave," he said flatly.

"We have to fight this," she said. "Keep your head

down and just do it. Don't look around. No one's watching."

Chad watched as the man stepped forward and slowly retrieved her gear. Neither of the two noticed his wonder.

Abby had her phone out. "Give me your number."

Geronimo frowned.

"Just do it," Chad said. "She stepped out the back to make your point. It's your turn."

They exchanged numbers.

Abby called him, right in front of him. The Hispanic looked at his phone. "Is this some white girl game?"

She held his gaze, her phone at her ear. "Just keep talking to me, focus on getting my stuff to the bike, then come straight back here. That's all you have to do."

"I don't have to—"

She ripped open the front door, forced a nonplussed Chad through, and marched them both to the right. Over her shoulder and into her phone, she barked at Geronimo. "Out the door, head down, move, move, move!"

Chad looked back at her in astonishment, but she pushed hard at his shoulder with her free hand, facing him forward again. As soon as Geronimo was out the door, he tried to turn back, but she rushed back and pulled it closed, shouldering at the muscled man. She didn't have the brawn to much affect him, but she just kept ordering: "Move! Gear to bike! Move!"

She jabbed a finger for Chad's benefit. "We're going to the hotel!"

"Why-" Chad started.

"We just are." It was almost totally windless, and her

hair felt like spider webs.

"I could grab my car," huffed Geronimo.

"No!"

"I'm clo—"

"Bike! Gear! Move!" She turned as she ran. "I said NO! Not the car! Run to the diner! GO!"

Tears stung Chad's eyes. He forced them on the hotel down the road. A doorway went by.

The houses registered less than the doors. Once, Abby started to veer to one of them. He pulled her back on course. But she did the same for him twice. Somewhere nearby, dogs were barking. Then he was inside and felt hollow. It took him a moment to realize that it was the emotional echo of having slammed the door behind him. It opened again almost immediately.

Abby demanded, "What are you doing? We need to kee—"

Even as they were breathing hard, they had to plug their noses. With the blood rushing in their ears, the buzzing was also slow to get through to them. They glanced at each other as they stepped past the living room. There were pictures, books, and figurines with a pirate theme, as well as some posters, maps, and travel books. "We need to..." and she walked, hypnotically, towards the buzzing.

She knew she should get out of the house. She knew there was nothing those flies could show her that she'd want to see. She pictured herself returning to the front door. Bullets smashing through it, feet and black clothes and shouting. Something erased. Fire and guilt.

Stars were gathering in her eyes before she realized

she was holding her breath. She was at a threshold. One hand pinched her nose and covered her mouth so she could keep out the thickening cloud.

She felt sick, but she had to know. Steeling herself, she hastily stepped into the doorway.

A body hung from the ceiling of a walk-in closet. Mercifully, she couldn't get a good look with all the flies about. Back in the living room she found Chad listening to the answering machine.

"...we're sorry about the inconvenience, but please stop calling about the barking. We're a dog pound. Consider finding a more suitable..."

She tuned it out as she headed for the front door.

"Geronimo?" she said thickly to the phone shaking in her hand. He'd hung up. When had that happened?

Chad was the white of ice as they reached the door.

Her hand was on the knob.

"I don't have his number," Chad muttered.

"I can't..." her voice cracked. It was just a door. The sunlight was lovely. No wind and a stray cloud or two. In the distance, barking.

"Close your eyes," Chad said.

"What?"

"Look, I don't know how you got us this far, but I think you were on to something about working together. Turn the knob, Abby."

Her breathing was heavy because she was standing in front of an open door with her eyes closed.

"Follow the wall," she said. "We'll both have to keep our eyes closed."

He hadn't realized he's stepped backward. His heart

fired a hard pulse of embarrassment.

Bordering on hyperventilation, she clung to the wall with most of her right side, pushing the door as far back as it would go while she slowly wormed her way over the threshold. All the while they talked: "Did you get Geronimo's number too?"

He kept moving. She heard him fumble for his phone. "No, but I'm getting messages."

They made it to the corner of the house. Ahead was a T-section. From somewhere to her right, she could hear jingling metal, accented by panting or the sound of lapping water. "I think I found the dog pound. This town is really quiet."

"Except the drones."

"Yeah," she said. "Are you okay?"

"I...I can't do this."

"Yes, you can. What were the messages?"

"I can't right now. I need to focus on..." He fidgeted behind her.

"...whatever's keeping people indoors," she finished for him.

Abby had her face pressed against the siding of the house. She was hugging the corner with her eyes closed. "All right," she said, "I'm gonna cross the str-..." she swallowed. "...the street." Taking two deep breaths, she opened her eyes and ran for all she was worth. Chad was beside her. They did their best not to look at the houses. Her eyes were on the sidewalk.

When she looked up to get her bearings, a lovely blue door caught her eye. She was through it before she even realized what she was doing.

"Abby? ABBY!?" burst through her focus. It was coming from Chad, outside.

There was a soft, feminine sound from the stairwell around the corner from the porch where she stood. It was like a high-pitched groan, almost a whine. "I...um..." she said to while she walked the five or six feet it took to investigate.

"Come back!" Chad said. "We can't stay inside!" He had his eyes closed, body pressed against the wall, fighting the urge to go in.

"Oh my god..." Abby whispered as she turned to find an old woman crumpled at the bottom of the stairs. She looked like a poorly bagged bundle of broken sticks. The woman looked up at her and suddenly all pain melted from the senior's expression. There is a glint in a person's eye when they are ready to sleep, and ready to say goodbye. Like starlight on black water, it shifted just once as the elderly woman noticed the young one.

Then it was still.

Abby raised her hand to her mouth at the heartbreaking sight, only to notice the air in front of her rippling with rapidly growing waves of heat.

Chad felt it. "Abby?"

Something was wrong.

Thatcher paced his basement, running the fingers of both hands through his head of hefty but clean hair. He hated the stereotype of the unwashed nerd. His fingernails were meticulously filed and his hair well-brushed. Almost giddy with nervous energy, he'd cleared away the garbage in the basement, vacuumed and dusted, and was now struggling with what to do. He'd tried a dozen games to distract himself, including the MMO Eve Online and some roleplay chat rooms, but the situation was irking him. A file for an e-book in the niche genre of litRPG sat open but unread on the left screen of his computer setup.

The right screen showed Instagram. He'd phished to get access to a townsperson's account so as to remove their post about all the drone activity, then changed their password so they wouldn't be able to do it again. Something was wrong in this town, and he needed all his ducks in a row to deal with it. How had he come to be responsible for so much? It was like people were only driven when he was, and they withdrew when he did.

But that was ridiculous.

The centre screen now showed a message from Kagami, an albino Japanophile he knew from his circle of drone friends. Her message said that a redhead and a blond had been seen running from a house that was now on fire, according to a friend who'd messaged her. Still no answer from Crossbones, the cynophobic fan of pirates.

He'd started pacing after a surge of problems: a fight had broken out in the hospital. Someone barred the mental health ward in an act of cowardice that he thought was barbaric. People were panicking. The hospital's Internet went down, and no one was sure why. A massive rat problem had cropped up around the grocery store because it had been unattended for so long.

Thatcher was furious. What was everyone hiding from?

He marched over to the ground-level window and peeked out through the curtain. No more rock doves. Upstairs, he went to the guest room, where he kept his drone.

Daylight cast a slightly blue hue through the closed curtain. Now that he was finished with maintenance and battery charging, he brought it out to the front door and set it down in the porch. The blinds on the door were closed. Returning to the basement, he began his flight routine, changing all the screens of the computer display to the drone's cameras.

He was proud of how skilled he'd become. He was able to make it lift off, open the door, and close the door behind it.

Geronimo was finding it harder to stay outside with every door he passed. He rounded a corner, considering jumping more fences. He was back on the street he started and realized that the hotel was far in front of him. Beyond that would be the place where he'd been staying.

"Who the devil are you!? Get off my lawn!" someone shouted at him.

A drone, sidelong to Geronimo, flew out of a house on a side street. Smoke was rising from a couple of blocks away. He was running, trying to get away from a cloud of drones that kept bombarding him with questions. He was wearing a ski mask he kept in his pocket in case he needed to quickly cover his face. They couldn't know who he was. That was critical.

Chad and Abby, meanwhile, ran at the hotel. It had floor-to-ceiling windows. People inside were staring. They made a mad dash for the front door.

Thatcher guided his drone toward the pillar of smoke and rose higher to try for a better view. *What was taking the fire department?* He cursed the warm, dry weather. The fire had spread. Messages started popping up on his screen.

He couldn't keep up with most of them. One was disturbing:

Shore: Crumb's drone just dropped out of the air!

He noticed then that there were several rooftops with drones on them. Doing nothing. One was near solar panels. Was it charging? There could have been any number of reasons. But with so many drones in the air, he shouldn't have been that surprised — what goes up and all that. At least two houses near the fire had caught. Was Crumb in one of them?

He flew to the closest house, where he saw someone in the living room window. What was that glitter? As he approached, the figure disappeared. Nearing the front door, he was shocked when it whipped open and projectiles began bouncing off of his precious drone. The man in the door was wearing — Thatcher couldn't believe it — a tin foil hat.

An actual, straight-up, tin foil hat.

The man was shouting: "I KNEW YOU'D COME! But no alien's takin' Ashton James!"

"Stop it! I'm not—"

"I know you're putting that fear in me! Well, I'M NOT AFRAID OF YOU!"

Thatcher didn't bother pointing out the contradiction. "Your house is on fi—"

"Yeah! Tryin' ta smoke me out! IT WON'T WORK! Ain't no alien probing me!"

"Listen! Stop!" But even as he shouted, Thatcher had to withdraw. There was too much going on. Even as he backed it out and away, his fingers flew over the keyboard.

He was looking for the town fire department, trying to get in contact with the hospital or an ambulance service, reaching out to his drone friends, and flying his own drone in search of the newcomers who've been making ripples in the grapevine since that morning. Then he remembered: there was a woman from Humdroid. Was this about competition with a drone company? Would they do that?

He turned his drone toward the hotel.

Abby was in the lobby. Meredith entered from a hallway, wondering what all the commotion was about.

"Lady," said one of the tenants, "you're loco. We don't have to go on a field trip with you!"

"I'm not saying all of you need to leave! Just one of you! Anyone!" Abby had both hands in front of her, pleading with a small gathering. Chad stood closer to the door, struggling to come up with a better game plan than simply getting people out of doors until things make sense.

The clerk had stepped out from the counter and was busily sweeping the area and washing surfaces. He checked his mask obsessively and tried to only be around people when he was behind them.

The black man Meredith met in the corridor when she arrived stepped forward. "Young lady," he said, "I think perhaps you're having some trouble with the sun…"

"Stop calling me lady!"

Meredith wended her way through the group. "Excuse me," she said with well-honed business tact, "but may I ask what it is you're looking for?"

"I need help," Abby replied.

"Obviously," someone snarked beneath her breath.

Abby ignored the other woman.

"I just docked my drone to charge," Meredith said. "I noticed a fire…"

Abby's lip quivered. She shook her head. "That's gonna have to be for the fire department," she replied.

Before she could continue, a passing maid said, "They won't come. Bunch of lazy good-for-nothings at town hall…"

There was general assent. "People here are weird," said a young Hispanic boy. He was holding the hand of the man who'd called Abby "loco."

"I'm just waiting to get my affairs in order," said a middle-aged woman who was checking her cell phone compulsively. "Then I'm out of here."

"Yeah," said a teenaged girl. "If I could breathe a little better, I'd be gone too."

"But you got the air tank you said you were waiting for," pointed out the black man's daughter.

Incensed, the teenager folded her arms. The oxygen tank was in her bookbag, and tubes led from there to her nose. "I can't drive with that thing hooked up to me. I'm waiting for my family."

Meredith stepped closer to Abby as the rest of the group began getting into similar stories and questioning each other. "I need more cleaning supplies!" the clerk called out to the same maid, who was now headed in the other direction.

"What kind of help did you need?" she asked, leaning forward to be heard over the rising din. Snippets got in: something about insects. Another person didn't trust the chemicals in the air outside, complaining that the highway should be patrolled for trucks with questionable products.

Abby opened her mouth, unsure of how to respond. A woman started crying, saying there were predators and that she couldn't leave "while the police were lazing about."

Someone kicked over a chair and started shouting. Abby grabbed Meredith and pulled her to the door. "Something's wrong," she said simply.

"Yes, I got that," Meredith said, "but please don't yank on me. Stop. No, wait!"

But Abby nearly dragged her to the door. "Step outside."

Chad put a hand on Abby's arm. She locked eyes with him and realized that she was feeling the same distress. She released the other woman.

Meredith took in the lovely sunny day. A butterfly flew past the windows. Drones danced distantly in the sky. "What's this about?" Meredith objected.

"We're not sure yet," Chad said.

Abby added, "Just step outside."

"We should get this—" Meredith started, turning toward the frothing of the crowd.

"We need to go," Abby cut her off.

Meredith looked at the door — and through it — with frustration. She glanced at Chad, Abby, and the crowd behind her. "Some of these people have been here for weeks…"

"You're new here?" Abby asked.

The Humdroid employee nodded.

"That explains why you seem more level-headed…"

Chad mused aloud.

"I'm a professional," Meredith bristled. When neither moved, a fog of doubt descended upon her. And there was a sense of urgency she couldn't explain, like she had a thousand things to look into and no one to help her. She ran a hand through her hair. "I'm not really staying to make a better business case for when I leave, am I?"

"Probably not," Abby agreed. Then: "Hold my hand."

People started throwing punches. A hollow and muffled metallic *ding* rang out as the girl with the oxygen tank hit the floor. Chad watched the crowd with mounting horror. Meredith blinked at the redhead, but she slowly complied. Then Abby locked elbows with Chad.

The crowd was getting out of hand. Two children were crying. Someone was screaming. The clerk was shouting for them to stop.

Meredith and Abby stood by the door, a window set in a wall of windows. Some pigeons landed on the ground to the left of the door and congregated with a calm that Abby couldn't understand. Couldn't they see the fighting? Why weren't they concerned?

"Look at me," Abby said.

"This is crazy," said Meredith.

Abby nodded. She and Chad began barrelling them all through the door. "No one stays behind," Chad said.

Every time one of them was about to give up and turn back inside, the others pushed forward.

On the fourth attempt, they got out of the hotel.

Thatcher was torn. He'd just caught sight of the entangled trio as they half-shambled, half-ran in the middle of the road. They looked ridiculous. He followed them as they went right from the door, eventually turning right again — onto his street. He couldn't tell what they were thinking.

As the trio made that turn, Chad looked up and huffed, "Is that Gerry?" The mask didn't hide the outfit, the build, or the style of movement.

Thatcher mostly just saw the cloud of drones. They seemed to be harassing someone, but they were too far away for him to identify. He cursed the drone cameras; if their resolution were a little better...

He spun the drone around to see if there were anything else in the area, just in time to see another one. "Look out!" he shouted uselessly as there was a collision. His screens turned to snow.

In unison, the trio wailed in dismay and tumbled all over each other. "What was that!?" Chad sputtered as he and the others picked themselves up.

Abby said, "You felt it too?" And immediately felt stupid; they'd all wailed.

Meredith watched this "Gerry" use his size twelve skeleton key to enter two doors down. Without thinking, she yanked the others once and simply ran after him.

As soon as they were inside, Chad savaged his way down the second set of stairs to the left. The first went up. The front door was broken behind them, and something primal made the lower levels radiate safety. Abby clung to the closest thing she could find. It was the rail. Gerry was in the kitchen ahead of them, turning and looking back at them with heaving lungs. Meredith was sprawled out on the floor. Everyone had a flood of emotions that included terror and…

"Are you…does that…?" Meredith struggled to pull herself up from the floor and the panic.

"It's like…" Abby wiped her eyes and nose "…like, I dunno, puberty or something. It's all coming at me at once."

Meredith was nodding as they both heard Thatcher. He was standing in the centre of his basement room, regarding Chad with outrage. "Who are you, and why are you in my house?"

Chad's hands were up, palm out. "Listen," he started.

The two women stepped down to the half-landing, so that they had to crouch to see Thatcher over Chad's shoulder. The three intruders were visibly trembling. Thatcher's eyes were glassy with suspicion and fear.

"I know you!" The Hispanic's voice was higher in pitch because of his mounting panic. His breaths came shallow and quick, and sweat beaded his forehead. "Chad and Abby!" He pointed at them frantically.

"Incenio," Chad's eyes widened as he spoke. "Why are…how did…" The card aficionado was looking at the three-screen setup behind Thatcher with a kind of awe. There was nothing but snow, but still: what had the Hispanic been up to?

"You're not how I pictured you from your voice," Abby remarked. Chad turned, and both he and Meredith regarded Abby with incredulity. "…what?" She asked. Her speech, like Chad's, was tight and strained.

"I get that a lot," the pilot of Incenio replied dryly. "Now, what the hell are you doing in my house?" With Herculean effort, he was suppressing his terror with glib humour.

Someone's phone was vibrating.

"Aren't you going to get that?" asked Meredith.

Thatcher noticed that these three seemed to be calming the more that he worked down his fear, controlled his breathing, and strove to come across to them as poised. In fact, they seemed to be mirroring him. But that was ludicrous. He was just thrown off by their presence.

The Hispanic gauged the three intruders. They did not seem eager to hurt him. His nervousness jangled with every vibration of Chad's phone. Abby and Meredith both shivered the way that Thatcher wanted to.

"Are you the one doing this to Towerton?" Abby asked. Meredith merely watched the Hispanic. Chad furrowed his brow.

"Doing what?" Thatcher asked. He mused about how he might fight the three of them off. The Internet was his best and most comfortable weapon, but it didn't use bullets.

"You're not gonna tell me you didn't know something's not right?" Chad scoffed.

Thatcher regarded the intruder with open hostility. "Yeah. Like, why are you in my house?"

The three looked at each other, suddenly abashed.

Thatcher pressed his advantage: "Get out and I'll give you a head start before calling the cops."

"Okay, okay, let's not get ahead of ourselves…" Meredith chimed in.

"Maybe we should all sit down?" Abby offered.

Thatcher frowned. "This is my house. What are you gringos doing?"

"Hey!" Chad stood up a little straighter.

"Get," Thatcher punctuated, looking the other man in the eye, "Out."

"Please," Abby said. It came out with Thatcher's hostility, which confused her.

Chad decided to take a gamble: "Look, we came here because something's wrong. It's been noticed. And now that we're here—"

"I don't care," Thatcher interrupted. "For the last time," and his voice rose, "Get! Out!"

They all felt a ballooning mixture of anger, fear, pride, and outrage. But there was also an awkward, embarrassed flush. Chad stepped forward to speak, and then there were footsteps upstairs. "Hello?" called Geronimo's voice.

Unaccountably, everyone in the room had a cold shock run from heartbeat to rising hair.

Thatcher frowned and looked up at the stairs behind the trio, muttering, "Geronimo?"

The well-muscled Hispanic man appeared at the top of the stairs just as the trio began talking at once. Everyone turned to face him.

"Who are you?" asked Meredith.

Then there was an impossible flare of rage. Everyone's knuckles went bone white with it, though four of the people there didn't know where it was coming from.

Thatcher roared, "WHAT ARE YOU DOING HERE!?"

"So, it's true!" Geronimo declared as he bulled his way down the stairs. The women had to flatten against the wall to get out of the way, and Chad stepped aside.

"GET OUT!" Thatcher roared. He looked around,

weaponless.

To everyone's surprise, Chad stepped forward and slugged Geronimo in the face. He nursed his hand as his target, barely phased, stared at him in surprise.

The muscular man said, "What was that?"

"I...I don't know," replied a throbbing and baffled Chad.

Every heart in the room pulsed with confusion and electric anger.

"Why is everyone treating my house like Town Hall?" Thatcher demanded. "And how dare you?" He was looking at Geronimo.

The well-muscled Hispanic regarded the pudgy, pale Hispanic with a closed fist, a tense jaw, and eyes that shone with sadness. "I have some explaining to do..."

Thatcher barked a mirthless laugh. "Finally catching on, huh?"

"You never would call me Dad..." the man sighed.

Thatcher flared. "A foster father isn't a father!"

"I suppose I should introduce myself," Geronimo replied. "My name is..." he managed slowly.

"Geronimo," Thatcher interrupted. "Yes, yes, now tell m—"

"...Soto," the man continued. Abby and Chad had a moment of small, static emotional shock. Then it was as though everyone's skulls were suffused with thunder and blood. "Soto Verra," he finished with obvious gravity, turning back to Thatcher.

The younger Hispanic never said a word, but the other three exploded in rage. "Why did you lie to us!?" Abby demanded. Tears burned their way down her cheeks. Yet here she was, in Thatcher's house, an intruder furious at an intrusion.

Meredith was silent. Her expression shifted as she looked at each person who spoke. Everything had gravity, as if the situation were hers personally. But she didn't know these people. There was no context for the anger, resentment, shock, and so on. What was going on?

Chad was experiencing a different transportation of wrath. He stood stock still and stared at Soto as though seeing into or through the other man. Everyone was white-knuckled.

Thatcher cursed. Once. In Spanish. Everything grew still. There was a crashing sound in the distance. People were shouting, but it was so faint as only to be heard in quiet.

"I had to protect you," Soto said.

Everyone felt sick inside. Chad remained a colossus of stillness.

Thatcher, too, stared at the older Hispanic. "That's your play? You weren't keeping me in a bubble, Gerry."

"Son, please—"

"I am not your son!"

Soto held out an ID card. Thatcher wasn't interested, but Chad could see it from where he was standing. Soto Verra, Shane Industries.

"What's going on here?" Meredith said.

Soto sighed. He turned to the trio. "I'm his father."

"Bullshit!" Thatcher erupted. "You fostered me when I was almost old enough to move out!"

"I chased you in the system for years."

"Chad?" Abby stepped forward and laid a hand on

his shoulder. He didn't respond.

Soto searched Chad's eyes. He looked at the women. "Please, let us have a moment of privacy."

"No," Thatcher said sharply. Suddenly, the strangers were less frightening than just being alone with...Soto. "Enough is enough. I'm a grown man now, and I'll have answers."

"Seems we're all kinda lost," Meredith remarked.

There was another brief silence, punctuated by distant shouts, crashing sounds, the shattering of a door, and screams.

"I really am—" Soto started.

Thatcher's interruption was harsh and sudden. "You there. What are you staring at?" Abby had to shake Chad's shoulder before he blinked, frowned, and looked at her. "Answer me!" pressed their host.

Chad looked between Thatcher and Abby, then sheepishly watched his shoes. "I'm...I'm not sure. I mean, I wanted bad luck for...uh...Soto, but..." and he ineffectually rolled his hands a few times as if to wring words from the air.

Soto was shocked. "Whatever for?"

"We're all angry at you," Abby said, looking around at everyone. "I think you're even angry at yourself." Her voice hushed and took on a hollow tone: "...but I don't know where that's coming from."

Chad's mouth worked, but he didn't have any answers. Luck should be either good or gone. He was remembering coming home once to his door ajar. He'd never forget that feeling of the world falling away from under him. That's what bad luck meant to him. What could have made him so angry that he'd wish that on someone?

Soto had turned back to Thatcher, who spoke with poison. "I can't blame you guys for instantly finding him gross. He's a slimeball."

Abby was the only one to notice that Soto's spine had stiffened at that remark.

Soto never said a word.

The younger Hispanic pressed his case: "Now, for the last time: why are you people here?"

"We ran," Meredith said simply.

Chad wiped his brow. With every word, every action, new emotions kept washing over them. They were breaking into a cold sweat trying to make sense of it all.

Abby took a chance: "We're part of a group that goes to places with…trouble."

Both Hispanics turned to regard her anew. They spoke at the same time.

Soto: "You never said…"

Thatcher: "What kind? Why?"

Chad swallowed. "There's something wrong with this town," he responded. "Getting outside is terrifying for some reason."

Thatcher frowned. "That's ridiculous."

"It's true," Soto said, turning back to the younger man. "I've been here for weeks, but couldn't get to you because I couldn't leave the house."

"But you managed to get a house," Thatcher pointed out.

"It wasn't his," Abby and Chad said together.

Meredith had her hand to her mouth. Her eyes were darting at each of them, and out the window.

"It was the one I turned to when I couldn't take it anymore. I even skidded to a stop right on the front lawn." Thatcher's eyes widened with recognition, but he didn't interrupt. "But I came here alone. So once I got inside, and found the owners were out, I had to stay." Soto clenched a fist. A bead of cold sweat travelled down the side of his head. His nostrils flared.

So many questions.

Thatcher's jaw tightened. "What did you mean when you said you found me?"

"I put you in foster care, ran, and changed my name," Soto explained.

"Guys," Meredith started.

"Why would I believe you?" Thatcher said. "My parents are dead."

Soto's voice was hoarse. "Your mother was missing. Reported dead. That's not the same. I don't know if she is or not, but I've been trying to find out."

"I was in the system for a decade before you showed up," Thatcher spat. "Why then? Why are you back? Did you follow me, you creep?"

"We have a prob—" Meredith tried again.

"I was involved in..." Soto sighed, gestured inarticulately, and tugged at one ear. "...look, I came back for you. But I had to protect you."

"You can't protect me if you're not around. Even if you are my dad — which you're not."

Uncertainty was an acid inside of everyone in the room.

"I had to be far from you to keep you safe. Look, there's a lot—"

"GUYS!" Meredith finally shouted.

Everyone turned to her.

"Don't you hear what's happening?" and she stood tall now, every bit the proud corporate professional. "Don't you smell it?"

There was a pause. Thatcher sniffed. "...smoke?"

The group looked at each other and ran upstairs. The haze as they hit the top step was a stark contrast to the sheltered basement. They went into the living room. Chad and Abby each took a curtain and pulled them wide, revealing the street to the whole of the window. Ashes were in the air. People were weeping, shouting, screaming. But there were only a few people outside.

And they were surrounded by drones.

There must have been several dozen, flitting about in a frenzied cloud.

There was a loud but dull, cracking crash.

"I've heard that sound before," Soto said. Thatcher looked at him and everyone surged with mistrust. Soto put a hand to his heart and his eyes widened even as his lips thinned to a line. His gaze fell on his son. "I knew you were gifted. This explains a lot."

Thatcher's expression was hard to read. Everyone felt tugs of confusion and curiosity.

"I've heard that sound too," Abby spoke, more against the unknown than for anyone's benefit.

Chad was getting overwhelmed, but decided to move things along: "What was it?"

"A falling beam," Soto answered quietly.

"The whole line of houses must be going up," Thatcher mumbled as he wrestled with Soto's words. He watched as several drones disappeared to the left of his window, towards the neighbour's front door. He cursed in Spanish. "They're pulling the people out!"

Hope. Shock. Pride. A thin fear, like metal wire laced under the surface of the skin. Several of them started coughing.

"We need to get out," Meredith declared. The group moved toward the hallway and found themselves facing the front door.

Drones were flitting about outside, and several of them blared from speakers. "Can anyone make sense of that?" Chad asked.

"I'm hearing some Spanish," Thatcher said, "but there's too much noise."

A drone hovered into view through the broken door. Meredith had a thrill of recognition. "That one's from the hotel!"

Its mechanical wrist twirled and one of its fingers completed a beckoning motion. The group looked amongst each other. "Ladies first," Chad said with a grin in his mouth, not his eyes.

Meredith and Abby both stepped forward. They placed one hand in the other's and the free hand on the front door frame. Soto and Thatcher each looked upon this scene in bewilderment. Chad looked between the pairs and said to the Hispanics, "I don't get it either. But Abby has a way of coming through."

Neither man replied. Thatcher had his eyes glued on the open door, and he was sweating profusely. Everyone started to periodically cough. Soto had a flat expression and folded arms. His eyes went from Thatcher to Chad to Thatcher to the ladies and back to Thatcher, over and over.

From the drone came a female voice none of the men recognized. "All right, I'm gonna grab you now. I'm not here to hurt you, but you have to get out."

The women nodded. Gradually, they took their hands off the door frame and held them out. The drone grabbed them by the wrist. Chad could see that their held hands were becoming white at the edges.

Slowly, the drone began backing up. At first, its progress halted. The women resisted. Then it became an odd sort of wrestling match, as each woman tried to push the other forward. They never said a word, and the drone struggled not to go too much one way or the other — all while continuing to pull them out. Inch by unwilling inch, they made their way beyond the threshold.

Soto looked into the living room, since he was the only one now standing at the edge of the wall of the hallway. Edges and circles were blackening their way into the wall, and smoke was thickening with every passing second. Not far past the front step, the women disappeared into a choking fog.

Chad met Soto's eyes, and they both looked at Thatcher. He was still watching the door.

Another drone appeared in the doorway. "Hey, guys!" came an oddly cheerful male voice. "I've got some friends here. You might hear some windows breaking. Nothing personal, but we need to get you out."

"This is my house!" Thatcher declared with outrage.

Windows broke. There was a burst from the living room. Soto didn't bother to look and stopped Thatcher with a hand on his shoulder when the younger man tried to turn. Both Chad and Thatcher looked at him with venom in their eyes.

Chad shook his head and rubbed his face with one hand. Drones flew in from the back door and upstairs. Thatcher was shouting between coughs, and vainly throwing his untrained girth against Soto's honed muscles. Chad was weeping silently, and not just from the smoke. He put his back to the wall and his head in his hands.

Two drones emerged from the basement, and a female voice remarked, "That's one hell of a computer setup!"

Thatcher shook his fist at that drone, but could only cough incoherently. The hallway was filling with merciless grey. No less than three drones appeared as if coalescing out of the smoke that was the living room. They could hear the raggedness of fire. The drone in the front door was shouting. Chad dimly registered that it had been talking for a while.

The drones could no longer afford to be gentle. In a cloud, they started bullying all three men. Chad gave Soto a glance and they both nodded in agreement. Thatcher was pushing for the stairs back to the basement. They couldn't make out much of what he was saying, other than snatches like "gotta," "rig," and what might have been "life."

Soto and Chad rushed him.

Chad wasn't strong enough to force against Thatcher's sheer weight, but he was making it much more difficult for the other man to get back to the stairs. Soto was suddenly a colossus.

Icy fear gushed beneath the skin and pushed them to blindly fight for their last coherent thought. Thatcher was swarmed by two men and a group of roaring machines. The broken front door banged again and again as the cluster of humanity, both flesh and machine, fought to simply step outside.

Every second of delay was punishing their lungs. Snatches of daylight were peeking through the now billowing smoke. As heat sank into their skin, it sickened them in a claustrophobic way. It was dry but somehow sticky, as though they were drowning in the home — not the house — that melted around them.

Chad could barely register anything anymore as pure panic became his personality. From here on, it was snatches. The smoke changed, thinner but more…everywhere. How had he gotten separated? His eyes stung along with his lungs, and he had the surreal feeling that he was breathing through his blind gaze. In and out, details swirled.

Screaming, weeping, shouting, cursing, crowding. He looked up in time to see a fire truck narrowly miss a cluster of people nearby. It had at least half a dozen drones flying around it, including some of those maintenance ones that had been handling garbage. And was that a mechanical arm at the steering wheel?

More than one drone lay broken in the street. As he continued to run and stumble, he heard them. The smoke was getting a little thinner. He was beginning to see more.

A house.

He ran for it with wild abandon.

A drone crashed nearby. It had simply rained down, as if the battery had died in the air. He slammed into someone else who was running. A lanky man who stumbled heavily after the impact but, unlike Chad, kept his feet. Chad stared at the dead drone next to him, shock warring with everything else. It took him a moment to realize it wasn't the drone he mistrusted.

What did trust have to do with this?

Voices everywhere.

He'd never wanted a basement so much in his life. Anger flared from nowhere.

Chad picked himself up. He stared in wonder for a moment as he looked back the way he'd come. The entire row of houses was a centipede of orange and red hunger, wearing black smoke like a profusion of hair. The fire was ravaging two other blocks at least, from what he could see. As he made a 270 degree turn, five more drones at random intervals simply dropped.

"It's not their batteries..." he couldn't help muttering.

In the distance, past the crowd, he could see Thatcher and Soto fighting at Soto's car. Fear, rage, and something unexpected struck Chad in the spine so hard that he threw up. Even as he heaved, Thatcher was inside the car. Then Chad registered what that unexpected thing had been:

Relief.

It was short-lived: some of the people in the crowd were separating, either from drones or others in the crowd, and running back to the buildings. They were running back inside. Even as the fire spread.

The crowd's eyes were savage. They gleamed with all the wrong kinds of light. The shock of this as he got up from vomiting called him back to the urgency of escape. Dimly, he was aware of Soto's car tearing over lawns and screeching down the other street. The crowd was not people, but oozing humanity, and Chad fled in terror. He was not the only one.

An explosion in the distance didn't much register, but shortly afterward some clattering made him look up as he ran. It was the drone that had helped Thatcher out of the front door, and it had hit the ground at an angle.

Chad stopped for a coughing fit. But the crash of the drone had gotten through his panic enough to make him look around. Not ten feet away, there she was.

"Abby!" he rasped out a shout.

She was on her motorbike, in her bike gear, and looking around. She flipped up her visor when she caught sight of him. Her eyes were wide and a little too still. Chad was running, stumbling, heaving, arms flailing in his desperation. He didn't quite reach her before she turned around and gunned her engine.

She was out of the diner's lot by the time he scrambled into the car. His door was still swinging, the alarm demanding a seatbelt, when he hit the gas. They were out of town, Abby well ahead of him, when he remembered his phone. He tore it out as he drove, swerving a little past the centre line while he checked it.

Seven missed messages, all but one from Tasha.

One missed call from Victor.

"F-," he started, and lost the rest of the word to a coughing fit. Looking up through cough-teared eyes, he could see Abby's shoulders rack and heave. Her hand went up to wipe at her visor.

They both pulled over. Chad opened his door, sitting sideways with his feet on the ground. He wept openly, holding his phone out for Abby. She swung off her bike, lifting her visor up. She'd sprayed it with spit from coughing while she was rushing to get it on. As she absently relieved Chad of his phone, her eyes were on the town.

Smoke clouds outgrew and outnumbered the clouds of drones, which were in a flurry. There were little pops and bursts as buildings collapsed on themselves and various things — like BBQ propane tanks in back yards — were exposed to the unchecked fire.

Meredith was dead centre in the crowd. She watched a drone get caught by three members of the mob, who tilted it downward and proceeded to slam it, camera first, into the street. Only a few minutes after the car containing the two Hispanics had roared away, everything had shifted. That nameless urgency had vanished. Everyone else, though, was filling a vacuum. She could see it: they'd lived with whatever had been here, and now that it was gone, the hole needed filling.

She watched the windows of a house let out a scintillating scream, but couldn't tell what made them explode.

Soto's wild driving began to ease once they got out of town. They were on the highway by the time Chad and Abby left the diner's lot. "In through your nose," he said, "and out through your mouth."

Thatcher was huddled into himself, coughing and wiping at tears and mucus. "What?"

"Focus on your breathing," Soto said through a half-suppressed cough. His fitness meant that he didn't struggle as much with the smoke damage.

"F-," Thatcher started, and coughed again. *My rig. My life. All of it. All I have are my clothes!*

"Breathe in. Count for six seconds. In. Breathe in.

There you go," Soto continued to coach as he drove. It was keeping his hands steady on the steering wheel. "In for six. Hold two. Out for four. Mouth. Out of your mouth. Start again. In six. Use your nose. I know it's hard right now, but just focus on this. There's nothing else. Nose six. Hold two. Mouth four." He continued this litany for almost forty-five minutes, interrupting whenever Thatcher tried to speak or do anything else.

The routine was hindered by their coughing. They'd need attention. Soto noticed in the rear-view mirror that emergency vehicles from a nearby town were heading out. They must have caught word of the disaster. "You've kidnapped me," Thatcher said, but he found he just couldn't muster the rage he wanted. He stared at the man he'd known as Geronimo, unblinking and resentful, and wanted very much not to have to keep following this breathing routine.

"I've saved your life," Soto corrected. He was exhaustion in human form. "Agoraphobia is a slow poison."

Thatcher was watching the windshield, no longer paying attention to the road. On the windshield was a scratch, most likely from something they'd plowed through in their panicked escape. He stared at it. "I don't have any phobias," he bit out.

"The whole town had it. I had it when I came, that's why I couldn't get to you sooner."

They argued about what happened for hours, and argued more when Soto refused to go to a hospital or a hotel, but insisted they'd need medical attention. Food. Rest.

"What's your plan, then?" Thatcher demanded.

TIMELINE II

I can recall with perfect clarity the day my wife died.

I woke up in my bed alone. My eyes snapped open staring at a too-bright sun, smelling the fatty strips of bacon on the air, and hearing the "da da da's" and "la la la's" of Jennifer singing to herself as she prepared our eggs.

I pushed off the covers and planted my feet on the floor. I resisted the urge to bolt down the stairs as naked as the day I'd been made, as making haste would do little. I dressed as quickly as I could, stumbling several times the way one does when one is rushing a simple task. As I was pulling on my pants, I yelled down the stairs. "Jennifer," I said, not angrily but assertively. "Take the food off the burner!"

I was still adjusting my shirt when I turned the corner in the kitchen to see that Jennifer was still at the stove. She smiled at me quizzically when I saw her, having heard what I called but having paid it no mind.

When I saw that smile, tilted to one side quirkily, her hair falling onto her shoulders in wisps, I had to stop and kiss her, and cup her tiny chin in my palm. When I made myself pull back from her, I took the handle of the frying pan from her gently and moved it to an inactive burner, then turned the stove off altogether.

"What are you doing?" she asked, rightfully irritated but also slightly amused at my odd behavior.

"We have to go into Signet," I said as I rested my hand on her hip and led her away from the kitchen. She followed me, trustingly. We trust each other in that way.

"Signet? We're going into town today for—"

"There's something wrong with the baby," I interrupted. She stopped mid-step in the middle of our kitchen, no longer obeying my gentle coaxing toward our front porch. She stared at me for a long, bewildered moment, then moved with as much haste as her cumbersome form would allow and went with me to get ready. She didn't ask how I know, not then. As I said, we trust each other.

We drove the Jeep through the York Market quicker than was safe: faster, honestly, than I had ever seen anyone do it. There were curses and yells behind me, and I saw fists shaking in the air several times when I glanced in my rear-view mirror. Anyone who recognized me — and to be sure at least one would — would give me a hard time the next time I came to trade, but I would explain about the baby and they would understand... or they wouldn't, I cared not at that point. Jennifer was all that mattered, Jennifer and the baby.

I drove through town, an area typically devoid of any vehicles at all, doing 120k. Jennifer touched my arm several times to try and slow me down or at least broach the subject, but never vocalized it. There was something in my eyes or in the tense way I held the wheel perhaps that told her not to — or perhaps it was her own hand, which I saw in my peripheral vision travel to her stomach more than once and press tightly.

She could feel something. Had she felt it before and ignored it? Or was this some sort of psychosomatic response: my assertion that there was something wrong with the baby causing it to be true? Driving at the upper edge of 120k through tight streets left little time for such philosophies, and they were gone from me as quickly as they'd come.

When we escaped York and entered the hills between it and Signet, I put on even more speed, careful to ease off as we topped each hill for fear of catching air and causing an impact that would affect Jennifer's unknowingly delicate condition. We passed a Reamer on the half-way mark who turned on his lights and moved, briefly, to follow us, but quickly gave up the chase. He was far outside his usual posting and alone, and likely in no mood for the sort of chase that I would be. Somewhere, in the back of my mind, I registered his presence and wondered what could have taken him so far outside of Parse on a day like today — but like the worries of my abilities to trade, they were gone quickly, eradicated by the needs of the winding road before me.

We arrived at Signet by late afternoon. The Signet Clinic was a low, long building from before the world went to shit, and it stood out among the salt-box houses that made up the rest of the town. It had been well cared for: the cracked brick of its exterior replaced when they came into disrepair, the tar on the roof kept well-applied. The people of Signet knew that the Clinic, and the people that worked there, were their chief export. People who could not pay in money paid in goods and services, and those goods and services made their way through the town. Signet was a community that thrived on the wellness — or in some cases, the sickness — of others.

I pulled the Jeep into the Emergency entrance and left it running as I rushed around to the other side to help Jennifer out. Her hand had found a permanent place at her side now, and I deduced that whatever had gone wrong last time she had started to feel much earlier than when she had woken up and chosen to ignore. How often was that the case, I wonder? How many small aches and pains and discomforts did my wife endure on a daily basis to bring our child into the world, and how many of them were normal? I was at a disadvantage to answer either question.

An orderly in stark white scrubs came out through the glass doors with an annoyed expression on his face, no doubt to tell me I couldn't park where I had parked.

I was picking Jennifer up as he did, holding her weight and my child's in my arms and feeling the strain of their life against my muscles. "Preeclampsia," I snapped at him as he opened his mouth, and he stopped dead in his tracks. I carried her toward him. "Complicated by acute anemia!"

He snapped out of whatever trance my sudden declaration of diagnosis had set upon him, and turned to run back into the Clinic. "Get me a gurney and a cart!" he yelled at someone out of my view, as I passed from the harshness outside into the smoothly conditioned air of the Clinic.

Jennifer's nails dug into the back of my neck as I laid her on the gurney that came out to meet us.

The Clinic had one sole room that could be used as an Operating Room in the event of an emergency. I hesitate to actually call it an operating room without qualification. It had the stirrups for the mother to bar the heels of her feet into while giving birth and it had some tools and it had drugs, but at the end of the day, a clinic was a clinic. It was a large room, I'll grant it that, largely empty so that people could come and go without tripping over one another. One wall was glass from my waist up, with chairs behind it for viewing. I sat in the first one that touched the back of my legs as I backed up. I couldn't take my eyes off of Jennifer.

There was a bag with cloudy fluid hanging near her like a sad stomach, thick with the weight of itself. A young doctor had come in and hung it after the blonde nurse had, on the third try, successfully gotten the IV into her arm.

Jennifer turned away from the needle as it went in, and her eyes found me. She was crying large, shimmering tears that came out weightless, finding their way to the gurney beneath her by divine will rather than gravity. Her eyes did not leave mine once they found me, and every so often I would catch her mouthing something to me. I couldn't understand what she was saying, some silent plea for mercy, so I nodded each time, not knowing what I was agreeing to and not caring — whatever it was

I would do, all she had to do was come out of this alive on the other side.

There was a young male nurse whose only job seemed to be the periodical check of Jennifer's blood pressure. It was highly scheduled: any time he wasn't performing the task he was standing off to one side, staring at the clock on the wall and waiting five-minute intervals. Every time the minute hand touched one of the twelve markers, he went back to Jennifer, to the sphygmomanometer strapped to her arm like a limp pillow, and pumped it up. He would then watch the dial as it deflated, look at the clock again, and write something on a clipboard. I know now and would have known then that the 'something' he was writing was her blood pressure and time, but at the time my brain would not process that. It was caught in the loop of the surrealism of this whole endeavor, my eyes locked with Jennifer's and sometimes drifting into the nothingness just beyond her, my mind lost upon itself.

Jennifer's feet were in the stirrups and the blonde nurse had just injected her with something, when the young man with the sphygmomanometer checked her blood pressure again, noted it, then turned to the doctor and showed him the clip board, motioning to this newest trend of numbers.

As though it had been waiting on some cue I couldn't recognize, the room sprang into action all at once. The gurney was turned and brought to the side, one of the nurses dragging the IV with it, making sure to keep the plastic vein that connected it to my wife slack and secure. The male nurse moved with the gurney, always at Jennifer's side now, constantly pumping the sphygmomanometer and letting it deflate. Pump, deflate. Pump. Deflate. He was no longer marking down the numbers, he was calling them out. I could see the lower half of his face moving beneath his surgical mask.

I stood up and walked to the window, clenching my fists so tight that they dug little arcs into my palm. I never took my eyes off Jennifer and she never took her eyes off of me, even as they rolled the gurney into different positions.

They smeared some brown liquid over her abdomen that seemed to stain her skin. The entire process seemed medieval, although I know it wasn't. There are some things that will always seem alien to those of us that don't do it every day, I think, and the image of a sharp small knife opening your wife's abdomen is, certainly, one of them. I watched it happen with disjointed awe. The body of the male nurse taking her blood pressure bisected Jennifer, separating her looking at me from the doctor that was now making an incision in her uterus. My mind latched onto this bisection I think, processing them as two different people: I don't know who that poor woman is being sliced down the middle, but my Jennifer looks upset.

I saw our child for the first time as it emerged from its amniotic sac, which clung to her with strong suction. She came out as though Jennifer's body were trying to hold onto her, a last attempt to provide the care her body had been designed for.

She. Her. Our child was a girl. I could see her tiny vagina now as the blonde nurse snipped the cord, her face red and covered in blood. We're all born covered in the blood of our mothers. It's one of those truisms that seems alien and important to say, but ultimately means nothing.

I stared at her, at the weight of her in the doctor's arms until he brought her to the table along the wall and his back shielded her from view, snapping me out of my trance.

I had stopped looking at Jennifer when my daughter had come into view. When I turned back to meet her eye they were not where I'd left them, leaving white sockets in their wake. Her eyes had rolled back up into her head, red veins creeping up from her lower lid and reaching skyward like the pious in mid-prayer. Her head was slack against the gurney and the male nurse had ceased taking her blood pressure and was now pumping at her chest frenetically. My eyes welled up and I begged, *begged* for her to move again.

I should have been more specific.

She began to seize. Her body shook and her limbs flailed, and the nurse had to stop what he was doing to hold her to the gurney so that she wouldn't flop off like a fish. Blood, already everywhere, splashed anew. The nurse that had been attempting to close Jennifer's abdomen pulled back with her hands in the air, not wanting to puncture her more as she twisted and shook on the table.

In the flurry of motion, something that should have been inside my wife moved through the open cavity in her abdomen and was suddenly on the outside. I cannot identify what it was, nor do I have the inclination to inquire as to what it was, but it was at that moment that my mind and body rebelled, unable to hold its grip on last night's supper anymore. I vomited all along the wall of the observation room, a healthy portion of it ending up on the glass itself.

It was the preeclampsia, of course, although they called it eclampsia. Apparently once the seizures start, they drop the 'pre' prefix. They'd done what they could going in to circumvent the anemia I'd reported, that's what they'd been taking steps to do right up until her blood pressure couldn't take it anymore, along with trying to coax her body into healthy labour. They didn't have a proper OR though, and when her blood pressure spiked, things had gone downhill quickly. Cause of death, I was assured, had been a stroke, brought on by strain and medication to reduce the acute anemia — a sort of Hail Mary situation. I nodded my way through their explanation, trying very hard to pay attention to each detail but finding it impossible.

Our daughter was premature and underweight, and her lungs had not fully developed. There were tubes in her every orifice and some new holes they've made for her — so many tubes that there seemed to be more tube than child. I held her, once, before she was gone too. Her breath was haggard against my chest. I don't think she ever opened her eyes once during her short life.

The blonde nurse had apologized tearfully: they just hadn't had the facilities here for the sort of care my daughter had needed, those clear boxes they keep them in, clean rooms, who knows.

Our daughter followed Jennifer out of this world a day and a half behind her, but it was all one day to me. I hadn't slept or eaten, moving from Jennifer when she had lost the ability to make eye contact with me to her, staring at her small face and waiting for her to look up at me with her mother's eyes and resume the task. She never did, not even as her tiny lungs relinquished their last breath.

I can recall with perfect clarity the day my wife died, even as it bled into the day my daughter died.

REPTILIAN

James Porter sat in the operations room staring hard at the computer screen. He rubbed his knuckles into his eyes, the vivid glare of the screen making them sore. Darkness lurked outside, the streetlights flickering against the dim horizon, and the sun still hiding behind the mountains. He had been fighting sleep to stay up all night, preparing for the lengthy, grueling days that awaited his special security squad. A vial of eye lubricant rested at the edge of his workstation. He couldn't resist any longer. Two drops in each eye. Then he blinked repeatedly, seeking to moisturize his fatigued eyes. He was eager to get outside as sitting behind a desk grew boring; he had grown to despise it. James needed to be out in the field, not stuck filling out the paperwork as others carried out the actual work.

The air in the room grew stagnant. It made him sick to the pit of his stomach. His facial hair tickled his neck after he had let it grow over the past twenty hours. Now it was tormenting him, and the itchy feeling wouldn't go away no matter what he tried. He scratched at it, the tiny hairs digging underneath his nails. Normally he wore his hair in a tight, meticulously trimmed undercut, but it was now a shaggy mess of matted brown. Sweat drenched his hair, clumping it to his head, and tangles formed in the mess. The walls of the room sweated from the humidity. His shirt clung to his sweaty body, and every vein stood out on his muscular forearms. A deep blue vein ran up his bicep like a major road with several smaller roads running in all different directions over the peak of solid mass.

His employer had hired the team weeks ago, giving them the assignment of tracking the former General Freemantle's operations. Hostility with the southerners had boiled over and reached an all-time high. His team of elite operators turned their focus on the research facility in Stapleton. Other firms struggled to gather intel on the erratic behaviour of the man simply known to some as *"The General"*, and his research site. Where others failed miserably, James Porter was the only individual who managed to unearth the slightest evidence. It all tracked back to two seemingly unconnected incidents. One was an odd purchase from a foreign bulk pet store, a rare breed of iguana paid for by Freemantle himself and shipped to the medical facility. The other was a phone call made on his personal phone cell phone to Pharmakon Industries, asking a very peculiar question: *"Do you think their blood will fill in the gap?"*

James still didn't understand how those two events related to what was happening here in Stapleton. No matter how many times he listened to the recordings, he got the same strange feeling. Something in Freemantle's voice caused his skin to crawl, like a thousand insects were crawling beneath his skin.

Two weeks ago, James set up his command centre in

the basement of a municipality on the outskirts of Stapleton. His wife, Kendra, and daughter, Alicia, reluctantly made the move with him under the guise of having moved from the next city over so he could work in the mines. The members of his team would visit, pretending to be aunts or uncles, making sure not to raise any suspicions from their neighbours. They would have backyard barbeques, drink beers, and laugh long into the night. Most nights ended with an exchange of information through the use of code words. Sometimes Fred or Angie would leave behind notebooks with vital intelligence. But on the nights that concluded with nothing more than cheerful banter, James envisioned how the other half lived. Yearning to settle down, those nights passed by quickly, leaving him with a dreadful longing to live a happy way of life. All he wanted was to spend time with his daughter. At the conclusion of those evenings, he made himself a promise that he intended to keep: this would be his last mission.

James covered the walls surrounding him in white boards with intel and pictures gathered from their reconnaissance missions. He arranged a picture of General Freemantle wearing a clean-pressed white suit in the middle of the room. Lines of thick, red string led to other pictures of the scientists under his command and various other high-ranking government personnel to link everyone together. Far off in the distance, James scrawled the word *pet store* and *Pharmakon*. The only connection between the two outside entities was Freemantle.

The world didn't look kindly upon espionage, but they never caught James Porter and his team. They were like phantoms to the outside world. The team didn't exist on any government pay roll or list; only those who had the highest security clearance were aware of their existence. They didn't collect a pension; they didn't have health care coverage. No one would record their missions; their accomplishments would not make it into the history books. When they died, their families would only remember them for who they professed to be. They would never understand what it was they did for a living. Although they had often ended the most dangerous conflicts around the world, society would never recognize them as being heroes. Only people with the means and desires to hire men like James Porter and his organization knew they existed for situations that needed a more direct approach that other agencies couldn't match.

James was expecting for a report from Angie King and Fred Thistle. They had parachuted into the nearby woods surrounding the laboratory just before midnight and had been trying to expose the reason for the increased activities outside the base. In the news briefings from the base, they cautioned the public that they were conducting night training. James figured something else was taking place behind the scenes. A chemist by the name of Devin Dysart had suddenly arrived at the base in Stapleton. This simple fact produced a lot of suspicion. Based on recent intel gathered on Doctor Dysart, his high pedigree and work with infectious diseases, the chance of it being just a coincidence was far too suspicious. This genius wasn't here for just another training night with the troops. James had put in the request for a background check on the talented doctor. Gut instinct told him that the doctor was, or at the very least, had recently worked for Pharmakon.

James would soon uncover the link between Freemantle and the pharmaceutical giant.

Fred Thistle was the communications expert for the team and a computer genius, and Angie thought his unique skills would come in handy if they found any technical equipment. They had to go in with no communication devices because the risk of getting discovered increased with any GPS or any form of radio wave. Angie and Fred had gone dark, but James believed they would handle themselves if shit went south.

James leaned back in his chair, waiting for any intel. He was growing impatient, yearning for a shave and shower. A sudden sharp ding alerted him that a message awaited him on the closed channel. "Finally," James muttered out loud to himself as he opened the email. It wasn't from his crew; it was a direct message from the man paying his salary. James knew this had to be important. Under normal circumstances, the email wouldn't contain actual names. Everything was out there for anyone to see. It was all out in the open now.

Top Secret
James Porter
Operative Terrence Baker has been under cover at
Stapleton Army Base and has made contact.
Dangerous biohazardous weapon ready
for human experimentation.
Base security tracking two foreign security
members near test facility.
They have issued shoot to kill orders.
Terrance Baker moving to extract your
operators in the area to safety.

James read the message in disbelief and raced to throw on his gear. He had to get his team out of there now before it was too late. If his employer already had a man on the inside, there would have been no need to infiltrate the base with blind eyes. It had become clear that being a ghost in the eyes of your employer made you expendable. They had kept valuable information from them and now their lives were in danger of being extinguished and no one would ever know what transpired. James rushed out the door without saying goodbye to his wife and kid.

A glaring orange sun beat down on Devon with relentless fury. Without a cloud in the sky to shield him from the sweltering heat, his skin felt like it was burning. The sunlight was so brilliant, the sky appeared to be white hot, with only the slightest shade of blue remaining. Sweat had already soaked through his undershirt underneath his grey work coveralls. The cotton fabric stuck to his back and every time he stretched, it would slide up his stomach and bunch up awkwardly, his beer belly poking out underneath. At least his shame was covered up by the coveralls, and most of his coworkers made him look like a rake, anyway. Devon had gotten expelled from school for fighting, and his parents had enough of his shit. They dispatched him to live with his uncle in Stapleton, hoping the rough miner would help straighten him out and make him into a respectable youthful son, or at the very least, keep Devon out of the public view. His father was running for the mayor's office and wouldn't suffer the embarrassment.

Devon had lived in Stapleton for four months now, and he still couldn't adjust to the extreme fieriness of the unforgiving desert. His skin burnt and blistered every day, as he still hadn't developed a tan. The air was dry, and his mouth parched. His cracked lips were sore. It hurt too much to eat most days, but his uncle informed him he would adapt to the hot weather. His only relief was the extraordinary cold deep down in the mines. His uncle was the superintendent of the Stapleton mining enterprise. He twisted the rules and got Devon a job driving the supply tractor, for which he was eternally grateful. Even though he detested his work, he couldn't deny what a marvellous man his uncle was.

Devon rested both palms on the lid of a rusted metal drum containing sixty pounds of fuel, dreading the gruelling task ahead. None of the other miners struggled with the barrels like he did. Most of them would watch and laugh at him as he wrestled to get the cumbersome containers into the back of his tractor. The burden of the heavy gas barrels caused the corroded metal edges to cut through his work gloves and dig deep into the tender flesh of his hands. His uncle encouraged him that he would grow calluses, but he was still waiting, watching the blood from his hand smear the rim. Devon hoisted the barrel up to his mid-thigh, the awkward and considerable weight seeming to buckle his spine. Each step he took threatened to break the bones in his legs and feet. When Devon got close enough, he would fall forwards and let the weight of the barrel crash into the pan of the tractor, causing the heavy metal beast to rock back and forth vigorously.

Footsteps crunched on the gravel as someone approached the fuel yard. A deafening crash caused Devon's heart to skip, and he spun around to see his uncle standing in front of a tipped over gas drum. His uncle Geoff's stature would intimidate a bear, standing seven feet tall and his chest nearly the same size as the barrel resting at his feet. His burly beard and tanned skin made him look like an animal. The stone crunched under the weight of his behemoth frame as he rolled the drum towards the tractor on his side. If Devon's checks weren't so burnt his uncle would have seen him blush, embarrassed he hadn't considered doing that himself. It would have saved him the incredible pain in his back and shoulders. With ease, his uncle hoisted the container into the back of tractor and placed it down with the delicacy a parent would place his newborn child into a crib.

"Thanks." Devon tried to sound grateful, but the sun had drained him of any enthusiasm and gratitude. The remark fell hastily from his lips.

His uncle wore a reflective yellow safety vest over his white wife beater. The veins on his bulging arms stuck out and ran over his skin like mighty tributaries. "They will need that gas today, Devon. Get in the cab and I'll load the rest. I don't have time for this today. A couple of birds must have flown into the ventilation duct and we need to get them out of there before they cause too much damage." Geoff's eyes started impatiently back at Devon.

"Sounds like a problem." Devon tried to sound empathetic, but it came across sounding more sarcastic.

"Yeah, it is. The worst thing is we are all too big to get into the shaft and we don't have time to wait for animal control to get here." A sly grin peeked out from underneath Geoff's beard. "Well, everybody except you."

Devon tried to protest, his mind hunting for the perfect excuse. All he could do was stand there flabbergasted. He gulped loudly before hopping up into the cab and turning the key in the ignition. The motor rumbled to a start and air conditioner kicked in. He sat behind the wheel waiting for his uncle to join him, still trying to come up with a valid excuse of why he shouldn't crawl into one of those ventilation shafts. The only alibi his uncle would accept would be a severe physical injury, and Devon trembled at the thought.

Baker raced through the woodland towards the testing facility. He recognized that he was running out of time. Branches snapped beneath his feet, and leaves rustled as he sprinted past. He jumped over decayed logs and roots without a second guess. His feet seemed to have eyes of their own now. They carried him over the dense forest floor without a single thought, his footsteps reverberating in the silence that blanketed him. This ability allowed him to focus on the task at hand while pressing through the thick foliage and planted trees that had no right being in the desert. They transplanted the fake forest under the guise of a beautification project by community leaders, but the actual reason was something insidious. The desert offered scarce privacy, and they implanted the forest in place to allow covert, exceedingly dangerous scientific operations to continue without intervention.

They discovered the operatives James had assigned to observe the 1054th Regiment. General Freemantle had successfully developed a new biological weapon that he could use to dismantle the entire infrastructure of a city with ease. His top-secret testing facility was concealed from public knowledge and had not appeared on any satellite images or blueprints of the facility. Members of a special forces unit that his boss had selected were now unknowingly walking into an ambush in the woods near the laboratory. They were being stalked by the 1054th soldiers. If he didn't reach them in time, they would slaughter them on the spot. He sent a message to Mr. Hicks to warn them. There wasn't enough time to wait for James Porter and the rest of his team, they needed action now.

He fired off his rifle wildly into the air, a desperate attempt to draw the enemies towards his present location. Even with that hope, he wasn't hanging around, vanishing like a ghost by the time they got there. Gunfire echoed powerfully in the forest and spilled outside and into town. No one in the township of Stapleton would even bat an eye at the thunderous clap of automatic fire. Living next to an infantry unit would make you numb to the melody of machinegun fire. Just another noise that integrated into your daily routine, like birds singing or the garbage truck making his rounds.

The edge of the forest came into view: the moon was sneaking behind the mountains, and the sun wouldn't rise for another two hours. Trees disappeared behind him as he ran towards an old dirt track that would lead him straight to the testing facility. Branches lined either side of the road, forming a narrow corridor. Tall grass grew in the ruts of the tire tracks. An intense light behind him cast his shadow down the long road for a moment before a set of lights turned on just ahead of him.

"Place your weapon down, Terrence Baker," a commanding voice boomed from a megaphone. "If you don't, your men will die."

Two silhouettes knelt in front of the green truck, their features obscured, making it difficult to identify, but he saw the red laser sights on their chests. Baker looked down and cursed himself for not being more vigilant. Multiple red dots floated in tight circles on his own chest. He unbuckled the shoulder strap of his AK 47 and let the gun fall to the ground in front of him. It landed with a metallic *thunk*.

"Now raise your hands above your head." The man approached as the two men in the headlights stood up and joined him.

He wanted to dive for his weapon. He couldn't believe he had fallen for their trap. The muscles in his abdomen and legs tensed. He thought about lunging for his machine gun, but the red lasers on his chest acted like chains holding him in place. He wondered if Fred and Angie had gotten themselves captured yet, or if they were somewhere in the woods nearby. They would be his only chance of salvation now.

A shudder raced down Devon's spine from the chilly mine air. It wasn't the same as air conditioning; the air down here was damp. The coldness wasn't just a momentary reprieve from the immense heat; it settled into your bones. It stretched out in your tissues and if you stayed down in the mines for too long, you would pine for a glimpse of the sun above. Devon and Geoff had driven their way down to the fourth level of the mine which was two kilometres beneath the earth's surface and far from the reach of the blazing sunlight. Bright halogen lights fought against the blackness to reach every blackened crevice. In the far corners of the lights' dying reach, Devon swore that the walls slithered with insects from the prehistoric ages, causing his skin crawl. Even with the headlights of the tractor glaring against the darkness of the wall, creatures remained concealed as they writhed in the shadows.

Six miners leaned up against an alloy tool shed, most of them taking long puffs of their cigarettes. The dull amber glow at the tips of the cigarettes struggled to remain lit down here in the dense air. "It's only been two hours and you can already tell the difference down here without the ventilation working." Geoff's voice was full of concern for his employees. "This is your chance to be the hero to these guys. You know, maybe you will fit in a little more around here."

Under normal circumstances, Devon wouldn't want to be associated with any of these hooligans and thugs, but it would make working in the mines a little easier. "So do I shoot the bird?" Devon spoke in his roughest voice, but he still sounded out of place amongst men like his uncle. Geoff's lips cracked a smirk and his uncle let out the heartiest laugh Devon had ever heard from his uncle. "What's so funny?" The sudden outburst annoyed Devon.

"You want me to give you a gun to go kill some pigeons or a rat?" The laughter dangled off every word.

Devon furled his eyebrows in frustration, vexed because he couldn't identify anything wrong with his comment. "Yes."

A thunderous roar swelled from deep in Geoff's belly. "I said, this is your chance to be the hero." His uncle wiped a tear from his cheek before it soaked into his beard. "They will write tales about your bravery, my boy." His uncle reached behind the seat and dragged out a wooden broom handle. "Your sword, my gallant knight."

Devon tried snatching the broom out of his uncle's sturdy grip, but he cemented the broom in his grasp. "I got this." Devon stared into his uncle,s eyes trying to prove his insults didn't intimidate him. His uncle eased the broom handle into Devon's grasp and deliberately climbed out of the cab.

Devon watched as his uncle approached the other laborers, his chest thrust forward making his posture even more intimidating than normal. "Listen up, lads, Devon has volunteered to head into the air vents and clear them out for you guys." Devon noticed that some workers chuckled at that. "In the meantime, I want you guys to head top side and get some fresh air, it isn't fit to work down here." Now Devon received their gratitude. It was no wonder everyone in the Stapleton mine respected Geoff. Devon found it hard to find any faults in the man even after his uncle insulted his manhood.

The workers made their way towards the old Chevy pickup. As they prepared to depart, the engine's thunderous roar rebounded off the cavern walls of the mine and blasted Devon's ears. He cupped his hands over his ears until they drove away, and the eerie silence crept back.

"Come on, Devon, we don't have all day."

Devon looked over at his uncle as he removed the cover to the access tunnels into the airshaft. A faint thumping noise rattled from somewhere inside the shaft. Another icy shiver traveled down Devon's spine even though he had grown used to the chilly air deep down in the mine.

The bright lights of the truck hid the man's face, but his outlandish dress uniform left no questions who had orchestrated the ambush. His perfectly pressed white suit allowed the polished brass to dazzle in the radiant light. Baker could see his reflection in Fremantle's shoes. Years of hard work had established a permanent sheen on the toes, a perpetual gloss that would fend off any dirt foolish enough to tarnish his boots. The former general had formerly been a hero for his country's army. Now he was the evil villain, motivated by greed and money in the private sector. He had been scrutinized attentively for years, finding unique ways to keep his true work sheltered from those that took any interest. Baker's admiration and disdain for the man muddled his thoughts, complicating his perception of the man standing before him.

"Thanks for coming to your better senses," Freemantle spoke, mocking Baker with his sardonic tone. "Now what shall we do with you?" He was hiding something behind his back, an odd shape added to his shadow.

"I don't have time for games." Baker needed to keep the general occupied for as long as possible. He had to buy James Porter enough time to gather the rest of his company. Someone needed to stop Freemantle before he unleashed his biological weapon. "I understand you will not let me live; I just need to know what you've been working on before I die."

"You will not deceive me with that tired old cliche." Freemantle leaned in close enough that Baker smelt the coffee on his breath. "I won't tell you what we have been working on here, but I will show you." He reached out and fixed his grip on Baker's neck. His bony fingers were frigid and deformed, reminding Baker of the grim reaper.

Baker tried to resist, but a guard grabbed his head and another man wrapped him up in a bear hug, pinning him in place. "You won't get away with this," Baker snarled. Spittle flew from his mouth, drops of saliva landing on the polished shoes and immediately wicked off.

Freemantle moved his hand out from behind his back to reveal an enormous syringe. He worked his fingers to locate the vein in Baker's neck and plunged the syringe deep into his jugular. Baker suffered a painful pinch followed by an intense burning sensation that started in his neck and rapidly spread to his heart. He tried to shriek, but a peculiar noise grew out of his esophagus. It was a short, squawking sound that passed his lips in short intervals. No matter how hard he tried, his voice only produced short clicking noises that dwelt in his throat.

"Now to spread this disease we will bring you to the hospital." Freemantle turned to one of his men. "You there, get over here and shot this man in the stomach. We don't need the doctors to discover what's actually wrong with this man." The soldier drew his pistol and took aim. "Wait you idiot, you'll get blood over my uniform. Make sure you don't kill him either, they'll stick him in the morgue if he's dead and the virus won't spread fast enough." Freemantle turned around and strolled away. Two guards accompanied him to his vehicle while the soldier waited for him to get in the truck.

Once the door slammed shut, the man fired a round into Baker's stomach. Baker cried out as the bullet tore through his intestines, his entire midsection set on fire. A tremendous surge of pain coursed through his veins, straight from his chest to his wound. Whatever Freemantle had injected into his body was reacting to the wound in his body. The foreign substance in his blood carried pain to every part of Baker's body. Every nerve in his entire body started firing off signals all at once. Baker couldn't handle it anymore. Stars danced around his vision until all he saw was a bright light. Waves of red-hot pain swept over his body, his nervous system shifted into overdrive.

James didn't have time to say goodbye to his wife Kendra or his daughter Alicia. He felt responsible for saving the lives of his team; it was his fault they found themselves in this plight. It should have been him. He cursed himself for allowing himself to get caught behind a desk. After devoting years' worth of training and practicing with his squad, they had grown into much more than just acquaintances, they had become his family.

His wife had never accepted what he did for a living, even though she had no issues spending his wealth. She had grown to resent to the attention he gave to his work. It drove her into cruelty; it contorted her personality into something essentially evil. Days would pass without them speaking, weeks passed by without her lifting a hand to help their daughter. She spent most of her free time drinking away her talents. Most days she drank until she stumbled around the house, unable to articulate a clear sentence to him when he got home from work. Recently they had grown apart to where they lived in the same house as strangers. He blamed her drinking; she blamed his absence. The only thing that kept them together now was their daughter, Alicia. James hired a nanny to monitor Alicia throughout the day and keep the house tidy. He couldn't count on Kendra to accomplish those things anymore. Her mood varied depending on how hungover she was that day. Sometimes it depended on what she had to drink the night before. If she drank bourbon the night before, James would disappear with Alicia in the morning. Kendra would curse and lash out at them after consuming too much of that amber liquid.

James jumped in his familiar red pickup truck and turned the key. The motor rumbled to life, and the cab of the wagon rattled as the diesel engine turned over. The streetlights flickered in the darkness, casting a dismal yellow light over the neighbourhood. Most of the lawn sprinklers sputtered water across the dry lawns, set on an automatic timer, to preserve the green grass. Sunlight scorched this city in the daytime, drying up the yards, and turning the neglected grass yellow. Most days were far too warm to find yourself out of the shade. Even now, James was sweating from the warmth, his undershirt clinging to his body. He rolled the window down and let the air flow through the cab. The plastic dashboard of his rig had been jet black, but since he moved to Stapleton, the sun turned it a much lighter shade of drab grey. A local radio station kept cutting in and out, the signal shouting out static on the outskirts of town. In an alternate reality, the town of Stapleton would have been a beautiful place to settle, if it wasn't so damn hot all the time. The houses reminded him of older times. Most of the homes were the quintessential American dream, with white picket fences and the large storm shutters over the windows. This wasn't just another city; it was a community that the residents took great pride in. Everyone kept their lawns trimmed, the bushes pruned, and the flower gardens alive with colours. It reminded him of the tiny town that he had grown up in, the perfect place to raise his daughter.

The truck engine roared like thunder as James sped through the desolate streets, the quiet townsfolk still nestled snuggly in bed. Exhaust sputtered out of the tail pipe, and large, blackened clouds drifted up towards the sky. He abruptly made the turn onto the highway that ran alongside of the army base outside of Stapleton. The rest of his team would meet him at the designated emergency extraction zone they picked when they conducted a reconnaissance of the base. They chose that location because there were enough trees to camouflage them from view. It was also close enough that could reach the key area of the base in under thirty minutes. The other members of his team would be late, but that would give him enough time to cut the fence with his wire cutters and get his bearings.

Devon found himself crammed into the air shaft, making it burdensome to maneuver. His back pressed against the frigid metal shaft every time he moved. His knees and elbows banged against the narrow confines of the ventilation duct. A loud, rhythmic clunking echoed further down the shaft, just out of sight. From the distance, soft blue light splashed into the shaft, pouring over the metal like a river. The tunnel made a sharp left corner where his uncle told him the blockage would be. Some poor creature had fallen into the duct and had gotten injured by the blade that propelled the filtered air into the mine. Devon struggled to contort his body to every angle, working to discover the swiftest approach to proceed around in the stuffy air shaft. Claustrophobia settled over him like a heavy coat. He sucked in mouthfuls of stagnant air, finding it laborious to breathe.

Violent knocking sounds grew louder as he approached. An ominous shadow flickered in the blue light on the back wall of the air vent. Devon tightened his grip on the wooden broom handle and wished that he had something a little sturdier. Whatever animal was around that corner had more life than he had expected. He thought about breaking the handle in half so he would have a sharp point that he could use to stab the animal. As he listened to the sound, he wasn't confident he wanted to get so close and personal with the critter.

The thrashing sounds stopped without warning, and an eerie silence fell over the ventilation shaft. Devon waited for the thumping to start again, but the animal had hushed. The injuries that the animal had suffered must have taken their toll and it had succumbed to their wound. Devon wasn't looking forward to cleaning up that bloody mess. The only positive thing about this was that at least he didn't have to take the life of a living creature. He slowly made his way towards the turn and the light became brighter. A flicker of bright sunlight blinded him momentarily before it completely faded. "That's strange," Devon muttered to himself. He crept towards the corner, making sure he didn't lose his grip on the broom. A strange odour wafted through the shaft. It reeked of damp fur and death.

Devon navigated himself around the corner and felt sick to his stomach when he saw the crow. Bile raced up his parched throat, burning the lining all the way up. The crow was gnawing at an extensive wound on its own neck, tearing hunks of viscera out of the vicious wound with its beak. Strands of gory flesh dangled from its mouth and had formed a greasy mess beneath its talons. The animal caught wind of Devon, its head jerking to the side to pick up the scent. The crow craned its neck towards Devon without moving its body, the creature's spine contorted at a terrible angle. Devon gagged, another surge of bile rushing up his throat at the sickening sight. He tried to turn away but backed straight into the corner. The crow shuffled towards him, jutting its head in unnatural angles, keeping its eyes glued on him. The crow tried to shriek at him, but strange noises came out instead. It was a low, wet clicking sound unlike anything Devon had ever heard before. The crow spread its wings, the tips touching both sides of the shaft. The animal moved faster and faster the closer it got to him. A frothy white spit spewed from the crow's mouth and dripped all over the feathers on its chest.

"Jesus Christ." Devon dropped the broom and frantically tried to reach down to pick up the handle. The crow kept rushing towards him with its wings spread out wide. The animal tried to squawk but only spittle ran out, the warm froth landing on Devon's hand. His fingers finally located the wooden handle, and he clutched it rigidly in his fist and swung the broom wildly. He whacked the crow backwards momentarily. The rabid animal absorbed the blow, continuing to approach Devon without hesitation.

"Get away from me!" Devon screamed. He swung at the crow again. This time the crow absorbed the blow, but just kept inching forward.

Devon was close enough to see the creature's black, wet eyes gazing at him. Devon kicked his steel toe boot into the creature's beak. Neck bones cracked and splintered as its head spun around from the force of the blow. Devon watched in horror as the crow thrashed around in the metal ventilation shaft. He looked on in horror as it dragged itself towards him with its wings. The crow's head dangled to the side, bobbing against its shoulder as it crept methodically towards Devon. It had stained its beak, its jaws constantly snapping open as streams of dark red blood gushed from its mouth. Devon pressed the broom handle against his knee and snapped it in half. He drove the splintered point into the crow's body. Devon suffered a sharp pinch on his wrist. He looked down at the torn flesh that dangled from his wrist, blood flowing down his forearm mixing with the sweat on his arm.

"Fuck," Devon muttered out loud as he tried to remember if they had found a cure for rabies. "You have got to be kidding me."

The crow's head continued to flail back and forth trying to get a taste of flesh. Devon used his boot to press the creature against a side wall and stomped repeatedly. Bones broke, and fluids spilled from the creature's ears and mouth. Devon didn't know when the crow died and he didn't care; he pumped his legs until the creature's body stopped twitching. Devon put the crow in a garbage bag and made his way out of the shaft. His temperature was rising, and his skin was tingling all over. Whatever disease afflicted that crow, Devon now carried it in his bloodstream.

Louise used her fist to hammer the dashboard of her old Civic. "Just work," she pleaded with her car. The air conditioner sputtered on and off. Waves of heat washed over her; it was getting to her now. At least she was on her way to work at the mines: the sooner she got underground the better. She felt disgusting, with perspiration pouring out of every pore on her body. Her deodorant wasn't strong enough to fight against the body odour in the cramped confines of her car. She smelt like she hadn't showered in days when in fact, she had showered just before she left for work. Sweat matted her black hair to her head, and it had now an unnatural sheen to it. Mascara was running down her pale cheeks, sinking her eyes deeper into the sockets. She had worked at the Stapleton mine for so long that she couldn't handle the extreme warmth anymore. Her pale complexion agreed: she belonged underground. She shouldn't be so close to the sun; she burnt too easily.

The desert seemed to stretch for miles around here as the trees surrounding Stapleton disappeared behind her. There was nothing on the horizon except the blaring sun. The sky appeared such a light shade of blue that it could have been mistaken for white, even without a single cloud anywhere. Sunrays beamed into the car and heated her faux leather seats, causing the material to scorch her legs. At least her CD player still functioned, she thought gratefully as she listened to the techno remix of her favourite pop songs. This had become her ritual during her drive to work. She would listen to her music and sweat like she was on the dance floor of her favourite club.

Louise made the turn off on the main highway but maintained her speed down the single lane road that led to the mine. The quarry was worth so much money, yet they refused to maintain the road. Louise bounced up and down as her tires crashed into the deep potholes that cluttered the pavement. Dust clouds formed behind her car as she sped towards the gate. Everything was so dry out here: what the sunlight didn't burn up, the mine had destroyed over the years, leaving the entire area a desolate wasteland. Louise drifted past the gate, rushing towards the work yard, and forced to slam on the breaks. The miners lined up outside of the pit, having a coffee break. Her car skidded fifteen feet before it came to a halt, Louise sensed her pale skin flush red with embarrassment as her coworkers stared at her. She eased off the brake and rolled across the parking lot towards her parking spot. At least Geoff wasn't there to witness that, but she knew he would hear about it. Soon everyone in Stapleton would know about it.

Kendra awoke in an empty bed again. It didn't bother her anymore; she had grown used to that. Once upon a time it would have broken her heart. Now she had grown accustomed to the freedom. Her husband disapproved of her drinking, but she wouldn't have to worry about his complaining today. Kendra looked in the mirror with admiration. Her blonde curly hair draped down to her shoulders, and her bronzed skin agreed with the warm Stapleton sun. Her white nightgown hung loosely from her delicate frame, with the strap dangled from her left shoulder.

"Alicia?" Kendra called out to the living room. She wasn't certain what time it was, but she knew her daughter wouldn't leave the house without permission. She thought of an image of Alicia glued to the television, not acknowledging her mother calling out to her. Kendra left the bedroom, wandering down the hallway towards the kitchen with her feet scraping across the hardwood. Family pictures hung from hooks on both sides of the corridor, most of them bringing back fond memories from before James had lost himself in his work, before she had searched for him in the bottom of a bottle.

Bright, yellow rays of sunshine beamed through the open kitchen window. It reflected off the lustrous finish of the hardwood table, the cloudless sky cast across the surface. Kendra shielded her eyes from the glare and shuffled her feet across the tiled kitchen floor towards the stainless-steel refrigerator. Grabbing a package of Fruit Loops from atop the fridge, Kendra opened the door and shivered as the chilly air caused the hairs on her arms raise. "Do you want a bowl of cereal for breakfast?" Kendra could hear the television in the next room, but her daughter still hadn't replied. "Earth to Alicia!"

It took a moment for her eyes to adjust to the dull light in the living room. Kendra saw Alicia's pink, fuzzy blanket in a heap at the foot of the recliner, an empty bowl left on the arm of the chair, and the television left on the kids' channel. Giant red curtains bordered the enormous screen door, left open to allow a breathtaking view of the rear veranda. It was still relatively chilly on this side of the house, as the morning sun wasn't high enough in the sky yet to heat it up. Kendra walked across the living room and pulled the sliding door open. The cement blocks were still cold against her feet, the shadow of the house protecting them from the sun's intense heat.

"Alicia, what are you doing out here by yourself? You know you can't just leave the house without telling me where you are." Alicia stood back on at the edge of the grass. Kendra smiled, happy that she passed down her blond wavy hair to Alicia and James had added just a kiss of fire to her beautiful locks. Alicia's curls rested just above her big silver belt that she wore with her black khaki shorts.

"I'm sorry, Mommy." Alicia's tone was feeble and shaky. Her daughter was doing her best to stifle a sobbing cry.

A surge of regret washed over Kendra. She didn't think she had raised her voice that much. "It's okay, honey. You just worried me, that's all." She made sure that she kept her voice soft and made her way across the patio towards

Alicia. "Are you crying?" Low, suppressed sobs spilled from her daughter's lungs. Alicia turned around, bearing her left wrist with her other hand. Blood oozed out between her fingers from a mangled gash on her arm. "Oh no, sweetheart, what happened to you?" Kendra rushed to her daughter's side.

"I saw a dog roaming through the yard, and I came out to play with it." Alicia wasn't crying because it hurt, her entire body trembled because she thought she would get into trouble.

"Let's get you to the hospital, you'll need stitches." Kendra put pressure on the wound and felt the warm blood trickling out from the profound wound. It was a deep, gnarled gash exposed the bone, the white surface poking through beneath the blood.

Devon slung the garbage bag out of the vent and it skidded across the gravel road. Wet, sloppy sounds permeated the mine as the contents of the bag sloshed around inside. Sweat was spewing out of his body from every pore and steam rose off his skin in palpable waves. The icy air of the mine did nothing to lower his body temperature. Devon tried to ease himself down from the shaft, but he was experiencing trouble getting his motor functions to work. "That fucking crow." Devon collapsed to his knees. His bones felt like glass, and every action was excruciating.

"Hey!" his uncle shouted out from behind the wheel of his large bulldozer "What's going on with you?"

Devon crawled towards the garbage bag. He wasn't

sure why, but his stomach was rumbling, and he was frothing at the repugnant stench. The rocks cut into the flesh on his hands as he dragged himself towards the decaying crow, its scent driving him delirious with hunger. He snatched the bag and tore it open with his bloodied fingers. Blood and white spittle coated the crow's feathers, a cascade of gory juices spilling between Devon's fingers. Unwillingly, he craved a taste of the dead animal, he was ravenous, his mouth watered with anticipation.

Devon jumped backward. The ground shook as Geoff jumped down from his seat, and he bolted towards him. "Are you okay?" Geoff moved fast for his stature, but not fast enough to stop Devon.

Devon scurried away from his uncle with the crow gripped tightly in his clutches. Flesh lodged underneath his fingernails as he dug them into the dead animal. Desperately, he tried to call out to his uncle, but no voice left his throat, just a high-pitched clicking noise. He crammed the crow's stomach into his mouth and chomped down on the soft flesh, tearing into the stomach lining of the crow. Tearing his head back, the warm, viscous contents of the crow's guts spilled down his neck and splashed into his mouth. Devon glanced over his back as Geoff twisted his face in disgust at the sight of him. A rage filled Devon, and he twisted to confront his uncle. That crow wouldn't be enough to satisfy his thirst for blood.

"The fuck is wrong with you, kid?" Geoff tried to knock the crow out of Devon's grasp, but he wasn't swift enough. Geoff took another swipe before Devon could react, and his fist smashed into the crow. The animal exploded in a bloody mess, sending a shower of guts all over his face.

"Fuck!" Geoff roared as Devon lurched forward and sank his teeth into his rib cage. Geoff grabbed Devon by the shoulder and sent him hurtling into the rock wall behind them. Surprised, peering down at his chest, Geoff watched as blood leaked out of the teeth marks that had penetrated deep into his flesh.

Devon stood up deliberately. He rubbed his cracked collarbone, the jagged surface jutting out of the skin, slashing through the flesh without a hint of pain. A bloody froth spewed from his mouth as he opened his jaws. He crept methodically towards his uncle and observed the horror build in the terrified man's face. A surge of energy built up in his legs as he prepared to make another lunge. Geoff caught him off guard as he pounced first, his heavy frame pinning him to the ground with ease.

"What the fuck are you?" Geoff struggled to keep Devon pinned down as his jaws continued snapping open and shut. The only responses that left Devon's esophagus were the same indistinct clicking noises that the crow had been making in that shaft.

James didn't know what was taking his team so long. With their time running out, he couldn't wait any longer. He used his wire cutters to cut through the chain-link fence. The sun, already climbing high in the sky now, hinted that it would soon be noon in Stapleton. He wasn't sure how much time Angie and Fred had left; the clock had been ticking for a long time considering it was a life and death situation. Now, they didn't even have the cover of darkness to remain concealed. The outskirts of Stapleton were a barren stretch of desert on one side of the highway and dense woodland on the other. Freemantle would stop at nothing to disguise his top-secret activities from the world, even going so far as to create a forest in the middle of a desert.

James took a moment to listen for approaching vehicles. He heard only the cry of some nearby birds singing their song, a dreary melody, as if the woods spoke through them. Pacing back and forth, James determined that the only thing worth attempting would be to head in on foot by himself. At least that would be quicker. Of course, if he ran into any trouble, he wouldn't have enough fire power to fight his way out.

The ground grew rugged, and dead branches littered the forest floor as the sun claimed several victims over the endless seasons of warmth. These trees suffered in this environment, they belonged in the Northern forests; the sun was far too robust in Stapleton. He hastened across the rough terrain, his eyes guiding his feet over the obstacles before his brain registered what it was processing. Dirt kicked up from his shoes, skittering across the ground behind him as he raced across the rough terrain, doing his best to avoid the natural ruts and dead branches. James had pushed deep into the forest without stumbling once and had soon come across the old dirt road that his satellite imaging discovered. If he was correct, he would have to follow the road north towards the top-secret testing facility. He believed if he would locate his team, that would be the best place to search.

A tall man wearing a jungle green tunic and wood-land camouflage pants leaned against the building, smoking his cigarette. Even from this distance, Fred envied the man, yearning for a cancer stick of his own. He braced the fire exit open with a dead tree branch. The guard stared up into the sky, not paying any attention to the world around him. A cloud of smoke danced around his face as he tried to blow smoke rings into the air. He failed miserably, but he didn't realize anybody was there observing him. His light brown hair stood up, gelled into a faux hawk, and he trimmed his moustache thinly. His gaunt frame on full display, his sweat-soaked shirt clinging to his body. Veins ran over his sinewy forearms, his jugular standing out prominently like a route heading straight from his heart to his brain.

Fred and Angie had reached the research facility un-detected. They waited patiently for an opportunity to gain access to the building. Both of them laid in a pile of dead leaves behind a decayed tree stump, camouflaging themselves from view. Moss had grown over most of the wood, and tiny bushes had sprouted up all around the dead log. The soldier savoured his last drag, then flicked his butt towards the trash can, missing it. "Air ball," the guard muttered to himself. Fred had to stifle the laughter that wanted to escape his lips. The man hung his head low and headed back inside, not bothering to pull the door closed behind him. Lady Luck was finally on their side. Fred jumped to his feet and sprinted across the clearing. He jammed the barrel of his assault rifle into the opening before the door sealed shut.

Angie patted his shoulder to let him know she was right behind him. "Open the door, I'll cover you," Angie whispered harshly.

Fred edged the door open to reveal a long, empty corridor. "Where do you think he went?" Fred asked, his heart beating fast. The possibility an ambush weighed heavily on his mind. Something was telling him they were walking into a trap. It had been too easy to get to this facility.

"There are a lot of doors in the corridor. Stay alert and cover your corners." Angie pointed down the hallway: all the doors rested on the left side except for one large double door at the edge of the hallway. The light that flooded through the windows on those doors were the only source of light. Brick walls lined the corridor. Ominous stains littered the cement floor all over. It looked more like a torture chamber than a research facility. Fred could see bloody handprints on the shiny metal doors. "Are you seeing this?" Angie walked towards the first door; she was doing her best to dampen the sounds from her footfalls.

Fred looked closely at the door frame. "It looks like someone tried to claw their way into that room." Deep scratches etched into the steel ran the length of the door. Long, jagged lines that began thin and turned into deep caverns further down the frame.

"What the hell was going on down here?" Angie placed her hand on the doorknob and tried to open it, but it didn't turn. "Do you think someone is alive in there?"

Fred leaned in close and placed his ear against the door. "It sounds like a crow trying to caw, but that makes little sense." Slowly, he backed away from the door and walked down the hallway towards the next door. He heard nothing behind this door until he tried to open the locked doorknob. Then he noticed the same strange squawking noise start up. It reminded him of a bird choking on water, if that was even possible.

"They must have experimented on animals." Angie walked down the hallway, passing the next two doors without stopping to check them. "We should head deeper into the facility and try to find some answers."

Fred turned to join her when he saw the soldier at the end of the hallway. The last thing he noticed was a queer smirk on the guy's face before he cast the corridor into complete darkness. The locks on the doors thudded open, and the enormous metal doors along the hallway creaked open. Fred felt trapped, the loud clicking getting closer as a wave of heat washed over him from the opened cells.

"I'll be right down!" Louise called out to the group as they headed back down into the mine. "I just have to punch in." She headed into the trailer that served as the primary office, consistently a mess. Today it was worse than ever. The table was cluttered with newspapers and empty coffee cups from the laborers. Normally, they took their breaks down in the mine, but with the ventilation system broken, Geoff allowed them to take their break in the office. It would have been far too hot to wait in the Stapleton sun. It looked like they took full advantage of the comforts of the office. Louise grabbed her white hard hat and reflective vest from the hook on the wall, then swiped her card through the punch clock. It beeped at her to emphasize she was late. She sprinted back outside, hoping that the truck had waited for her, not surprised to learn they had left without her. Not wanting to waste time, she reached into her pocket and pulled out a package of earplugs. Ripping up the pack, she threw the plastic on the ground and balled up the earplugs so she could stuff them in her ears. The heavy machinery had been to blame for her hearing loss, not the loud music she listened to in the car. At least that's what she told herself.

Louise broke into a half sprint, speeding down the gravel road to get out of the sun's scorching heat. Once she crossed the threshold to the mine, it was like plunging into a cold pool. A wave of frigid air engulfed her. "At least the ventilation system is functioning," she muttered to herself. The bright florescent lights on the ceiling illuminated the roadway, yet somehow left the walls of the mine in dark shadows. Darkness made maneuvering the tunnels difficult, deep ruts crisscrossed all over the road. It gradually sloped downward, allowing people to adjust to the descent. The first floor of the mine was suspiciously empty. They had used it for the storage of non-essential equipment, discarded and forgotten and left behind to perish.

The walk was long and lonely, leaving her with nothing except her wandering thoughts. She couldn't wait to see Devon. Today would be the day that she told him how she felt about him. She was psyching herself up, gathering every ounce of courage she had. The stories she had been told by the others didn't concern her. She would forgive his past. All that mattered now was how she had fallen for him, despite his shortcomings. Even if he was oblivious to it. Before she recognized it, she had cleared the second floor and was heading down the steeper path towards the third floor. She could see a red glow coming from around the corner. Maybe the alarm hadn't registered that the ventilation system had turned back on. The emergency lights signalled evacuation. No one was making their way out of the mine.

Louise thought she heard a man scream. She paused for a moment to take out her ear plugs. Instinct held her in place. She stood in silence, trying to determine the source of the anguished cry. Without waiting to know how severe the injury was, she rushed towards the first aid kit at the entrance to the third floor. Another blood curtailing wail stopped her dead in her tracks. It took a few screams before she registered that there were multiple sources of the agonizing screams. She broke into a full sprint to reach the scene of the accident, not paying enough attention to where she was going. In a panic, she lost track of her location on the road and she tripped up in the deep rut as she rounded the corner. She wasn't agile enough to break her fall, and her face smacked off the road. A gush of blood burst from her nose. The coppery gush of blood flooded her mouth as she bit through her tongue. She felt a wiggly hunk of flesh slide down the back of her throat.

A blood curtailing scream made Louise look up. Twenty feet in front of her, a theatrical production of carnage reached its pinnacle. Almost impossible to comprehend, the workers were fighting and tearing each other apart. Flipped over on its side, the truck she had tried to catch had crashed into a stack of mining equipment, with the chassis facing Louise. Men were chasing each other around like barbarians. Geoff's arms pumped relentlessly, using meaty fists to club an employee's head to a bloody pulp, splintering the smaller man's skull with ease. Eyes dangled from the sockets of the man's skull, darkened oozed flooding from his nose and ears. Geoff reached down and grabbed a handful of the red paste and shoved it in his mouth, relishing the taste. The light shined on his grotesque face, a splatter of brain matter dangling from his chin.

Louise's stomach rolled over, causing her to urge as bile filled her throat at the gruesome sight. She did not understand what was happening down here. The only thing she knew was that she wanted no part of it. Her only chance was to turn around and run before anyone noticed her. Cautiously, she stood up as quietly as she could, and started to turn when she looked at Devon. Frozen in place as their gazes met, her jaw dropped open, spilling out a single word: "Fuck."

Devon tilted his head to the side, his earlobe touching his shoulder. His lip curled into a wicked snarl that bared his blood-stained teeth. Blackened spittle flew from his lips as he opened his mouth to scream. A low, gargled clicking noise pushed through the phlegm in his throat. Louise turned to run just as Devon made his break towards her. Fate was working against her. She stumbled over the rut again, barely catching herself before she crashed to the ground. She scampered up the road, trying to get to her feet as the footsteps closed in on her.

Fred raised the sight of the machine gun to his eye

so he could see using the night vision. A darkened room exploded to life, a verdant hue illuminating everything. He wanted to make sure he didn't get surrounded, so he thrust his way towards the open door, astonished to see a malnourished man barring his path. Deep scrapes and bite marks covered the stranger's body. He remained in the doorway, his jaws snapping, black drool oozing past his lips and down his chin. "Get down on your knees," Fred warned.

The man lurched towards Fred, his head bobbing up and down with every stride he took. He was struggling to scream, his mouth wide open and neck muscles tensed. A complex, wet sounding grumble escaped his throat.

"I said, get down on your knees." Fred was giving the man a second chance.

When he didn't acknowledge, Fred took charge of the situation, driving his combat boot hard into the man's diaphragm. Nearly breaking his fragile frame in half, Fred sent the man tumbling backwards, collapsing into his cell in a crumpled heap. Fred stepped into the room, overwhelmed by the decaying stench. A slight trickle of light penetrated the chamber from a pinhole in the ceiling, the sunlight working against the night vision. Covered in decomposing animal carcasses and human waste, the floor was a disgusting mess. Fred watched the man scurry to his feet. Quickly, he twisted his gaze back towards him, his nose sniffing at the air to help him locate his assailant in the darkness.

Gunshots rang out in rapid succession from the hallway, the deafening barrage of the AR-15 amplified by the narrow corridors. Metal clinking joined the chorus of gunfire as the shells bounced off the cement floor. Fred found it challenging to count the number of shots Angie fired, but heeded the warning. Without hesitation, Fred fired two rounds into his target. The first round opened a dark, gaping red wound on the man's chest, and a second sent a spray of bone and blood flying out of the back of the man's skull. The victim twitched violently before he buckled into a lump on the soiled floor.

"Are you alright?" Angie startled Fred. He spun around to see her standing in the doorway. Gore covered her shoulder length hair, fragments of brain embedded in her black hair.

"I'm fine." Winded, the last syllable was drawn out as Fred tried to catch his breath.

"We need to get out of this hallway and find out what the hell is going on here." Angie slung her rifle over her shoulder and clasped her left wrist.

"You okay?" Fred pointed to her wrist.

"I'm fine," Angie snapped. "One of those fuckers bit me." She turned and headed down the hallway, out of view without waiting for her partner.

Fred made his way out of the room and stepped into the hallway. He spotted Angie at the end of the hallway. The floor was littered with the fallen corpses from her encounter with the prisoners. All of them had one thing in common: the scars on their bodies. There were woman and men laid to rest in the hallway, and Fred was determined to find the source of their strange behaviour. He made his way down the hallway. Blood spilt out of the freshly opened wounds and over the concrete floor making it slippery.

"Here, I'll get that door open." Fred reached into his pocket and took out his wallet. Using a credit card, he tried to jimmy the lock open, but a magnetic lock sealed the door.

"You know how to get through that," Angie asked impatiently, "or would it be quicker to go around the building?"

Fred only had one solution that would work because of the time constraints they faced trapped in this hallway. "Step back." Fred took aim with his rifle and discharged several bullets into the door until he heard the magnetic field let loose. The door groaned open to reveal another empty corridor that ran perpendicular to the one they were in. This corridor was adequately lit with a nice marble tiled floor. The walls were pristine white with nice paintings of various nature scenes hung in an orderly fashion. Air conditioning filtered through the grates overhead, an extreme opposite to the hellish, hot dungeon they had just left behind.

"Well, this is more like what I expected when we entered." The hallway reminded Fred of Freemantle. Everything was perfectly in place and polished, which made it stand out just like the former eccentric general.

"Which way do you think that soldier escaped?" Angie peered down the hallway.

There was a single door at either end. One of them was painted black and the other was white. Fred turned around and noticed that someone had painted the double doors black. He didn't want to risk facing more of those savages. "Let's try going this way." Fred pointed to the white door, and they both made their way down the hallway in formation, on edge from the eerie silence. The door wasn't locked. As Fred turned the knob, he stumbled into the room.

The door opened into a science laboratory. Jars of varied coloured liquids rested in the open cupboards that ran along the back wall. There were four stainless steel tables in the centre of the room, each with its own sink and built-in cabinets underneath. Two patient beds covered in white bedsheets were on either side of the tables. Each bed had thick leather restraints attached to the metal frame that could restrain the arms, legs, and the chest of the poor victims of some mad scientist's experiment.

Angie rummaged through some journals on one table. Fred opened various drawers and looked for anything that looked important. "Have you found anything?" Fred asked.

"Nothing that I understand. It's all science formulas and gibberish to me." Angie tried to turn on a computer to find it locked by username and password. "Have you ever seen this logo before?"

Fred walked over to look at the employee login screen: the words *Engen Laboratories* ran along the top of the screen. "I've never heard of it." Fred wheeled over a chair and sat in front of the computer.

"Do you think you can hack into this computer?" Angie scanned the room for anything else she could use.

Fred hit enter on the keyboard to see what would happen. *Incorrect username and password* popped up on the screen. Fred clicked on the question marks that followed the phrase. "Maybe someone wrote their username and password somewhere. It appears to be their last name and initials."

Angie rummaged through some notes in a drawer, hauling out journals and binders. "I don't think the people that work in this office are the people that need to record their username and password."

Fred knew that she was right, it would be pointless looking around for that information. "I guess we will have to do this the old-fashioned way." Fred turned the power off the computer tower and turned it around so he could unplug all the chords. "Can you unplug a computer for me? I want to have a backup in case something happens to the CPU chip I take." Fred took out his multi tool and flipped out the screwdriver to remove the back of the computer. Once he got the back off, the hardware exposed, he found the hard drive. He removed the memory chip and placed it his chest pocket.

"It's unplugged for you." Angie walked away from the computer and began searching through the paperwork.

Fred retrieved the hard drive from the other computer. "Do you find it strange that it's so quiet here?" The building was dead silent, except for a low, electric hum. He looked around the room and noticed that everything was packed away for the day. Every workstation was tidy, and the building appeared to be empty now.

"You think it's a trap." Angie was thumbing through the pages of a binder, her eyes scanning back and forth, trying to absorb the information.

"It can't be a coincidence they leave alone us to rummage through a top-secret facility. Something is going on here." Fred looked back at the door expecting to see that soldier peering in at them, but the door was still shut. "I mean, this place was swarming with activity when we got here, I doubt they went home." Fred opened the cupboards and rummaged through the different containers. Most of the labels contained several severe warnings and seemed dangerous. "What do you think about all of this?"

"You need to come look at this," Angie responded.

Kendra closed the car door and jumped into the driver's seat. Adjusting the rearview mirror, she watched Alicia squirm in her car seat. Her daughter's face grimaced in pain, making her look wretched. The engine sputtered as she turned the key; the car jolted and knocked as she pressed on the gas pedal.

"Mommy, it hurts!" Alicia cried out, kicking the back of the passenger seat.

"I know, sweetheart, we will make it all better soon." Kendra's nightgown, smeared with crimson blood, clung to sweaty skin. Some of Alicia's blood had rolled down to her thighs, tarnishing her pale skin. The car vibrated as Kendra accelerated down the barren street. She had done her best trying to wrap her daughter's wound in gauze, but the red fluids had already soaked through.

"Mommy, please!" Alicia screamed shrilly. Kendra raced through the streets, speeding past the stop signs, refusing to slow down around the turns. Alicia's shrieks were becoming high-pitched and erratic with every passing moment.

"We will be there shortly, just hold on okay." Kendra looked into the mirror and saw a spew of white spittle spraying from her daughter's clenched lips. Alicia was trying to scream through her teeth. Kendra's heart sank as a somber thought crossed her mind. *What if that dog had rabies?* Was there even a treatment for that now? Kendra punched the steering wheel in anger and frustration. The jolt sent a wave of pain up her arms until it faded at her elbow.

High-pitched squeals quickly turned into a rapid squawking that sounded like a bird chirping. Kendra turned around just in time to watch Alicia bite her own arm. Alicia jerked her head back, tearing a large mouth-ful of flesh out of her bicep. Red fibres dangled from her mouth as deep red blood gushed out of the nasty gnash.

"What are you doing?!" Kendra screamed out in hor-ror. Alicia chewed on the hunk of meat in her mouth as Kendra looked on in shock, unable to take her eyes off the horrific sight.

A resounding smash abruptly stopped the car dead in its tracks. The airbags deployed, and the force knocked Kendra out cold. The car was a wrangled wreck: all the windows had shattered sending glass over the grass and asphalt as the car smashed into a tree. Alicia continued to gnaw at her restraints, working to free herself, but her teeth were doing more damage to the flesh on her arm. A trickle of blood turned into a thick stream that cascaded down her arm and soaked into her car seat.

James followed the road from fifty metres in the woods. He had uncovered a pair of footprints in the ex-posed patches of earth on the forest floor. The imprints might have belonged to Fred and Angie, but it was nearly impossible to know. Combat boots were common across most military units regardless of nationality, purchased from any local surplus store. That was where James had bought most of the gear for his team, from an old white bricked building down on the waterfront of his hometown. It was an absurd image that he struggled to push out of his mind's eye. With everything that was going on, it made little sense to be thinking about something so insignificant. Maybe it was his brain's coping mechanism to deal with the stress of the situation.

The sun was at its highest point in the sky now; James had been running for two hours now and he still hadn't reached the testing facility. The shade of the forest canopy had kept him sheltered from the sweltering Stapleton sun for the better part of the morning. A wide clearing presented itself just ahead of the road. This had to be the secret test facility.

A tree branch snapped just ahead of him, and James dropped to the ground, forced by the hand of instinct. He scanned the clearing ahead for any sign of movement.

"James, we need to move!"

"Thistle?" James called out, he recognized the voice. "Where's Angie?"

"She's securing a vehicle. Let's move it, we got to catch up before it's too late!" Fred Thistle called out, a sense of urgency heavy in his voice.

"What do you mean?" James asked. "What's going on at that testing facility?"

Fred emerged from behind a shrub. His black-framed glasses rested low on his nose and his stubble had grown in thick and dark overnight. "They have created the biological weapon we've all suspected. If they use it on a city, everyone will tear themselves apart. They will take us out without firing a single bullet." Fred's combats were soiled by blood, and James saw the carbon buildup in the barrel of his AR-15.

"Where is the General?" James rushed forward to join Fred.

"He's headed into Stapleton. They have already unleashed the virus. If they aren't careful, this disease will spread much faster than they are forecasting." Fred spoke hastily, barely pausing long enough to catch his breath.

A Jeep raced down the dirt road, sending up a cloud of dirt behind it. "Why would it spread quicker than they are predicting?"

"They used a strain of reptile genome that will spread amongst most animals. Angie has already identified three crows with the plague and before they recognize, what's happening, the infection can transmit from town to town." Fred favoured his back as he dashed towards the Jeep. "They have a convoy ready to transport the pathogen and if we don't prevent the spread, it will consume the North before we can even get out of Stapleton."

The Jeep screeched to a halt at the edge of the road. James rushed towards the vehicle and jumped into the passenger's seat. "Jesus Christ, are you okay Angie?"

Angie's ebony hair stressed how pale her skin had become. Large beads of sweat covered her broand w, her blue eyes were bloodshot and sunken in their own sockets. "I'm fine, don't worry about it." She coughed into the crook of her elbow.

James looked her over again. "You look horrible." He

could swear he could see waves of heat pulsating off her body in the dry heat of Stapleton.

"Don't worry about me, you just make sure you're ready for a fight." Angie put the Jeep in drive, the gears grinding as she moved the gear-shifter.

"We will be outnumbered and overpowered." Fred spoke up from the back.

"I love a good fight." James was never one to shy away from any conflict. His primary concern was to prevent this epidemic from spreading, by any means necessary. His daughter's face super-imposed over Angie's. He had to keep her safe, no matter the cost. They weren't an official government entity, just a group of wanna-be heroes. He could feel his heart racing with anticipation, and every nerve ending sending chills through his body as the adrenaline flushed through his system.

A sickening crunching sound startled Kendra back into consciousness. She tasted blood and her neck was pulsing in pain from the whiplash. It took a moment for her to comprehend that she was still in the car. The front windshield had shattered, and shards of jagged glass embedded in her soft flesh. Kendra turned her head and nearly threw up at the sight of her daughter. Alicia had gnawed through the fat and tissue surrounding her upper arm and was now biting into the cartilage. Alicia's teeth weren't strong enough to get through the solid bone and were splintering into pieces in her own mouth. It wasn't stopping her from trying, however; she gulped down a mouthful of shattered tooth fragments and blood.

"Please, stop that, Alicia," Kendra begged her daughter to listen to reason, but her daughter continued to mutilate herself. Kendra reached down to unbuckle her seatbelt, but a sharp pain in her hand forced her arm to recoil. She looked down and watched the blood pour out of her hand. A large sliver of glass had sliced her hand wide open between the webbing of her index and middle finger.

"Fuck," Kendra cursed as she shook her hand, as if magically that would make the pain go away. The revolting sound of her daughter gnawing into her own arm was making her sick to her stomach. She peered in the rearview mirror, praying that her daughter had ceased chewing her own flesh. Everything went deathly silent.

Alicia had bitten through the nylon strap of her car seat on the right side — she lunged forward with her arm outstretched but the left strap held her in place. Alicia leaned her body awkwardly to escape the constraints of her chair and fell face first onto the floor. Her body was twisted, and she struggled to straighten out in the tight confines between the seats. She was trying to yell, blood spewing from her mouth preventing the escape of any sound.

"Alicia, you have to stop!" Kendra swept aside the jagged glass and unfastened her seatbelt. She shoved the car door open and tumbled out of the car. Her head was a foggy daze. She stood up. Bracing herself against the side of the car, her head spun out of control.

"Alicia, Mom is coming!" she cried out with motherly regard. Kendra used her gentlest tone to soothe her ravenous daughter. She made her way around the back of the car and opened the door. Alicia's face pressed against the car mat in a pool of her own blood, her jaw snapping open and shut. "Alicia, it will be okay." Kendra reached down and pulled her daughter out of the car.

The rumble of an automobile engine distracted Kendra as a van pulled up behind her. The tires crushed the dirt and pebbles near the curb of the road as it slowed to a stop. "Do you need help?" A woman's panicked voice cried out: "Oh my God!"

Kendra turned towards the car, and her eyes registered the hood of the red van just as she felt the sharp pain run up her leg. A wave of white stars twinkled in her vision as the immeasurable agony corrupted every sense in her body. "Alicia!" Kendra screeched as she stared down at her daughter's face buried into her upper thigh. Alicia hadn't just bitten her leg: she was chewing on it. Deep red blood gurgled from Alicia's mouth as she sucked in air between vicious bites.

Kendra tried to shake her daughter off her leg without harming her, but Alicia's grip locked in tight. "Alicia, you're hurting Mom!" Kendra couldn't take the suffering any longer; she kicked her leg with every ounce of strength she had left and sent her daughter tumbling backwards. Alicia's head smacked off the side of the car with a loud thump. She collapsed against rear passenger door and a maroon blotch streaked down the car as she fell. Her eyes closed and her head slumped into her chest, blood dripping down her face as her jaw fell open.

"What are you doing?" the woman wailed as she rushed past Kendra and scrambled to Alicia's side. She was a short, stalky woman wearing jean shorts and a black tank top that was too small. Her love handles poked out of her shirt as she bent down to check on Alicia. The scent of the woman aroused Alicia, and her nostrils flared wide open. Alicia's eyes sprang open as the woman leaned in to check on her. A ferocious rumble stuck in her throat as her head sprang forward.

A tear ran down Kendra's face as she watched her daughter's teeth sink deep into the nape of the stranger's neck. She wanted to rush to her daughter's side but her muscles refused to listen to her brain, her impulses firing in all directions but failing to register. "Alic...!" Kendra's scream stuck in her throat. "Ali..." The word fell back into her larynx. She took a deep breath and tried pushing out her voice with every ounce of strength, her diaphragm forcefully pushing against her lungs. Only a muffled choke escaped.

Everything around her seemed to fade into the distance. The bright Stapleton sun dulled, the sounds of the city distorted, and she could only focus her sight on one disturbing, disheartening sight. Fear forced Kendra to watch her daughter devour the stranger, tearing apart her victim with a gleeful smile, her once innocent face smeared with blood. Without knowing it, Kendra's lips curled into a wicked snarl and she salivated at the ghastly sight.

James Porter bounced around his seat as the Jeep's tires bounced over the curb. "Angie, we need to be in one piece when we catch up to them." James knuckles turned white as he gripped the handle at the top of the door frame. The Jeep was weaving in and out of traffic as Angie sped through the city streets of Stapleton. Her complexion was ghastly, the white of her eyes had changed completely red with burst blood vessels. Crowds of people ran through the streets, chasing after each other with crazed eyes. James shuddered, realizing that Angie was turning into one of the bloodthirsty monsters Freemantle had created. The infection passed from host to carrier through a bite. "Angie, pull over."

"There they are, just ahead." Fred pointed towards the convoy just ahead.

Angie's head drooped as she slammed down on the gas pedal. "Angie, you need to slow down." James reached out towards her shoulder, but she smacked his arm away. He glanced out the window and observed as the back of the giant green Dodge Ram approached. James and Fred both leapt towards Angie to wrestle control of the vehicle away from her. It was too late. The grill of the Jeep crashed into the back bumper of the giant truck at a right angle, sending both vehicles swerving out of control. James felt the force of the impact as his neck jerked forward violently; the seatbelt nearly broke his collarbone with the whiplash. The Stapleton sun spun around in his vision as the Jeep's tire smashed into a high curb and rolled over. Sounds of crunching metal and shattering glass was deafening, enclosing them from the horrified cries in the streets. James rocked back and forth, fixed in his seat until the Jeep came to an abrupt halt on its mangled tires.

The crash disoriented him enough that it took a few minutes before he realized they had smashed through the enormous glass window of a pharmacy. A splatter of blood ran down the windshield and flowed down towards the source. Flailed over the hood, an elderly man laid motionless, his legs bent into impossible positions. Long grey hair, smeared with blood and fragments of brain matter, concealed his face. The man's face was pulverized beyond recognition. The impact had toppled shelves and pill bottles over and scattered about the pharmacy storefront. A pharmacist stood behind the counter with his jaw dropped open in a stunned gasp. Drops of blood from the car crash stained his white lab coat, and a splash of blood soaked into his goatee.

James looked over at Angie and nearly threw up. Her collarbone had snapped in half and the jagged edges tore through the soft flesh at the nape of her neck. Blood spewed from her mouth as she forced out a seething, gargling screech. James looked around for his rifle. It had become lost during the accident. Angie reached out for him, her nails digging into James' shoulder. She worked to shred her nails down his arm, but the nails bent backwards and peeled off from the root.

"Angie, what the fuck are you doing?!" James screeched in agony. He looked into his old friend's eyes, shocked to find the devil's eyes staring back at him. Wet, black eyes gazed back at James, staring at him like a ravenous dog when food hits the floor. The seatbelt struggled to keep Angie's greedy, snapping jaws out of James. An explosion of gunfire exploded in the streets outside of the drugstore, and James heard the roar of diesel engines rushing towards his location.

The seatbelt snapped, and Angie lunged for James. A high-pitched hiss escaped her throat, piercing into his ears with her fiery breath on his face. He tried to put his hands up to defend himself, but it was too late. James closed his eyes and waited for the end. Agonizingly moments passed by, even though time seemed to stand still. Angie didn't sink her teeth into his throat. All at the same time, a resounding pop echoed and Angie's unconscious body collapsed onto his shoulder. Her dead weight rocked the Jeep.

James opened his eyes and peered down at her devilish grin, those cold eyes peering back up at him with animalistic ferocity in them. Fred had twisted her neck at an impossible angle, a portion of her spine jutting from her neck from where her head should have rested.

"We need to get the fuck out of here right now." Fred held his hands in front of his face and observed them trembling uncontrollably.

"What the hell is going on here?" James turned back to look at Fred, a look of guilt and regret washed over his face. Sweat and dirt smudged his five o'clock shadow.

Fred pushed the door open and slid his way out of the backseat, holding his back and grimacing in pain as he tried to stand upright. "We don't have time to stick around." He held up his hand, gesturing for James to listen. The heavy echoes of footprints and gunfire raged through the streets. "The virus has spread beyond our control and if we don't get out of Stapleton now, we will die."

James wouldn't leave Stapleton with his family trapped in this chaotic scene. "I can handle putting down these crazies."

"I'm sure you could if you had time, but you can't outrun the napalm strike that's headed our way." Fred opened James' door and held out his hand. "This was an experiment gone awry."

"I can't leave Kendra and Alicia." James stepped down

from the Jeep, the bruises in his abdomen tightening.

"I can't stop you, but I need to get back. Good luck." Fred nodded his head and turned without saying another word. Both men knew what they had to do, and neither man would convince the other any differently. James watched as Fred ran towards the exit with his gun raised, the muzzle flashing three times before he disappeared outside. James pulled out his cellphone but there was no reception. He would need to hurry.

Louise ducked into the abandoned emergency exit and scampered behind an old storage container. She lifted her palm to cover her mouth, trying to dampen the sound of her heavy breathing. Her lungs pressed against her ribs and she sought desperately to catch her breath before Devon caught up to her. No matter how fast she ran, she couldn't shake him. The other miners had blocked her escape up the main shaft. Her coworkers had gone completely demented, fighting with each other and tearing into each other's flesh in some sick orgy of blood and gore. She angled her head and stared at the old cave wall in terror; she had wandered into a trap. They had pushed the old scrap container against the wall, and there was no other way around.

Louise heard the shuffle of footsteps approaching. She cowered behind the metal container and shook vehemently. The scuffling steps halted, the low, clicking squawks shattering an abrupt silence. Louise had to fight back tears of fear. Her muscles twitched and stiffened as a flood of adrenaline tried to propel her forward. Held in place against her will, her legs remained glued to the ground.

The strange, disturbing clicking sounds stopped and an eerie silence weighed heavily in the room. Louise's heavy breathing seemed that much louder now, and the only noise louder now were snorts and sniffing. The slow but steadily growing sounds of dragging feet crept closer and closer to Louise. She wanted to run, but her legs wouldn't budge; she found herself trapped.

Devon appeared as he staggered past the corner, his sly smile smeared with blood. "Devon, stay back." Louise's voice quivered and tears rolled down her cheeks. His wet black eyes locked in a death stare with her terrified ones, his ravenous jaws salivating at his captured prey. Devon fell on top of Louise, crashing into her and pinning her to the ground. She couldn't see his face anymore. The fear escaped her body as Devon's ice-cold hands delved into her stomach. She felt his fingers dig farther into her gut and a warm rush of fluids gushed out. A white fiery flash of pain flushed throughout Louise as she lost her vision. The sickening sounds of Devon chewing on a shredded portion of her intestines made her cackle and she died with a sadistic smirk.

James wandered down the street, not realizing how long it had been when he noticed the unmistakable golden glow of his daughter's hair. He would have recognized it anywhere. The pandemic transformed the town of Stapleton into an apocalyptic nightmare. Vile creatures who had once been human roamed the asphalt jungle. Their thirst for bloodshed and flesh was far stronger than anything he had ever experienced. His daughter stood out like an angel amongst those ghouls. The warm sun glowed in Alicia's hair, and her bronzed skin radiated with it. Gore sullied her clothes, but that wouldn't hide her beautiful aurora. Deep down, James knew that his daughter, who he had loved more than anything in the entire world, wasn't standing in front of him. He refused to acknowledge that he had let anything so awful happen to her.

James knelt down on one knee and held his arms out for one last hug. Just like all of those times, he would come back home from being away for work for a long time. She rushed straight for him with her arms outreached. He couldn't stand to look at those wet, black eyes. James closed his eyes and visualized his sweet little daughter rushing in to give him one last loving embrace. "I'm sorry, Alicia." The words gurgled out of his throat as her teeth pinched off the noise.

The echo of jet engines rumbled in the distance, which meant they were closer than the noise let on. James opened his eyes. Three fighter jets passed overhead, silhouetted against the pale sky. He did the only thing a parent would do in a situation like this: he wrapped his arms around his daughter tight, doing his best to protect his baby girl from the napalm strike.

Fred walked through the airport terminal with his head held down low. Deep down inside, he would regret abandoning James Porter and the rest of his team for the rest of his life. But money talked, and he took orders from people who paid him enough to retire. He didn't know if they had made it out alive. That was no longer his concern; there was no looking back now. Forward, that was the only direction left for him to travel. He cursed himself for allowing them to get caught in this terrible nightmare, but he needed them to help him achieve his aim. The intelligence he carried was worth much more than his current employer would pay, so he was taking it elsewhere. Money talked. Nearly finished, this deal would allow him to walk away from this nightmarish line of work. In two days, he would sit on a beach, drinking his worries away.

Not having to wait in line at the Southern Sky's kiosk, Fred walked up to the counter. An adolescent man wearing a red blazer over a yellow dress shirt sat behind a computer. His blond hair was slicked back and there was way too much gel holding it in place. "Can I help you?" The man's voice was deep, which startled Fred; he'd been expecting a cheerful voice.

"Yes, I'm looking to book a flight home." Fred took his wallet out of his jeans pocket. His thumb traced the hard plastic case of the USB drive. He kept it in his pocket but felt reassured by its touch. The information on this drive was worth hundreds of millions to his newest employer.

"You don't have a ticket?" The attendant furrowed his brow.

"No, I don't." Fred took out an onyx credit card, as he did a business card fell to the floor and landed face down.

The credit card caught the man's attention. "Very good sir, and where would home be?" His attitude was suddenly much more upbeat.

Fred bent down and turned over the card, a smile spreading across his face. "A little place you've never been before," Fred said as he flipped the Pharmakon business card over in his hand. "Fox Island."

TIMELINE III

I can recall with perfect clarity the day my wife died.

I woke up in my bed alone. The sun was harsh on me, and the air was thick with both the familiar scent of bacon and the sound of Jennifer singing to herself.

I got up and got dressed in the same clothes I had every other day: clothes I had thrown out as they had been stained with my wife's blood, but that now were back and perfectly clean. I was still adjusting my shirt when I turned the kitchen corner to see Jennifer standing at the stove. She smiled at me when she saw me, that sideways smirk that always calmed me and excited me all at the same time.

When I saw that smile, tilted to one side quirkily, her hair falling onto her shoulders in wisps, I had to stop and kiss her, and cup her tiny chin in my palm. When I made myself pull back from her, I took the handle of the frying pan from her gently and moved it to an inactive burner, then turned the stove off altogether.

"What are you doing?" she laughed, miffed at my behavior.

"We have to go into Parse," I said as I rested my hand

on her hip and led her away from the kitchen.

"Parse?" she repeats, stopping in her tracks mid-way through the kitchen. Her hand went to her abdomen unconsciously. "We're not going to Parse."

"There's something wrong with the baby," I said.

She stared at me for a long, bewildered moment.

"There's something wrong with the baby and there's nothing they can do at Signet."

Both her hands were now at her abdomen, as if she could somehow will the child to health. I hoped that the stress I was causing her would not cause more problems or aggravate her condition. Then all at once she came to life, moving with as much haste as her cumbersome form would allow and went with me to get ready. While we prepared, she asked me how I knew and I told her. I told her without telling her about York and Signet and everything else. I told her so little that I almost told her nothing at all but my wife was smart — it was one of the first things I truly loved about her — and she inferred the rest and broke down crying there in our porch. It took twenty minutes to get her back on track and out the door from there, and I decided that no matter what happened I would never tell her more or tell her again: this would be mine to bear, and mine alone.

Between the towns of York, Signet, and Goin that secured the coastline and the free city that was Parse was 300 miles of barren land policed by the Remers that no one went through without dire purpose or need: Reps territory.

I'd never seen them up close, but knew from those who had that I didn't want to. On one of my two previous trips through the territory, I had seen a herd of them moving along the horizon — their movement was not controlled and fluid like normal, natural creatures in motion; it was random and chaotic, factions splitting off and moving in different directions, others eventually seeing it and returning to the fold, picking a new direction that was nowhere close to their original path.

Also, 'herd' was not an apt term for their roaming, disjointed gatherings. If I had my way I would borrow from the crows and call it a murder. A murder of Reps, moving along the farthest edges of my vision as I wondered, frantically, if their sight was better than mine and if I could be noticed alone in amongst the desert sands as I was.

I heard that they had been men, once. If that was what they had been and what they could be called, they could no longer.

I made sure the Jeep was full of gas and that there were extra cans in the back, and my rifle. I did not, under any circumstances, want to get caught in Rep territory in a vehicle without fuel.

Parse was on roughly the same longitudinal line as York and my farm. The shortest distance between us and it was to head due west along the flat of the desert between the two toward the Remers guard wall that stood along Parse's eastern border, and so that was what we did.

Despite its danger, or perhaps even because of it, the desert had always been appealing to me in my youth. I heard folks from Goin talk the same way about the ocean, the difference being everyone knew the ocean teemed with life; in the desert, even after all these years, life was a secret. It seemed flat and devoid of anything — how could there be anything when everything could be seen and one could see nothing? But I'd wager a year's income that there was no square foot of sand you could plant your shovel into without finding *some* form of life: dung beetles or tics or red harvester ants.

It was that unknowable quality that drew me to make my home as close to its edge as I could — in being unknown, I was the only one who truly knew it. To everyone else, the desert wasteland between York and Parse was like the unexplored areas of the old maps: places where dragons slept. I named these unexplored regions with glee, even if I was the only one who ever knew their names. There was satisfaction for me in discovering that undiscovered country... the same satisfaction that I got when I laid next to Jennifer at night: this feeling was mine, and no matter how close anyone else got to this feeling in their own lives, it would never feel exactly the way this felt, right now.

One hundred miles into the desert we reached the outer ring of where I'd explored between my Jeep and my telescope. The shadow of Parse was a scant whisper on the horizon now — the land so flat that the city was visible hours before we would reach it. The desert was greener here, with more oases and small, scant rivers that cut their way through the sand like the Nile had in ancient Egypt. It was the dryness, the absolute desolation of the one hundred miles between this and my farm, that supposedly kept the Reps at bay.

Jennifer had been cradling her ample belly, supporting it with her left hand while stroking it with her right. The wind from our speed was catching her hair and making it dance all around the cab, and she looked like some heretofore undiscovered work from the Renaissance: Madonna in Jeep.

"It is a girl, yes?" she asked out of nowhere. Her voice was calm and serene, but the context was wrought with worry.

"...Yes," I answered, tentatively.

She nodded. "You named her Gwen then?"

I paused for a long moment which was just as pregnant as she was, if not more so. "What are we going to do in Parse tomorrow?" I ask finally, forcing a smile.

She watched me for a second, then smiled that quirky sideways smile that greeted me every morning. "Tomorrow. Tomorrow I will be bedridden in a hospital in Parse."

I nodded, then took a hand off the wheel as if to give an alternative point. "Okay, then what do you want to do in Parse next week?"

She laughed.

"There's always the theatre. We could take in a show."

"Please."

"We could go shopping. We'll need new clothes for you and the babe."

She laughed outright at that. "You *hate* shopping."

I shrugged exaggeratedly, and she laughed again. I smiled and she leaned in and kissed me on the cheek. She laid her head down on my shoulder and I turned to kiss the top of her head.

I slammed on the breaks and we both thrust forward against our seatbelts.

Twenty feet in front of us a vaguely human form was lying naked in the desert sand, his flesh bleached to a near bone white.

His flesh was taut to his slender form, all his ribs visible. Veins of deep purple made their way over a scalp that was devoid of hair yet dotted with scabs, as though someone had ripped it out at the roots. His face was turned away from us, showing only the deep bones of his spine and the slight cleft of his buttocks.

Jennifer hugged her stomach, and there was a moment when that was of the utmost concern to me: had I caused more damage to her or the child? That was something I did not think I could bear. She made a cough low in her throat, then sniffed back whatever pain she was feeling and turned to me. "We should tell someone in Parse about him. It's shameful for a body to just be left out there alone like that."

I turned toward her slightly, without taking my eyes off the man in front of the car. "That's not a body," I corrected softly. "And they're never alone."

As if on cue, one of its arms rose from the husk of it and planted itself into the sand. I heard the air in Jennifer halt abruptly as she watched it brace itself and slowly rise from where it had lay for god only knew how long. It turned to us, its face just as white as the rest of it save for thick red rings around its eyes and mouth, which hung open disjointedly. It stared at us with eyes that had burst all their blood vessels, the crimson of them so dark that the pupils were indistinguishable from the whites.

I pushed the Jeep into reverse and backed up as the Rep rose to its feet, its eyes locked on us from the second they caught sight of us. It was more than just the cold, calculating stare of a predator though: it was anger. That was the thing about the Reps and the stories that surrounded them that never ceased to send chills down my spine — from the second they saw you, they hated you. They hated you with the type of blinding rage usually reserved for child predators and tax collectors. The red rings around their eyes burned with it.

"I've never seen one before," Jennifer said, leaning forward and touching the dash. In the corner of my eye she was awestruck, that beautiful soft mouth agape and making her jaw round.

The Rep opened its mouth as the distance between us grew and emitted a low, guttural click not unlike a death rattle. It was inaudible beneath the slow drone of the Jeep's engine, yet in my memory I can clearly hear it, the *click click click* of the moist remains of the creature's tongue flailing for purchase against the roof of its mouth and the battered shards of its teeth.

She turned away from the horror as we backed up faster, widening the gap between us. Her face was full of wonder and I clung to it. She was afraid but she didn't let that fear block her from this new sight, this new experience of her world made real before her eyes. She was a wonder of wisdom set against the pale sand of the dune behind her.

Then the sand of the dune moved, and the arms of two more Reps came into view.

"Christ!" I yelled, jolting the wheel and making Jennifer jump. She screamed without being sure why, and one of the emerging Reps nabbed the metal skeleton of the Jeep before it was pulled free again by the momentum of my turn. I could see its sandy palmprint on the metal, including the gap where it had been missing its ring finger.

I let my turn bring us around one-hundred and eighty degrees until the original Rep was in my rear-view mirror and then I pressed down on the gas hard. The back wheels sputtered and spun in the sand for an instant before finding purchase and thrusting us forward, even as more Reps emerged all around us.

Jennifer turned and looked over the seat back at them as they rose to stand and in greater number, new ones coming seemingly out of nowhere until they formed a slowly advancing wall along the horizon. Her hair blew around the cab of the Jeep as we picked up speed, but she never blinked. She watched with one hand gripping the back of her seat and one gripping my shoulder.

We drove ten miles back the way we'd come before turning off of the normal straight longitudinal path between York and Parse we'd been taking. We ventured south in a wide arc that veered back towards the west and Parse's border wall, to make sure we avoided the Reps. They tended to move in large swarms, and I'd even heard that in Parse they'd started accounting for them the same way they used to the weather. I gave where I though the swarm was a wide berth while staying as close to our route as I dared: you couldn't get over the wall just anywhere, and I didn't want to add more time to our journey unnecessarily.

It did, of course. Either from the fright of the Reps or the roughness of our ride, Jennifer's water broke hours before it had on other occasions. The blood had splashed down her leg and into the seat of the Jeep and she'd screamed that scream I'd heard too many times and yet would never, ever get used to. It's a scream that can't be faked by any actor or caught by any recording device — the type that has to be heard in the moment by human ears, that makes you believe in a soul if only because you just felt it be pierced.

I sped through most of her agony, trying to still make it to Parse on time. The wall was well in sight at the end, not a glimmer but a discernible presence. No entrance was though: we'd been pushed too far south. When her screams reached their apex and she gripped my arm as though she were trying to stay above water, I stopped the car and went to her.

She fought hard. She pushed through the blood and the pain and pressure. Her face was a deep crimson from pushing and I tried to help her breathe. Towards the end I could see her, the child that Jennifer and I had chosen to call Gwen but whom I had not yet acknowledged as such. I could see the flesh of her crowning within my wife even as Jennifer's lips turned purple from the effort. At first, I couldn't fathom the odd shape of my child's head, and then I realized that she was breech. On top of everything else, my child was coming out bottom-first.

Jennifer died on her next push. There was no doctor involved this time, but the pressure had built to an aneurysm. She died with our child still in her, and there were several panicked moments as I cried and fumbled without knowing what to do before my hand found my knife.

My blade lingered over Jennifer's abdomen for a long moment. I brought it down and touched her flesh, then drew back. I did this over and over, unable to separate her and release our child from what had given it substance but was now its prison, its executioner's chair... but couldn't. And after a time, I knew too long had passed, and I knelt in the sand clotted with my wife's blood and mourned them both again.

I stayed that way until dark, and I heard the Reps shuffling in the distance, enticed by the scent of blood and the screams.

I can recall with perfect clarity the day my wife died.

NEW EMPLOYMENT

Alicia bubbled with excitement, squirming with delight in the cool, misty afternoon. It was time to use her skills again after weeks of waiting. She wondered why she had to wait. She never left any evidence after all was said and done. She sighed contentedly. That was unimportant now. In a few minutes, half an hour at most, someone would come along, and everything would be good. She giggled. Good for her, at least.

It wasn't long until a short, blocky car slowed down to where she was waiting. Inside the passenger side was a woman with a small round face and blue eyes, set off by her blue blouse. She had dirty blonde hair that poured off her head onto her shoulders. Driving was a man with a broad, square jaw covered with a thick, black beard. The beard tapered neatly into a short haircut, giving the man an impression of military power. Two people! How exciting! And both so fit too. Usually it was truckers on this road, ugly fat slobs who were more fat than meat. Alicia ran her tongue over her teeth as she walked over. This was gonna be good.

As soon as the man got a good look at her, he slammed

on the gas and sped off, catching Alicia completely by surprise. How rude! She adjusted her bust, wishing for a mirror to check how she looked. Even if she was hideous, to offend a hitchhiker like that! The man had to be a brute! And such fit people! Alicia shook her head. It was a damned waste, that's what it was. Then she calmed down. The voice is right, there will be more. Who would want such a mean brute anyways? He'd be no fun. He'd ruin the fun with the girl, in a matter of fact. No good at all.

She giggled again. The voice was always right. She wondered how she ever lived without it.

It was two or three minutes before a trucker showed up out of the mist. He pulled over and Alicia climbed in. He was fat, with multiple chins, and greasy mustache. She groaned internally. Fat louts were more fun than boney crackheads, for sure, but she was so sick of them. He was excited, at least.

"Where are ya' goin', little miss?"

Tossing her hair, she replied, smiling, "Oh, just into town. Me and my... ex-boyfriend got in a fight. He thought it'd be real funny to kick me out of the car all the way out here."

The trucker looked her over with an appraising eye. "What was the argument about? Must'a been pretty important, to kick such a pretty little lady out."

She laughed at this. "He was calling me a slut, for screwing 'every guy I met'." She could see it in the way the man's eyes traced over her again. He was almost there, just needed a little push. Then the fun would begin. He was already falling.

"That's a horrible thing to accuse a woman like you

of doing."

"Well, it's true." She adjusted her bust to show a bit more, and she had him, hook, line and sinker.

She couldn't hide her grin as she led the man into the woods. It was so easy to pull these lonely men to the cabin. One whiff of sex, and they were putty. If it had been the couple, it would have been much, much tougher. She could hear the man huffing and puffing along behind her as they went deeper and deeper into the woods. Soon, they came to their destination, a dilapidated, old, creaky cabin. Alicia ushered the man inside.

"Nice and private. You got good taste, mis- ARGH!" The man slammed to the ground, clutching his ankle.

Alicia rolled him over with her foot. "You fuckers are so predictable, you know that?" She played with the razor she had used to cut his Achilles tendon. She licked the blood off. "Now get in the fucking chair." She gestured to a chair with leather straps across where the waist, wrists, and ankles would be.

"I, I can't move my feet.."

Alicia grabbed him with her free hand and shoved him towards the chair. "GET IN THE FUCKING CHAIR!" The man was sobbing as she strapped him in. Her voice was softer when she spoke again. "What's your name?"

"B...Bill."

"Well, Bill, we are going to play a game, alright?" Bill nodded "If you can guess what bit I'm going to cut off next, you get to keep it. If you guess wrong, I cut it off." Bill looked terrified. Alicia decided to give him a bit of help. Pointless hope made the game a bit more fun. "I'll start with the little things. Ready?"

Bill nodded.

She giggled. "Well then, guess."

"L-little f-finger."

"Left or right?"

"R-right."

"Wrong."

She hacked off his left little finger and popped the gory morsel in her mouth. Bill was too busy screaming to notice. It was tasty though. A little bit fatty, but the man clearly used his hands a lot. She was going to savour those. As the screaming subsided, she could hear the voice again. She took the moment of calm to console the voice.

"No, no, that's not the game. He guesses, we either cut or don't cut. That's the deal. He'll scream plenty, don't worry." Bill looked up. He had pissed and shit in fear, and that smell of terror was a perfume to Alicia. Her voice was silky as she spoke again. "Guess."

It was night before Alicia was done with the fingers and toes. She had taken a break, and savoured every morsel. When she had been working for her brother, there had been bigger meals, but now she had to savour every bite. The floor was damp with blood. As she replaced the hatchet behind the door, she licked her lips. Then, the grin on her face began to form into a frown. The game was over, the poor man's heart was giving out. She began to unstrap him. Bill's eyes fluttered open.

"Are- you letting me go?" His voice was weak, horse.

But the glimmer of pointless hope in there made everything a little more delicious. She giggled.

"Nope."

Her eyes glimmered, her smile filling with crooked, jagged teeth. The last thing Bill saw was that massive, toothy maw engulfing his head.

As she sat, contentedly picking her teeth after the meal, she listened to the voice. Pickings were good here, that's for sure. But they were all the same. Fat louts. Greasy. Weak. Not like the two from today. Those two would have survived for at least the night. And she could have taken turns, forcing each to guess for the other. That would have been a good game. And the meat, ah, that would have been nice. She had to find new grounds. But where? It had to be somewhat secluded. They had to scream. That's what the voice liked. And what the voice liked, she liked. So cities were out. Unless... The subway systems in major cities. They had abandoned stations, she had read about that in the papers. She grinned. Something like that. Private. With plenty of pickings. Ohh, that'd be good.

As she stood to leave, she checked to make sure everything was clean. Seeing that it was, she giggled. Alicia Bond still cleaned up good.

COMFORTABLY NUMB

Cathy watched from across the park as smoke cocooned Xander's head, the blue grey haze captured against the night sky by the glow of the streetlamp. Her own breath hung in the air like a ghost, as if her soul was escaping through her lips. The morbidity of the past few months cloaked her thoughts now, as she watched Xander and felt the burning pit of anxiety grow in her chest.

His newest secret pleasure, walking the streets of Coral Beach late at night even when the Womb didn't force him outside, was ill concealed from her. Too many nights now, since she had taken to staring out her own window onto the town, had she seen Xander's hunched figure stooping to light a cigarette outside her house. He seemed completely oblivious to where his feet were taking him, and she found her concern outweighing her fears that he may not be entirely in control during his midnight wandering.

Cathy had been careful to be outside well before he passed by tonight, to avoid any chance that he would hear her drop down from her bedroom window to the lawn below. She had waited until after he reached the end of her street to creep out from behind the bushes she had hidden in, quietly making her way down the street after him.

Xander chain-smoked his way throughout Coral Beach: passing their school, the Factory, and by the houses of so many deceased friends before Cathy had finally felt some relief to see him take a seat on the creaking swings they had played on as children. His back to her, she could still recognize from across the park that his hands trembled as he held the smouldering butt of his last cigarette against the tip of a new one to light it.

He stayed there for some time, running his fingers through his hair and the cloud of smoke in such a way that it sent tendrils off his body. Cathy felt her stomach somersault as she was instantly reminded of the dark transformation he was prone to. The air was so still and crisp that under any other circumstances, in any other town, it could have been the perfect night.

Coral Beach was not the perfect town though, and as she watched Xander fuel the cloud around him, she felt distinctly unlucky to have ended up there. True, if she had never moved here she would not have met Mike, Xander, or even Sara, but she doubted she would have buried so many friends by this point in her life.

It's not that she hadn't loved her childhood in Coral Beach; even now she looked back fondly on games of hop-scotch with Mike and the long nights spent playing boys versus girls spotlight with he and Xander behind Sara's house. Hell, there was part of her that could almost smile at the time she had shoved Tommy to the ground when he had chased her and broken her headband in the first grade. Now though, she wondered more than ever what life would have been like had her family never moved here. She couldn't imagine any other series of events leading her to trail a friend through the streets at night.

Xander doused his cigarette suddenly, snapping Cathy out of her reverie. He was gone from the swings so smoothly they didn't even sway in his wake. Cathy's heart jumped up into her throat as her eyes darted quickly about, scanning the darkness as she crouched low to the ground. There was no way he was about to move like that without a reason. What if there was some unseen threat in the night that only he could pick up on? What if *he* was the threat in the night?

Cathy spun her head hoping she wouldn't catch a glimpse of blue or red shining in the night. She realized dizzily she had been holding her breath, and a small cloud escaped from her mouth again as she gasped for air. She barely felt her chest fill as a hand clamped over her mouth and an arm drew her body close.

"Shh," Xander whispered in her ear, muffling the yelp that escaped her lips. He smelt like a mixture of nicotine and leather, which she found oddly comforting, despite her revulsion toward his dirty habit. His warm breath on her neck was shallow as he pulled her even lower to the ground, flattening their bodies against the raised flowerbed she had been using for cover as she stalked him.

The black air of the night was suddenly pierced by the red and blue of police lights, a cruiser silently pulling onto the frozen fall ground of the playground. Xander relaxed his grip on Cathy as the sounds of two slamming car doors pierced the quiet night. He held a single finger to his lips, the dark circles under his eyes illuminated by the emergency lights in such a way that Cathy was suddenly struck by how emaciated her friend had become. Tonight, his eyes harboured a fear she had seen him push away time and time again. The fear was a warning: stay quiet, stay hidden.

Voices carried across the clearing, sullen and gravelly: "It smells like smoke, you smell that? We're not alone here."

"Friggin' gang bangers prob'ly hanging out here. God knows th' rest of 'em aren't dense enough to be out this hour anymore."

"You sure we're okay here tonight then? I don't want to get reamed by some punks when I'm trying to relax."

"Freakin' pussy. The lights scared anyone off. We're fine here. Get out the friggin' light before I light you up."

Xander motioned for Cathy to duck back towards the trees. "Keep low," he whispered, throwing a glance back over his shoulder. She peeked behind her and caught a glimpse of two pimple-faced patrol officers passing a glowing joint between each other. Hair fell across her eyes as she turned back toward the trees, scurrying past where the errant officers had any chance of seeing them.

Xander followed her closely, moving smoothly across the grass. Ducking into the darkness of the wooded area surrounding the park, he motioned for her to keep moving. The glow of the emergency lights faded as they moved deeper into the woods, until the two friends found themselves walking silently through the pitch black of night. Branches tugged at their clothes as they picked their way to sparser patches where the mask of trees and darkness might be more forgiving.

Cathy continued through the woods at an impressive pace, ignoring the stinging cuts she received in the process. Her heart was still in her throat; no distance seemed quite far enough away from the park for her to stop, and Xander's silent, corresponding footfalls only reminded her of having been caught once already that evening. She stole a glance back at him, hoping to judge his reaction to her activities, but shock sent her tumbling to the ground.

Xander lunged to steady her as her legs buckled on the uneven ground. His eyes had a wholly unnatural look to them, as the Womb's scarlet shimmer glossed over his own eye, but the look on his face screamed concern. "Careful, careful!" he murmured, looping his arm under her own and bringing her gingerly back to her feet.

"I...I..." stammered Cathy, completely lost for words as her eyes scanned her friend's face. Xander's brow furrowed, questioning silently if she was okay. She could feel the hairs on her arms stand at attention, the chill she felt catching her breath and leaving her mouth gaping as she stared at him.

"Cathy, are you alright? Say something," Xander said, pulling back from her and taking her by the shoulders so he could be face to face with her.

Finally finding herself, Cathy launched in on Xander. "What are you doing wandering Coral Beach? Are you looking for a fight? Christ sakes, Xander, your eyes are half red, dammit! Are you looking for a chance to have the Womb take over? You could kill someone! You could be killed!" she hissed.

Xander's look of concern faded in almost an instant, replaced with something that infuriated Cathy. A grin spread across his cheeks and, to her horror, a poorly concealed chuckle bubbled out from his lips.

"Oh Cat," he whispered, "leave it to you to be more concerned about me when you're the one who's gone and hurt themself."

She frowned, her brows knitting together and her mouth set in a thin line as Xander brushed her bangs away from her eyes.

"You realize I could ask you the same questions," Xander said, beginning to lead her through the forest again. "You're the one who followed me here. What would you have done if I had lost control?"

Cathy grumbled at his point. "Not much I could do, I guess. Still, it was either I follow you and find out what you were doing, and hopefully stop you from getting in trouble, or you wander about unchecked looking for a fight all night."

"Cat, you realize this is just my way of blowing off steam right? I can't smoke in the house. Mom would kill me. Besides, I might as well walk the streets. You saw how much interest the cops have in keeping the town safe," Xander chuckled, rubbing his brow. "Honestly, woman, you're like one of those little Pomeranians who bark at the bigger dogs."

Cathy scowled. "You think I couldn't hold my own in a fight?"

"Against a genetically modified killing machine, or even just one of the Tees or Omegas? Maybe not. You would definitely try though." He hugged her closer, as if he had reminded himself of her comparative fragility. "You've got your ankle pretty busted now, and I'd say you're covered in scratches. How're you going to explain that in the morning? What's Mike going to say?"

"Like you're not covered in scratches too!" she scoffed. Xander gingerly pulled back from her and held his arms out wide. In the dim light, it was clear he looked pristine. "Screw you and your healing factor!" She huffed as she said it, but a smile had already started creeping back onto her face.

She attempted to take a step and continue on out of the forest, but her unsupported bodyweight placed entirely on her ankle sent her knee buckling. Xander dove in once again, scooping her up under her arm and helping her continue.

They hobbled in silence for a little while, until the trees cleared and made way for the road. They had ended up back toward the Factory, and at the sight of it Cathy found herself craving a cherry Coke.

Xander echoed her sentiments almost psychically. "What I wouldn't give to go sit down right now or shoot some pool," he chuckled. "Actually," he amended, "nachos would be amazing right now, smothered in cheese sauce. I'm starved."

The Factory had long since closed for the night though, and all the staff had been home for hours. Cathy longed for the days when Roxanne had served them up fries, and she and Sara had gossiped while the guys played a round of pool. It had been so simple then. Now, she could hardly walk by the place without imagining what Roxanne's last moments had been like, or how Jamie had felt as he headed out for home one last time. She shuddered.

"You alright?" Xander asked. "Are you getting cold?

Do you need my jacket?"

Cathy forced a smile. "No, I'm fine. Just remembering. These streets seem haunted sometimes. The fog doesn't help," she said, gesturing around with her free hand.

Xander sighed. "I know what you mean. My biggest concern used to be whether or not you, Mike, and Sara were going to leave me on my own at a party. Now you're following me through the streets at night," he joked, trying to lighten the mood.

Cathy smiled, leaning her head against his shoulder. "You know, I'm sorry about that. Not the leaving you at parties... Well, actually scratch that, I'm sorry about that too. I'm sorry about jumping to conclusions tonight though. You've got a lot on your plate these days and I kinda forget you need to cool down sometimes too."

"Ah, it's not so bad," Xander lied, leaning his head against hers. "The job has some perks after all. I couldn't see nearly so well in the dark before, and look at me now! I can spot you tailing me in the pitch black a mile away."

Cathy's playful scowl returned. "You mean to tell me you knew I was following you all along?"

"Yep, why do you think I was stopping to light a cigarette so often? I needed to give you time to catch up," he joked. "Seriously though, don't worry about the whole gleaming reddish eyes thing. There are only so many times I can get up and go to the bathroom in the middle of the night freaked out because I've seen myself in the mirror before I get used to my lame night vision thing."

Cathy sighed, content for a moment, before another question flew into her brain and her head cocked to the side quizzically. "Wait, can you not turn that off? Isn't that going to really freak people out?" she asked, examining his eyes once more.

Xander laughed. "Cathy, would you want to walk around this town without glasses if you needed them?" She shook her head. "Well, that's exactly how I feel. Yes, I can 'turn it off', but when my friend is tailing me and we end up running from delinquent cops I'm going to take any advantage I can."

They turned the corner to her street in what seemed like no time at all, Xander with his arm still supporting her. Her long black hair was tangled and knotted, and Xander found himself picking leaves out of it for her.

"Xander, promise me tonight *was* just you blowing off steam? If there's anything else, you know you can tell me," Cathy said, hugging into her friend as they drew closer to her house.

"Cathy, I promise. Sometimes I just need to wander these streets and remember the good times. We used to be able to play here. We never used to worry about the things that go bump in the night. It's nice to just think back on those times."

Cathy sighed. "I know what you mean. Just promise me you won't get into any trouble? Mike and I worry about you. I don't know what we would do without you."

"Like I said, I promise. Now, how are you getting back inside?"

They stopped in front of Cathy's house and regarded the height between Cathy's window and the ground nervously. The porch seemed much more difficult to climb with a sprained ankle. "Pull me up?" Cathy suggested.

"Sounds like a plan," Xander replied, walking her

quietly across the lawn and helping lean her against the porch. He hopped up onto the railing lithely, pulling her up next to him, then made sure she was steady against the support beam before scaling up to the roof above. She reached up, and grabbing her arms, he hoisted her toward the roof. For a moment, she hung off the edge, just her arms and shoulders secure as the rest of her body dangled precariously, but with a great heave Xander brought her forward. The momentum sent her tumbling on top of him, and the two collapsed in giggles.

A light flickered on and shone through a window on the opposite end of her house. "Crap," she hissed. "We woke Mom and Dad."

"Get in quick then," Xander said, the hint of a laugh still in his voice as he pushed her through the window. She scurried and ducked under the covers quickly, watching as Xander pulled the window down and slipped off the deck. It was the most carefree she had seen him in ages.

Cathy Kennessy's bedroom door opened, and Karen stuck her head in, the same frown that had been plastered on her daughter's face for a majority of the evening now on hers. "Cathy?" she whispered. "Is everything alright in here?"

Cathy gave her best impression of sleepiness, mumbling and turning over in her bed. "Mmm, why wouln't it be?" she slurred, rubbing her eyes as the light silhouetting her mother assailed her eyes.

"No reason, I guess. Your father and I thought we heard a bang. Must just have been something on the street. You go back to sleep, sweetheart," Karen murmured, her features softening as she realized her daughter was okay.

She closed the door softly, heading back to bed.

Cathy listened for her mother's footsteps to fall away and for her parents' bedroom door to close, and then carefully sat up in bed. She turned on her bedside light, pulling away the covers and examining her ankle. She propped a few pillows under it to elevate it, hoping it would be better enough by morning that she could convincingly pull off that nothing was wrong with it. Grabbing a mirror from her side table, she assessed her cuts as well, relieved to find that it was nothing makeup wouldn't be able to cover.

Her secret, and Xander's, was safe. Did she regret jumping to conclusions? Maybe, but she cared much more that she had made sure Xander was safe. For the first time in a long time, she wasn't scared, and she felt a little better than comfortably numb. She switched off her lamp again and sank back onto her bed. Letting the warmth in her chest spread, she drifted off to sleep, feeling for all the world as if she had finally made a difference.

TIMELINE IV

She sat with a bowl of ripe cherries in front of her, her fingers finding each one as if choosing it carefully before plucking it from the teeming masses and pressing it between her lips. Next to her was a bowl of pits that was always empty: each time one was placed in it, it would be removed and placed in a receptacle that was out of her sight.

"I've been thinking about the Northland," she said to the young man sitting near her, with his fingers hovering above the keys of a typewriter. "I think we're due for some rapid expansion."

"Yes, Mistress," the young man nodded, clacking a note into the keys. The typewriter made a sharp chime and he hit the toggle and re-margined the set.

There was a sound next to her and she turn to her pet. It was moving listlessly from foot to foot and making shrill, whining sounds deep in its throat.

"What is it?" she smiled, pushing back her blonde hair and marking a lock in red.

It turned to her with its large green eyes slanted upward, its discomfort palpable.

"... Yes," she said after a moment's contemplation. "Yes, I feel it, too." She turned back to the young man at the typewriter. "Please contact the clerics. I need something investigated."

The young man nodded, then turned to leave the chamber.

She turned and rested a slender hand on her pet's scalp, her nimble fingers scratching deftly underneath its arched chin until its eyes narrowed and it returned to a state of semi-relaxation.

I can recall with perfect clarity the day my wife died.

I woke up in my bed alone. My eyes snapped open staring at a too-bright sun, smelling bacon and hearing the "da da da's" and "la la la's" of Jennifer singing to herself as she prepared our eggs.

I pushed off the covers and planted my feet on the floor. I resisted the urge to rush down the stairs as naked as the day I'd been made, as making haste would do little. I dressed quickly and as I buckled my belt, I yelled down the stairs. "Jennifer," I said assertively. "Take the food off the burner!" I paused a moment. "Quickly!"

When I turned the corner in the kitchen to see that Jennifer was standing back from the stove. It was off, the bacon slowly calming as it sizzled in its own fat and cooled. She smiled at me quizzically when I saw her, having heard what I called but having paid it no mind.

"We have to go into Parse," I said as I rested my hand on her hip and led her away from the kitchen. She followed me.

"Parse? We're going into—"

"There's something wrong with the baby," I interrupted. "Don't ask me how I know, please, I just do."

She stared at me for a long, bewildered moment, then moved with as much haste as her cumbersome form would allow and went with me to get ready. She didn't ask how I know, not this time, and I breathed a sigh of relief.

The angle at which we approached Parse had taken us about twenty miles south of the longitudinal line that connected our farm with it when Jennifer noticed it enough to say something.

"Why are we so far south?" she asked, letting her gaze fall over the slight raises in the sand dunes around us.

"Are we?" I asked, and am now unsure as to why I played dumb. I suppose I was trying to avoid the scene that had played out before.

"The sun is too far to my side," she said, not accusingly, simply noticing her surroundings. Her fingers were intermittently patting and drumming along the taut flesh of her stomach.

I looked at the sun, then at her, as our Jeep sped along the cleavage between sand hills on the way to Parse. I wondered in that moment, possibly for the first time, what I would do if this time it worked? What would it be like not to worry about today, but to worry about tomorrow again? If we got to Parse, and if she were fine and the baby were fine, would I ever tell her? Was that a burden I could place on her, even along with the knowledge that everything worked out in the end?

My mind pondered these thoughts even as we reached the Western Wall of Parse and turned to travel north along its edge, its tall stone lined with graffiti and art murals and PSA signage. It was gaudy and blatant and did nothing to distract me from those aching, lingering doubts... and yet, here we were, at the very mouth of Parse, and there had been no Reps and no labour pains and no blood. Even after the long detour south we'd made, we'd still arrived hours before when she typically went into labour.

When the doors to Parse came into view, it was like a weight had been lifted off my shoulders. The doors were massive and heavy things, with bolts in them the size of a grown man's head. They looked immoveable unless one had seen them move, their hinges creaking loudly in a way that echoed throughout the desert and never ceased to attract the Reps.

I parked the Jeep and let it idle, the vents billowing futile cool air at Jennifer. I walked the ten feet or so between the Jeep and the wall, just to the side of the doors. As soon as I stepped out of the vehicle, I learned just how wrong I had been about the futility of the Jeep's vents: the air was dry enough to suck the breath from your throat, and the sun reflected off the steel and concrete of the wall so that the heat of it came at you from multiple angles.

Alongside the doors on the wall was a small plastic box, barely the size of a hardcover novel. It was that greenish-grey colour that it seemed all military hardware was, close to the shade of the sand but not quite right. I unbuckled two latches on the side and opened it, revealing a keypad with large, gaudy numbers and a speaker grill the size of my fist. The pound key had been scraped down, replaced with a sticker that said 'Page.' It buzzed in that way speakers do, but then nothing happened. A voice should have come over the line asking me the nature of my visit, but none came.

I pressed the buzzer again, holding it down for longer this time. The harsh crackle rang out, but still there was no response.

"Hello?" I yelled, backing up a pace to see if any of the Remers that patrolled the wall were in shouting distance. "Who's on the gate?"

There were no Remers walking along the upper edge of the wall, nor were there the silhouettes of any in the Plexiglas towers that dotted the wall's edge.

I went back to the buzzer and held it again, and this time halfway through my press, the small, man-sized door that had been made within the larger door clicked its locking mechanism and swung itself ajar, opening to just enough of an angle that it could be seen. There hadn't been a voice and we hadn't gotten clearance, but here it was: the door to Parse had been opened for us, along with all the hospitals and medicines and painkillers that they promised. It was all there, inside the shadowed dark that lay just beyond that hanging metal frame.

They'd opened the door that a man could fit through, not one that I could drive through. They hadn't answered the damn buzzer to know I had a Jeep, so why would they. But then, why wouldn't they? Did they think I'd walked here? I wasn't in the mood to question these things. I went to the Jeep and shut it off and helped Jennifer into the sand, which burned her feet even through her shoes. We walked to the door and entered the dark, leaving our Jeep and the last remnants of our world behind us.

The buildings within the walls of Parse were tall and packed tight together, conspiring with the walls to blot out the sun unless it was at its apex. The buildings had been evenly spaced at one point, with enough land for everyone to enjoy... but initial dreams of expanding further and further into Rep territory as the city's population grew had been scuttled early on, and so new developments had been built between existing ones, until the communities on the borders of the walled city became densely populated ghettos that gave way to the shining metal of its interior.

On a normal day in Parse, it was difficult to notice just how eerie that hodgepodge nature of the buildings could be, with a tiny small house sprouting up like a weed between the spaces of two larger ones. It was difficult for the eeriness to reach you because of how densely populated Parse could be, with the streets lined with people busy to get to their jobs or get breakfast or go home from a long night's work. This was the first and only time I'd seen the streets as they were now: empty, with the only sign of human life the trash bins that still overflowed with refuse and discarded newspapers from the day before.

I swallowed hard as sweat found its way to my brow and trickled down my neck, the humidity of the world inside the wall finding me as my eyes darted from alley to alley, searching for any sign of human life.

We walked slowly, Jennifer with one arm wrapped over my shoulder. I supported her weight as much as I could as we walked the empty street down its yellow dividing line, as quickly as we dared but hampered by the growing disquiet in my wife's belly.

"Is it always like this?" Jennifer asked finally, her gaze moving frantically from one darkened window to the next, looking for even a light on behind a black curtain.

I swallowed hard and told her it's not.

We passed by several blocks, continuing straight each time. The hospital and all the major buildings were at a straight run downtown, and all main roads were like arteries that led back to its heart. I looked down the side streets we passed and saw more of the same: long rows of densely packed buildings with no life to keep in them. It reminded me of the fake towns the government had set up during bomb tests in the desert, populated exclusively by mannequins and tumbleweeds. The association made me shiver despite the intense humidity of the city.

We were five blocks in and the door we'd entered the city through was a small nub on the horizon, when Jennifer stumbled. It was as though her ankle had given way beneath the weight of her, one step fine and the next impossible. I caught her and hoisted her back to her feet and kissed her, and it was only when she was righted that I noticed that the hairs on the back of my neck were standing on end despite the intense heat.

There was a child's laugh on the air, an ephemeral giggle in response to my wife's stumble.

We continued down the arterial until eventually the wall we'd entered through had faded from view and the spires of the hospital began to loom on the horizon, a sharp point in what had otherwise been a collage of blunt edges. We travelled with Jennifer at my arm and me inspecting every shadow and side street worryingly. When the wall was truly out of sight, I broke out in a hot flop sweat, like a hunted animal who has lost sight of its only exit.

There was a child in the doorway to a tenement building.

I stopped suddenly in the middle of the street and staired at her. She was small — ten at most — and stood in the centre of the doorway with a bright clean blue dress and dirty cheeks. Her arms were limp by her sides in a way I'd never seen a child stand before; they were always leaning or fidgeting or touching something, the living embodiments of attention deficits. She just stared at me, her face as devoid of expression as a bakkara player.

Jennifer turned and saw the child and smiled. "Hello," she said in a flowery tone despite her discomfort.

The child continued to stare at me, not even twitching her pupils in Jennifer's direction.

"Is everything okay?"

I squeezed Jennifer's arm to get her to stop, and saw her jaw tighten when I did. The child just stared at us, and in the distance the same giggle that had laughed at my wife's misfortune returned. It hadn't come from this child, but even when I knew that it seemed to be wrong. It was like this child were laughing at us without raising her cheeks or opening her mouth, beaming the laugh straight into our minds.

Jennifer turned away from the child and looked at me, her face wet. "What's happening?"

I pursed my lips. On the air the giggle was joined by another and another, until it was an orchestra of disembodied laughter following us down the street. When there

were so many laughs that they became difficult to separate, one began to sing.

Red eyes bad
Green eyes worse
Beware the demon pain has cursed.
He tries to trick
He tries to sway
Don't be the fool don't be his prey.

Then another joined the chorus and another, but never
in time with one another, starting the tune at different intervals so that the sound came at you confusingly.

When I looked from Jennifer back to the doorway, the
girl was gone.

"We have to go," I realized suddenly, with a hushed
breath.

Jennifer looked at me with panic-stricken eyes, then at
the hospital spires in the distance, then back to me. One
arm clutched me while the other held her stomach up,
as though she thought that if she let gravity take hold,
it would drag her intestines out of her all at once. She
winced under the weight of it, likely feeling our child
move and squirm inside her. "Okay," she said finally, her
voice weak.

She said it as though she were accepting death, and
my heart broke.

We turned around, and when we did the girl was
back: sitting on the curb to our right not ten feet in front of
us. There were four more children with her now, most of
them older but one couldn't have been older than eight.

I stopped when I saw them, and it took the breath out

of me. The poem and the laughter was still on the air, but none of them were singing it, all their lips so tight their mouths way as well have been drawn on. I swallowed and started to walk past.

They were arranged in a not-quite-straight line, some standing and some sitting, all with their arms resting awkwardly and all of them staring me right in the eye. Their gaze moved with me as Jennifer and I hobbled past, migrating like those paintings designed to make it look like one eye always followed you.

They didn't follow us when we passed them. They barely even turned their heads to keep us in view as we passed the next side street, and then another. By the time we were approaching the third side street, I looked back and they were gone — although I couldn't tell if they had moved or if they'd just faded from view. At every side street I looked both ways out of habit, and at this one when I turned right there were at least thirty children standing in the street, all of them with clean clothes and dirty faces, and all of them staring directly at me.

"I'm not sure what's special about you," came a voice like springtime over the air. A loud voice. An adult voice.

I swallowed and my lower lip trembled. I knew who this was even though I'd never heard it before. I knew it from the way the children singing their poems in the distance halted the second she spoke, as if on cue. I knew it from the sing-song way she spoke, her words not tethered to a certain tone or inclination.

When I looked over my shoulder, back toward the hospital whose spires had promised such salvation only moments ago, a tall blonde woman was standing between us and it.

I let go of Jennifer. I didn't mean to, but my arms had lost all their power.

It was Celena.

She stepped forward, one powerful leg in front of the other, swaying back and forth in her red dress. Like the children, the dress was clean, and her blonde hair matted and tangled into frizzy clumps. She wore lipstick that matched the shade of her dress but had applied it with the reckless abandon of a toddler, smearing it past her lips on either side and into a Glasgow smile.

She approached us without direction, taking a step toward us one moment and then away the next. Next to me, I felt Jennifer quivering — she knew. I hated that she knew.

"There's something though," Celena continued, her actual smile twisting the one she'd painted on. "Something special. Something happening that made me notice you... or maybe the same thing happening more than once... is that a thing?" She turned to me when she asked this, as if wondering my opinion. Her eyes were emerald green and wandering, the left one flickering off to one side as if twitching.

I swallowed, unsure if I was supposed to answer. She was within ten feet of us now, well within striking distance. From what I'd heard, anywhere in sight was striking distance for her, but what I'd heard could well have been exaggeration.

She stepped yet closer, close enough that I could smell the sweet of her perfume and the rank of her breath all at once, the dichotomy making my nose curl. I fought the urge to let it, you didn't know what could set her off. She hummed contentedly, the same way Jennifer did when she sat in the sunlight stroking her pregnant belly. I hated myself for making that connection, but there it was, and as if to cement it, Celena reached out and touched her hand to my chest.

"Yes, a few times now," she said under her breath. She moved her hand to touch Jennifer as well.

"Don't," I said without thinking, the word coming out from between my teeth.

She stopped and turned back to me, smiling wide enough that I could see her teeth. She kept eye contact with me as she reached down and rested her hand on Jennifer's belly.

"Her too," she smiled.

There were hands on me then, and a kick to the back of my leg, forcing me onto my knees in the street. The hands on me were small and weak but many, working as one to keep me down. I turned as they did the same to Jennifer, and I saw the impact of her striking the ground ripple up through her in slow motion.

Her water broke.

"No!" I screamed, bringing an elbow up into the face of a small boy. He fell back in the splash of blood and snot and a new boy took his place almost immediately, piling on me and gripping at my shift and skin and tearing both.

The water that came from Jennifer was red again, as it had been before.

In the distance the chanting had started again.

Red eyes bad
Green eyes worse
Beware the demon pain has cursed.
He tries to trick
He tries to sway
Don't be the fool don't be his prey.

I lashed out again, hitting a little girl in the face so hard I felt her jaw shatter. It stopped me when I saw it, her dirty cheek hanging too low for the rest of her face. The image took the drive from me and I turned to Jennifer, who wasn't looking at me. She was staring at the ground in front of her, grabbing at her stomach and crying her tears into the pavement.

"Well, well," Celena sang, looking out towards the hospital. "Quite a trick we have here, isn't it?"

She stepped to one side and it was there, like a magician making a lady appear as if from thin air. There had been no mirrors here though, just the shadows and the black of the street that masked the black of its scaly, oily flesh.

When I saw it, my heart stopped. There was nothing — no rumour or tale — that could do the horror of such a thing justice. Anyone who had gotten close enough to see it — *really* see it — likely wouldn't survive to give the details.

It was hulking, a mass of winding sinew and muscle that went from nowhere to nowhere, defying anatomy with its anarchy. Its flesh was a slick black with scales that moved with its interest, rippling as it raised its bump of a snout to the air and snorted in the scents around it. It had claws, each long and sharp, the translucent yellow of cartilage. Its eyes were huge and cat-like and triangular, and a sickening shade of aquamarine green.

It opened its mouth to speak, the words coming out like vomit and smelling just as bad.

"Black Womb lives!"

It stepped toward Jennifer.

"No!" I screamed, lunging forward on my knees and scraping them badly.

"Now, now," Celena chided me, holding up a single finger. The smile on her face was death itself, some part of me knowing what was coming the moment I saw it. She stepped past the Womb towards me, but I didn't take my eyes off it as it lingered closer and closer to Jennifer, its claws twitching as more and more blood trickled from her thighs down into the street.

Celena took my chin between her thumb and forefinger with great force and twisted my head toward her. "You've been a very bad boy," she said in that cruel, singsong madness voice of hers.

My eyes darted from Jennifer to her for a second — only a second — and when they returned the Womb had opened up her abdomen in four long lines, spilling bowel and bladder out onto her legs. She screamed so loud I didn't even hear my own, but I swear I did.

I lunged forward but Celena and her brood held me, their grip startlingly tight.

"None of that," Celena smiled. "None of that will do at all."

Jennifer fell into the pile of herself that was growing in front of her in the street, her intestines unravelling like some sort of macabre magic trick. Despite all the times I'd watched my wife suffer, my mind still couldn't process that. There's something so foreign about that sort of gore — something so fake looking, so staged. The mind refuses to process.

The Womb climbed onto her and blocked most of what was happening. I saw its back rise and fall with some secret rhythm, saw my wife's blood appear in spurts then sprays then streams. I heard her sounds — first cries, then soft mewls, then eventually scant whispers — give way to silence. But I didn't see her, and on some level I'm thankful for that. Celena and her children held me in place and eventually I stopped fighting them, not by choice... the strength had just left me.

When The Womb was done, they let me go but it was like their arms still held me. I couldn't move.

The was so little left of my wife I couldn't even move her, once I found my legs. When I tried, she fell apart in my arms.

I can recall with perfect clarity the day my wife died.

A NIGHT TO FORGET

She could see a small bird struggling to keep its footing on the narrow windowsill as the wind tugged at its feathers. It wasn't particularly interesting to look at, but it helped her avoid having to look at anyone in the room with her. It wasn't until the police officer addressing her moved into her line of sight and broke her concentration that she finally clued back in to what he was saying.

"...so if any memory of last night, anything you can tell us about what happened comes to you, please don't hesitate to call this number. We just want to help find out what happened." He attempted to look reassuring as he placed a small card down on the bedside table. Lucy forced herself to nod as she continued to look everywhere but his face. Seeing that they weren't going to get any other kind of response from her at the moment, the two officers and the doctor supervising the talk finally turned to leave the room and, much to her appreciation, closed the door firmly behind them.

It was hard to believe that less then twelve hours earlier she had been out enjoying a night on the town with friends and was getting pumped for finally being free for the summer. Now she was sitting up on an uncomfortable bed in a dingy hospital, surrounded by doubt that life would ever go back to that carefree normalcy that she was enjoying just the night before. Ever since she woke up, confused and disoriented, in an unfamiliar room and surrounded by people who were all clamoring to know what happened to her, she felt completely bewildered and lost. It was as though someone had ripped her from her normal life and threw her into a chaotic mess where she was expected to straighten everything out without any prior knowledge of what was going on and what the rules were.

Here's all she really knew about the previous night, and this was only going by what both the police and doctors had told her since she awoke: She was out drinking and having a good time, but started to feel queasy and decided it was finally time to call it quits and get home so she could drink plenty of water in the hopes that she wouldn't wake up with a hangover. This much she remembered. In fact, she even remembered saying goodbye and stumbling out of the club and heading towards the general direction of home. She debated for all of a few minutes on whether or not to get a cab, but considering she already felt sick, felt it was better to get some fresh air and walk the few blocks back to her apartment instead. Deep down she supposed that perhaps, just maybe, had she swallowed her bile and caved towards getting the cab, none of this madness would have ever happened. Alas, she chose to walk, and that's where her memory of the night halted so abruptly that it made her head swim just trying to pull up the memories she should, in theory, have. According to the only witness who had come forward, she was spotted turning down a dark alley that was commonly used as a shortcut between the busier area of town and the far quieter residential areas. Moments after she vanished from view, a suspicious looking man quickly made his way down the same alley. Less than five minutes later, all sorts of blood-curdling screams tore through the air and the cops were quickly called to the scene. What they found was her lying on the ground, unconscious and completely unharmed but for a couple small bruises and one relatively small bump on her head. The creepy part? Well even though she was virtually unharmed, everything in the area, herself included, was covered in bright and sticky splashes of fresh blood. As for the stranger who had followed her down the alley? Well, he was nowhere to be seen and it was strongly believed that he was most likely no longer living if all the blood found on the scene belonged to him.

Hence her waking up in a hospital and being grilled by the police.

Grateful to have a few minutes alone with her own thoughts, Lucy slowly slipped out of bed and cautiously tip-toed over to the door. Thanks to the small window set in it, she could see that the hallway had finally been cleared of reporters and police. Now the only people going back and forth to various rooms were the patients of those rooms and the hospital staff. This peace wasn't going to last long though, as despite having been living away from home for two years now, her parents were on their way to collect her so she wouldn't be alone while recovering from the traumatic experience she didn't remember having. Personally, she wouldn't have contacted them yet as physically she was fine and capable of taking care of herself, but the hospital had contacted them before she woke up. By the time she found out this information, her parents had already been on the road for over an hour as they had to travel from the next town over to get to where she chose to live and go to school.

Finding that the door didn't come equipped with a lock, she sighed heavily and turned away. Adjusting the flimsy hospital gown around her so she wasn't showing anything embarrassing, she slowly made her way over to the window. Outside the day looked to be gloomy and overcast, a perfect complement to her ever-worsening mood. Despite telling both the doctors and police everything she did remember, she kept being given the impression that no one believed that she truly didn't remember what happened. The only thing she had going for her was that the main doctor taking care of her did admit that trauma could be the cause of her memory loss, but even he seemed to believe that she should remember soon and was frankly surprised that nothing they told her about the previous night even remotely sparked any recollection.

Placing one hand against the cold glass, she leaned forward to rest her forehead against it as well. It helped sooth the edges off the headache that she could feel forming behind her eyes, but sadly did nothing to help solve the more serious problem she was faced with. Someone had more than likely died and she, the only real witness to the crime, couldn't help at all with solving it. Hell, for all she knew the police suspected she had committed a crime and was using the memory loss as a way of hiding her guilt.

Closing her eyes, she forced herself to swallow back bile as her stomach decided now was a good time to start doing summersaults. They did show her a couple pictures of what the alley looked like when she was found, but until now she had been able to push the images to the back of her mind as though they came from a movie rather than real life. All of this was downright insane to her. She was nothing more than a mousy looking college girl with frizzy brown hair, a whole mess of freckles, hazel eyes hidden behind super thick glasses, a noticeable lack of fashion sense, and was just a bit too chubby to be considered attractive (in her own personal opinion). She was used to drifting through life in the background and barely being noticed by anyone. And yet here she was, waiting around in a hospital room while her hope that this was a bad dream was being dashed rather thoroughly.

Finally, it was the faint *pap, pap, pap* of fat raindrops splattering themselves against the glass she was leaning on that dragged her out of her bleak thoughts and back to reality. It wasn't like brooding over how unfair this situation was would actually do anything for her. She just had to follow the doctor's advice and try to relax and go about her life as normally as possible, and sooner or later her memory of the previous night would come back to her. There, that was a positive thought. The police did not think she was in any danger, though they were going to keep an eye on her, and she was advised not to leave town until the investigation was complete, but other than that she would be able to just continue with her regular routine. Sure, her regular life was boring, but that was better than thinking about this creepy murder mystery that she was caught up in.

Pushing against the glass, she slowly straightened up and started to turn away from the window. Even though the hospital bed was uncomfortable and lumpy, right now it was starting to look more and more inviting. It wasn't until she was back-on to the window that the hairs started to stand up on the back of her neck with the uncomfortable feeling of being watched. A shiver flowed up her spine as she abruptly turned back to the window to try to find out what was causing the feeling.

Down below her was nothing more than the back end of the parking lot. It wasn't even that full as most of the people still outside were rushing between the building and their cars in an attempt to get out of the rain as quickly as possible. Her frown deepened as she scanned all the people below. None of them even seemed to be looking up at the building, let alone up at her in the window. It would seem as though paranoia was really starting to get to her. Grasping the thin curtains to either side of the window, she yanked them closed with just a bit more force than necessary. "There, problem solved," She muttering softly to herself as she slowly made her way back to bed.

She just needed sleep. That would help her feel better.

Down near the back of the parking lot, a slender figure took one last draw off a smouldering cigarette before lifting one foot to put the cherry out against the sole of their shoe. If it weren't for the rain, a cloud of menthol scented smoke would be gathered around them like a cloak. Slipping a half empty pack out of their coat, they carefully stored away the cigarette butt before putting it away again. With one last glance up at the covered window on the third floor, theyslowly turned away from the hospital and started to walk away. The rain was soaking through their clothing, yet nothing seemed to bother them as they stepped off of the smoother concrete of the parking lot and into the mud churned up around it. Within a couple minutes, they were lost from sight in the sparse woods surrounding the lonely building.

The following morning Lucy was released from the hospital, and with the arrival of her parents, was led out to their car. She had insisted on being fine enough to get a cab home and have them meet her there, but to no avail. Instead, she was flanked on either side by her mother and father as they escorted away from the dreary hospital. In a way she felt they were going overboard and acting like bodyguards rather then her parents, but then she had just been through a traumatic experience. Even if she didn't remember it.

Sitting in the backseat, head resting against the window as they pulled out of the parking lot, she started to tune out the world around her. In the front of the vehicle, her parents were debating if they should stop somewhere to eat or prepare food once they arrived at the apartment. It was kind of funny listening to her dad insist that they eat out to help her recover from how crappy hospital food is, but she was having trouble staying invested in what they were saying. When the radio was switched off so they could properly debate the pros and cons without distraction, Lucy stopped listening altogether. It felt selfish to not care when they were just worried and trying to help, but everything still felt fake to her. This was more like a movie she was only half watching rather than her real life.

Turning her head to stare out the window, she sighed softly to herself as she watched a stretch of densely packed trees fly by. They were moving just fast enough that all the greenery was starting to blend together, so she made a small game out of trying to pick out various birds as they flew through the branches. It wasn't exactly fun, but since it was helping pass the time, she wasn't exactly upset about it. Just as her eyes were starting to hurt from straining them to see deeper into the trees, she suddenly caught sight of a flash of bright blue from deep within the woods. Even though she knew it was probably just a blue bird, seeing it made her feel like she had just been drenched in icy water.

"Sweetie?"

Lucy jumped at her mother's voice, causing the older woman to frown softly. "Are you okay, dear? You look rattled." The concern she felt was clear in her voice and quickly echoed in her father.

"Do you remember anything, Lucy?" Even as he spoke, he pulled into the parking lot of a small homey diner and quickly parked.

Raising her hands to try to ward off their concern,

Lucy frowned and shook her head. "I thought… no, I don't think so…" For a second, she could have sworn she was on the brink of something, but just as quickly it was gone again.

"How about this, we all go in and get some nice, warm food. Then, if you feel up to it, we can discuss this some more." Having turned in his seat to look back at her, he smiled as brightly as he could manage.

Her mother grumbled a bit as she exited the vehicle, but then that just meant she had been on the losing side of their debate. Gathering herself up, trying to at least look unfazed and ready for anything even if she didn't feel that way on the inside, Lucy pulled herself out of the car to join them. It was no longer raining out, but the very air felt like it could start again at a moment's notice. Hurrying to catch up with her parents as they crossed in front of a patiently waiting driver who was also looking to park, she couldn't help but pause as everyone else entered the diner. With one hand on the door to keep it held open, she turned her upper body to slowly scan the parking lot. Her heartrate was starting to slow from the random start she had in the car, but at the same time she still felt weirdly freaked out. Almost like she had seen something she shouldn't have. When nothing stood out to her as being off or suspicious, she finally stopped dragging her heels and entered the diner.

They were still serving breakfast, much to Lucy's pleasant surprise, and with her father offering to cover the bill she wasn't about to skimp on anything. Passing the wait for food with various small talk, she was almost able to trick herself into forgetting why her parents were visiting and pretend that everything was okay. It was even easier to pretend once the food arrived and she had a large plate loaded down with bacon, eggs, toast, and even a couple pancakes to distract her. Perhaps there was some wisdom to her father's argument that eating out would make up for the horrible hospital food.

It was that thought that shredded her attempts at pretending and forced her to once again think about the mess she was stuck in the middle of. Her father cleared his throat as she went from quickly gobbling down her meal to just pushing the no longer appetizing food around her plate with her fork.

"Lucy? Are you sure you're feeling okay?" His voice was full of concern as he looked her over. It was only then that it occurred to her that both of her parents had ordered only coffee and were watching her with an expectant air.

Leaning across the table, her mother reached out to give her hand a small, warm squeeze. "We know you're probably tired of talking about what happened, but you know we can't help but worry."

Inwardly Lucy sighed, but she didn't dare let that show. Instead, she put on a brave face and started filling them in on everything she had been told while in the hospital. Sure enough, they already knew most of it, having had an opportunity to talk to the police when they arrived in town, but they were polite enough to let her talk without interruption. In fact, the only breaks in their conversation happened when the waitress stopped by the table to refill their drinks and the occasional ding of the small bell attached to the door as people entered and left the diner.

"And now I'm just desperately trying to remember

anything that could help them discover what happened." Having gone back to staring at her plate while recounting the whole story for them, she found herself once again pushing her food around with her fork. "It's scary, what happened I mean, but since I can't remember anything, it feels more like a dream I had then something that actually happened." The more she thought about it and talked about it, the more her mind would drift back to the strange feeling she had in the car. Looking up at them, she frowned. "The only thing out of place that comes to mind is the colour blue." Seeing the confusion on their faces, she scrambled to elaborate. "I think I'm remembering something, but the more I try to think about it, the more my head hurts. From the description of the guy who followed me and the out of focus security footage of the guy, it didn't seem like he was wearing anything blue, and yet that color is stuck in my head."

Nodding slowly, her father seemed to muse that over. "Perhaps you saw someone or something blue right before anything happened."

Nodding in agreement, Lucy unsuccessfully tried to calm the butterflies that were starting to build up in her stomach. Once again, she found herself looking around in a paranoid fashion, as though expecting someone or something to jump out at her.

"Perhaps you should pass this information on to the police. I'm sure they'll be grateful for anything that will help put this to rest." Even though the small, older lady still looked worried, Lucy could tell her mother was starting to calm down now. In fact, now that she was really paying attention to her mother and father, they both looked a bit ruffled and tense. Then again something scary had recently happened to their daughter, so that was easy enough to explain away. The only issue was that their nervousness was making her feel incredibly on edge and the paranoia was only getting worse.

"I'll call the station once I get home." Pushing her plate to the side, Lucy tried her best to smile. It was a weak smile at best, but at the moment it was the best she could do. "For now, I would like to get home. I'm feeling… tired." She caught herself just in time. Had she gone with frightened or unwell, her mother may have insisted on staying with her for the rest of the day just so she could care for her. Even so, it took the entirety of the time for her father to pay and for them to make the trip out to the car to convince her mother that she didn't need them to stay over and that she would be fine. She was feeling so strung out that all she wanted was to curl up on the couch and watch movies with her roommates. After promising her mother that she would call if anything happened, or came to her, they got in the vehicle and slowly pulled out of the parking lot.

From inside the diner they just left, another person turned away from the window as their car turned a corner and was lost from sight. Getting up slowly, almost unfolding themselves from the small booth they had been seated at, they strolled towards the door and out through it without garnering a single glance from anyone else in the establishment. If it weren't for the ding of the bell at the door, it would have been just as well they hadn't been there at all. Pausing to one side of the door, they pulled out a box of cigarettes out of their jacket and fished about inside until they pulled out one stick that was half burned away. Pressing the butt between their lips, it only took a single flick of a lighter to get it burning and expelling minty smoke. Shrugging deeper into the worn leather jacket, they set off in the direction that Lucy and her parents just drove off in.

Having made it to the apartment building she lived in, and having also accepted that her parents weren't going to drive away until after they watched her walk up and enter the building safely, Lucy felt a sort of selfish relief as she watched them finally drive away through the small window beside the main entrance. Still unable to shake off the unease that had settled over her shoulders like a cloak, it didn't take her long to get herself moving and up to her apartment.

"I'm home!" she called out as she locked the door behind her, doing it more out of habit then anything else. She found herself being greeted by silence. Hesitantly moving down the hall to look around the connected kitchen and living room, she was disappointed to find a hastily scrawled note for her on the coffee table. A brief scan of it revealed that both of her roommates wouldn't be home, one because she decided to head home for a few days to visit her folks, and the other because of work obligations. So much for the relief she felt when her parents left.

While it was hard to deal with them being overly concerned and protective, she had been hoping an evening with her friends in the safety of her own home would help her push everything from her mind for a bit. Fetching her laptop from her room, turning on just about every light in the house in the process just to make the place feel warmer, she started boiling the kettle for hot chocolate while the machine took its time turning on. Setting the laptop up on the coffee table, she tried to make herself sit back and relax on the couch. Even if there was no one else home, the door was firmly locked and besides that the main door to the building was only accessible with a key, so there was no way for anyone to get in unless they lived there. There was no reason for her to be so nervous.

Or so she told herself before logging into social media. Having been offline for over a day, she had been expecting to have a lot of notices and posts to go through. What she hadn't been thinking about was just how much news and rumours would be filling her feeds to the brim. Even just scanning through the first dozen posts made her feel like a weight was pressing against her chest to the point where she was having trouble breathing. Not only were the more graphic pictures and reports of what happened making her feel like she was about to get violently ill, but the rumours, conspiracy theories, and speculation seemed to mostly revolve around the idea that she was responsible for the crime!

Slamming the laptop closed, she staggered upright and ran to the bathroom in an attempt to keep from getting sick all over the floor. It was all too much. She was the victim here, not the perpetrator of the crime! How could anyone think that someone as small and meek as herself would harm another person? It had to be false, and she wasn't going to rest until she got to the bottom of it. Wiping tears from her eyes as she shuffled back out to the kitchen, she only just remembered to shut off the kettle as she reached for the cordless phone that was actually resting in its stand for once.

Dialling the number supplied by the police, she forced herself to sit up and breathe normally while it rang. This was all just speculation and as soon as she remembered more of what happened, the easier it would be to figure out the truth and shut down the rumours that she had anything to do with what happened beyond being in the wrong place at the wrong time. It actually took her a moment to realize there was someone on the other end of the line saying hello. "Hello? Sorry about that, but I do think I've remembered... well, something anyway." She cringed as she said that, but honestly, she couldn't think of any other way to describe it.

"Alright, just try to explain it to the best of your ability. Anything you remember could help."

Nodding despite no one being around to see the motion, Lucy took a deep breath. "Well, it's not much, but for some reason my mind is stuck on the colour blue. I don't know if someone was wearing something blue, or there was something blue there when everything went down.." She was rambling, but then it wasn't like she had more to report.

"Let me stop you there." The voice on the other end of the line didn't sound too impressed. "The only thing found in the alley that was even remotely blue was the blood splattered shirt you were wearing."

Lucy could feel herself turning white. "No... I... I have

to go." Fumbling with the phone in her desperate attempt to hang up, she all but threw it across the room and onto the couch. Even though she had forgotten what she was wearing that night, it wasn't her shirt she remembered! That shirt was a light blue, and it was a bright blue that kept coming to mind. All but crying now, it felt like the world was crashing down around her head. No one was going to believe she was innocent if the only thing she could remember made it seem like she was responsible for what happened. Pacing back and forth across the room, she finally scrambled for the phone she had thrown. Calling up her parents, desperate now for anything that could help her feel better, she had trouble explaining why she wanted them to come over, but luckily she sounded panicked enough for them to drop everything and head over regardless.

By the time they arrived and rang the buzzer down by the main door for her to let them in, Lucy was a complete and utter state. While her mother tried to calm her while talking through the intercom, her father just looked stoic as he held the door open as another person looking to enter the building slipped by them. Without even acknowledging the other person in the lobby, they took off in a rush to their daughter's apartment. All but slamming the door off its hinges, Lucy threw herself into her parents' arms and sobbed about how she didn't do anything wrong.

It took a few hours of calming talk and her parents helping her close all the curtains in the apartment before she even started to calm down. They were concerned enough that they were even going to take advantage of the fact that her roommates weren't around and stay the night. No amount of calming talk and reassurance was helping her feel better though. "If only I could remember more.." Sniffling as her mother slowly led her towards her bedroom, she sounded like a broken record. By this point her mother was just making soothing noises as she put her to bed.

"Just try to get some sleep, dear. Your father and I are just out in the other room, and nothing can happen to you here, so you just need to relax and stop trying to force things. No one can accuse you of anything without proof, so you need to ignore what people are saying online and wait for the police to sort this whole mess out." Tucking her daughter into bed, something she hadn't done for years, the older woman fussed about the room and tidied up the dirty laundry scattered around before turning on the small desk lamp across from the bed. "There you go. Just try to close your eyes and relax. You can call out to us at any time." Kissing Lucy on the forehead, she finally left and pulled the door mostly closed.

Sinking down into the plush blankets and pillows, Lucy forced herself to close her eyes. Her mom was right. She just needed to relax. Having her parents come back was actually helping more then she thought it would, and perhaps getting some proper rest would help even more. With that thought, she finally let go and drifted off to sleep.

The pitch darkness of her sleep was punctured with

violent nightmares.

She was watching herself from a distance as her past self stumbled drunkenly down the street towards the alley, only it was no longer an alley and was instead a massive, gaping maw, full of sharp teeth and dripping wet. No matter how loud she screamed, she was powerless to stop herself from plunging into the darkness. Everything would go dark for a moment and suddenly she was her past self again, standing in the inky dark alley, back pressed against the wall, and tears streaming down her face as a knife came ripping through the darkness towards her. Darkness again, before suddenly she was standing in the alley, though now everything was bathed in an eerie red light. With a weird feeling as though she were suddenly in control of the dream, she turned to look in the direction she entered the alley from.

Standing just out of arms reach, a suddenly familiar person slowly grinned at her, the red light giving her the impression that they were coated in blood.

Jerking awake with a gasp, she almost fell out of bed with how fast she came bolt upright. With one hand pressed against her chest as her heart tried to bang its way out of her ribs, she clutched the bedsheets with her other hand, knuckles gone white from the force. Despite being awake, the dreams still clung to her mind, chilling her to the bone as she struggled to regain control of herself. She tried telling herself that it was okay, that her parents were just out in the other room, and in fact her mother left the door open...

The door was shut tight without any light even making its way around the frame. Now that she was aware of that, she couldn't help but notice there also wasn't a light on in the room anymore. With the horrible feeling that something was terribly wrong, Lucy slowly turned to look at the desk. It took a moment for the bit of streetlight cutting in through the gap in her curtains to help her see that she wasn't alone in the room. Casually leaning against the desk, seemingly carved from stone by how little they moved, was the person from her nightmare. On the tall side and weirdly lanky, it was only rips in their clothing showing off a bra strap that revealed their gender. Yet all Lucy could focus on was the bright blue streaks through their thick bangs that all but covered their eyes. They finally seemed to realize they had her full attention and just like that, their thin, bloodless lips split open in a grin. "Remember me?"

The forgotten night came back to her in a rush. Heading down the alley as a shortcut, hearing someone behind her and turning to face them, being grabbed and threatened with a knife by a rough looking man who demanded she hand over her wallet, and feeling like she was about to die. Then, as the fear of the man threatening her stole her voice and kept her from making a sound, she could only watch over his shoulder as the androgynous woman with blue streaked hair stepped out of the shadows behind him and held a finger over her lips as though to caution her from making a sound. Coming up directly behind the mugger as he started to shake Lucy to get a reaction from her, the strange woman opened her mouth wide, too wide, revealing far too many sharp teeth than should ever be in a human's mouth, and grabbed him tight enough by the arms to make him scream and lose his grip on both the knife and Lucy. Falling back against the wall, Lucy could only watch in horror as the woman drove her teeth into the man's neck, spraying crimson blood everywhere. It was only when the warm blood splattered against her face that her voice returned and she started to scream until everything went dark.

Mouth open, but unable to say a word, Lucy could only stare at the woman in growing horror. The blue haired woman simply sighed and shook her head. Her voice was rough to hear, as though she had some kind of throat injury that never properly healed, but yet she was making sure not to speak too loud and alert anyone else in the apartment. "You know I had hoped you would be like everyone else and simply forget I exist or write me off as a nightmare, yet here we are." They sounded almost as though they were chiding her. "I'm just other enough that people don't normally even see me as I walk past them down the street, or say enter the café they're eating at, or hell, even as they let me into buildings I have no business being in. And yet here you are looking at me with the same expression you had the first time."

Lucy turned to the bedroom door, thinking of screaming for help, only for the woman to suddenly push off the desk and was directly in front of her again. "Now, now, you don't want anyone else to be dragged into this, do you?" Waggling a finger at the terrified girl still in bed, the woman shook her head. "No, because I would have to do to them like I did to the man who tried to mug you. In fact, if I hear any news of my existence being passed around to anyone, I may just be hungry enough to make sure not only you, but your parents disappear the same way." Slowly her lips split open to show more and more teeth. "So be a good girl and forget everything. Got it?"

The last thing Lucy saw was that mouth opening wider and wider as it got closer.

Lucy's parents came awake to the sound of their daughter screaming hysterically. Scrambling down the hall, they burst into her room to find her sitting up in bed, mouth hanging open, just staring straight ahead without seeing anything.

Grabbing her by the shoulders, her mother gave her a shake as she desperately tried to calm her. "Lucy! Stop screaming! What's wrong with you?"

As though needing something to do, her father searched the room and even threw open the curtains to reveal that there was no one else in the room. "What's wrong, Lucy? Did you have a nightmare?"

All Lucy could do was stammer for a minute, babbling without actually saying anything until her mother gave her another shake. Finally, her eyes seemed to focus, and she stared back and forth between her two concerned parents. "I.." She had to clear her throat that was sore from screaming. "I don't remember."

THE PORT 13 MOTEL

They say that The Port 13 Motel is haunted.

"You know," Des says where he sits at the front desk, clicking on a grey mouse. He frowns at the ancient-looking computer monitor and clicks the mouse again. "Who exactly are 'they' anyways? All I can imagine is a bunch of men in suits sitting around a table spouting off so-called words of wisdom."

A woman around the same age as he frowns softly and touches the top of his head. His frown grows, and after a few seconds, he looks up. "Well, okay, so there could be women too but that's not the point, Quinn."

She frowns again, taps his head with a single finger, then slips away, past the front desk and through the "Employees Only" door.

Des clicks the mouse again. They have a reservation for tonight. Hopefully they don't cancel.

"Maybe we could play with it," Vincent says.

Des watches the knife Vincent is waving about.

"You know—" the knife points straight at the ceiling—

"re-do the whole decor!" The knife swings to the right. "Dark colours, dark curtains—" the knife points right at Des. "We could call you Igor!"

"Cute." Des glances at Florence curled up in the corner with the newspaper. She twirls a long, brown curl in one finger. "What about you, Flo?"

"You're not ugly enough to be Igor," she replies in a soft voice. "Maybe the passive butler, however…"

"Yes!" Vincent cries, swinging the knife back around to point it at her. "He can be my groom!"

"Who died and made you lord of the manor?" Des asks.

Quinn whispers by, her fingers brushing against the back of Des' hand. He blinks after a moment, and then bursts out laughing.

Vincent glares at them. "Hey! Don't leave us out of the joke."

Quinn quirks a smile and glides across the kitchen towards Florence, brushing a hand over her hair once she arrives. Florence's hazel eyes go distant for a couple of seconds before she chuckles — a low, thick sound.

Vincent points his knife at Quinn. "Rude."

She blows him a kiss and then floats out of the kitchen.

A vampire, a witch, and a ghost walk into a bar—

"Am I the bartender in this scenario?" Des asks.

"Oh, shut up!" Vincent throws a bread roll at him. It hits Des straight in the forehead.

"Ow."

Behind him, he hears the soft giggle of an unseen Quinn.

Their reservation that night does not cancel.

'Thank God,' Des thinks as a man, a woman, and two small children come in through the front doors.

He glances at the computer monitor and sees that the reservation for tonight is actually for a couple, not a family. Unexpected guests then. Even better—at least this time of the year. It'll be a different story in two months.

He looks back at the family. Their coat shoulders look wet. "Welcome to The Port 13 Motel," he says. "How are you guys doing tonight?"

The man readjusts his grip on his suitcase handle. "Uh, fine. We're fine. You, uh, do you have any rooms available?"

Des looks over the family, glances back at the computer screen. "You guys looking for—" and then stops because the woman is pulling one boy away from the other one while whisper-shouting at them.

The man's shoulders climb higher as this incident goes on and the woman's voice gets louder. He does not look behind him — just stares straight ahead, somewhere just past Des' right shoulder.

Des almost respects him. It's hard to respect a person when you're pitying them, however. "How about a room with a double and two singles?" he says instead.

Something shifts in the man's face. "That would be perfect."

"Well, Steven started it!" one of the boys shouts.

"Did not!"

"Yup, just give me one minute." Des turns back to his computer. The room hasn't been used in a week, but Quinn keeps a clean house. He's not worried.

He walks the man through check-in while Steven and Scottie (as the other boy is revealed to be) keep fighting. "We offer meals here," Des says. "We just require an hour's notice beforehand."

"Wait, you mean you do supper?" the woman asks, breaking through her sons' fighting. Her face is exhausted.

Des holds back a sigh and pulls out a piece of paper. "Here's the meal plan for the week." He holds it out to the woman.

She reaches for it, and their fingers brush. A bright red series of digital numbers, like those found on an alarm clock, flash before Des' eyes: **42:147.**

He forces his smile to hold as the numbers blink out as soon as they lose connection. "Vincent is a very good cook. Sometimes he goes off the menu though."

The woman holds the menu as if it is a piece of a treasure map. Her sons start tugging at her jacket, asking to see.

Des turns back to the man. "You guys are in room 210, just up the stairs and to the right." He holds out the card key, and when the man reaches for it, their fingers brush.

10:39.

Des' smile holds. "If you decide on supper, we'll need to know by 5:00. You can either eat down here in the dining room or we offer room service."

"Thanks," the man says. The family gathers up their

suitcases and the woman herds her sons up the stairs behind the man.

The moment they are gone, Quinn slips into the second chair at Des' left.

"You need to stop doing that," he says.

She reaches out and touches his arm. He glances down at her small, pale hand on his slightly less pale arm. **50:201** is slowly fading from view, the bright red turning pink and growing fuzzy along the edges.

"I'm alright," he says softly. "Honest."

Her fingers curl around his forearm and hold on. They sit there until he doesn't see the numbers anymore and the footsteps of the family upstairs has become background noise.

A vampire, a witch, and a ghost walk into a bar where a bartender mans the front desk with a decade-old computer at his side—

No. Wait. That's not how the joke goes.

And furthermore, Des has never been a bartender. He doesn't even know how to make a good martini—

"I will have to teach you," Florence says very precisely, in the way she does after her fourth glass of wine. One hand strokes his hair, and a blurry **31:192** buzzes before his eyes.

—and he actually doesn't like people as a general rule. They make him uncomfortable, and he makes them uncomfortable. Admittedly, he's rather good at reading people, but that was a survival skill. It's what one has to learn when one has a mute sister and no one else in the world.

Vincent flops down into the chair that Quinn has vacated two minutes before. "Please tell me I have people to cook for."

Des doesn't take his eyes off the computer screen. "You have people to cook for."

"Wait, really?" The chair scrapes across the floor as Vincent sits up.

Des shrugs. "Dunno. They seemed interested though." A light flashes through the front windows, and he glances in that direction. He's seen this kind of light motion often enough to recognize them as headlights. "Reservation?"

Vincent drops his elbows on the counter and then plops his chin in his hands. "Are they lovers?"

Des glances at him. "Does that matter?"

A massive shrug. "I like lovers. They give me hope."

"Vincent. You are a lover."

He glances at Des with smoky dark eyes and raises his eyebrows.

Des makes a face. "Man, stop. It won't work on me."

The front door opens and the chime dings. Vincent perks up like a dog about to get a treat or offered a walk. "Lovers!" he whispers-shouts.

Des swears he's wagging an invisible tail.

Des turns to face the couple walking across the room and pulls up a smile. "Hi there! Welcome to The Port 13 Motel."

"I admit that I am disappointed by their lack of creativity," Florence announces.

Des continues to set the table. Both the family and couple have requested supper in the dining room, which requires a large round table and a smaller square table. The four employees will eat in the kitchen as per usual.

"Uh huh."

"After all, to believe that Vincent is a vampire requires a leap of faith." Florence continues to speak to the pot on the windowsill, her fingers gently stroking the dirt inside. "And no one truly believes Quinn is dead, although I can understand how people may find her presence haunting."

Des frowns and taps the knife closer to the plate. There, that was better. Far more balanced aesthetically.

"But calling me a witch? Bah. Practically anyone can be a witch."

Des squints at the table. "Should I give them a candle?" The centre seems to be lacking something, and while candles are an easy and beautiful fix, he's not too sure if it'll work in this case.

Florence turns slightly, fingers still curled into the pot. "The couple? Yes. Not the family though; the boys will set the place ablaze."

"Can't have that." He thinks about maybe borrowing a couple of Florence's cacti for the family table — those are hardy plants. He looks over to Florence, and instead of asking her for the plants, says, "You sound more offended than disappointed."

She blows out a breath and waves a hand in the air. The tips of her fingers are caked in dry dirt that flutter off with her motion. "I just cannot help but wonder — are they calling me a witch because my father was black?"

As she speaks, the plant in the pot straightens like its being pulled up by an invisible string. The closed bud turns its head up to the light of the soon-setting sun and slowly opens, pink petals stretching and spreading out as if offering Florence a hug.

"That's pretty racist," Des says. "Even for Wisconsin."

Quinn is watching the couple with narrowed eyes. Des comes up behind her and pokes her in the arm. **50:201.**

"Stop that."

She turns her head, screws up her face, and sticks out her tongue.

Des rolls his eyes. "Well then, don't be so obvious about it at least," he whispers. "You're gonna give us a reputation."

She blinks big, blue eyes at him — a shade lighter than his own — and then gives him a very unimpressed look. She reaches out and pokes him on the nose, holding the pad of her finger there. **50:201** flashes into his vision again along with another vision: *Today's trashy newspaper; a focus on* The Port 13 Motel *story.*

He screws his face up. "Ha ha. Don't remind me." He swats her hand away, blinking away both images. "Vincent's looking for a taste tester; why don't you go make yourself useful?"

Her eyes light up, her well-known love for food overriding all else, and a second later she's gliding away.

"But why am I the vampire?" Vincent asks. He has a

pair of oven mitts on his hands — they're designed to look like bear paws.

Des doesn't even need to look at Quinn to know what she's thinking: "*Twilight.*"

Vincent rears up, the oven door left gaping open. "*Twilight*?!"

"It means you're beautiful, darling," Florence responds. She pours a thick, red wine into three glasses.

Vincent bends over to pull a dish out of the oven. He straightens, shuts the door with his knee, and then turns to the counter. "Flattery," he scoffs, tossing his head and hair. "Mere flattery."

Quinn creeps closer, eyes bright and focused on the food.

Des watches, shaking his head slightly. "It's because they've never seen you outside, numbnuts."

Vincent narrows his eyes at Des and places the dish on the counter with careful control. "Rude, butler. Rude."

"At least you're not a witch," Florence says, slowly twisting the cork back on the wine bottle. "A ghost and a vampire: there's something romantic about that. But a witch? Bah."

Quinn inches closer to the food; Des slips past her and reaches for two of the wine glasses. "I'll take these," he says.

Florence closes her eyes and brings the third wine glass up to her face. While Vincent's back is turned, Quinn leans her face to the food, closing her eyes.

They inhale.

They sigh.

"Oy! No breathing on the food!"

Des pushes the door open with his foot and steps back into the dining room.

It's raining in the morning.

Quinn presses her hands against the window to the side of the glass front doors. She leans in, and Des watches the back of her head.

Vincent comes out of the employee entrance, a large raincoat on and holding another in his hand. He casts a sour look at Des. "Florence is out back."

"Typical." Des glances at his computer screen. The family is supposed to check out in two hours and the couple is booked for another day. They have another two reservations for tonight. "Is she wearing a coat at least?"

"A hat. Under duress." Vincent stomps over to Quinn and shakes the second coat at her. "Here. You're not leaving without it."

She reaches out with one hand without turning her head. Her hand clamps onto his forearm.

A pause. Then: "Well, you kind of are," Vincent says. "In comparison to the rest of us, you definitely are."

Quinn sighs, her shoulders rising high and drooping low. She turns and takes the coat from him. She looks over, catches Des' eyes, quirks a smirk, and then slips past Vincent, out the door and into the rain.

Vincent blows out a breath and squares his shoulders. "Wish me luck."

"Luck," Des calls, voice bored.

Vincent inhales, rolls his shoulders, then opens the door. He takes a step outside, hisses like a cat, and then bolts outside, head ducked low in a charge.

Des drums his fingers on the counter and then slips off his chair. They were going to need a mat to keep the floor clean.

The Port 13 Motel is named after Port Haven, which is a small, secret school in California.

The four of them met at that university five years ago. Florence was a history teacher. Vincent taught art and led a cooking club for those students so inclined towards practical skills. Des was there to drop off his sister. Vincent had been there to welcome Quinn to the school; Florence had come around the corner with a student discussing the reign of Nero; Des had countered a point she made. When Vincent returned twenty minutes later from showing Quinn to her dorm room, Des and Florence had moved on to Constantine and whether Christianity was a political move or an actual spiritual reformation. Vincent had butted in with comments about the art of that century, and an hour later they were discussing the treasures of the Vatican.

That first night ended with Des getting ridiculously drunk with Florence and Vincent off of cooking wine. He has very little memory as to what happened that night and refuses to talk about the morning after. After saying goodbye to Quinn — and being scolded quite harshly by her for being so irresponsible — he left her at Port Haven until Thanksgiving six months later. He returned to find that Quinn had joined Vincent's cooking club and was one of Florence's favourite students. The teachers remembered him and welcomed him back with more wine and a thoroughly stuffed turkey.

The four of them drank a lot that night. They also plotted.

It was Florence's idea, Quinn's vision, Des' skills, and Vincent's talent that started it all. It was long-term and possibly impossible. But when they all awoke the next morning, they found the idea had merit. They agreed to try.

So Des left, and Vincent and Florence taught. Quinn continued to grow and, by the time two years passed, she was an administrator for the school.

And then Des called. He'd found the target.

Vincent put in his resignation the next day. Nine months later, Florence and Quinn gave their resignation and climbed into a minivan Quinn had bought eighteen months earlier. They spent another three months fixing up the property a certain woman had left her new husband in her will.

Which is how The Port 13 Motel opened for business twenty months ago: a series of coincidences acted upon by four ambitious, special people.

The second reservation of the evening is a pair of men with a suitcase each. One is in a suit with a pierced earlobe and a snake tattoo winding up the side of his neck. The other is wearing a very nice vest, pressed pants, and a curling smile.

Des squints at them. His chest feels tight, a gut reaction he's learned to heed. He glances at the computer.

Bliss and Touré. Interesting.

"Welcome to The Port 13 Motel," he greets as they near the front desk. "How are you doing tonight?"

The man with the snake tattoo grins; he has a chipped tooth. The man with the vest smiles and says, "Very well, thank you. Yourself?" He has a smooth voice and a soft accent.

"Pretty good, thanks," Des says. "Did you guys have a reservation?"

The man with the vest continues smiling. It looks natural on his face. "Yes. It should be under my name." He pulls out a wallet from his pants' pocket and hands Des a single card he fishes out with elegant fingers.

Their fingers don't touch. Des makes sure of it.

He glances down at the ID card: Daren Toure. "The reservation is actually under two names," he says, handing the card back. He looks back at the other man. "I take it you're Bliss?"

The man grins again. The chipped tooth glints back at Des. "Damn right. Not what you expected?"

Des just looks at him. "I work at a motel. I don't dwell on expectations." He looks back at Toure. "You've got three nights reserved."

He nods. "Yes, just in case. We have business in town." And the smile stays.

Des looks at the two men. "Hope it all goes well."

"Thank you."

Des takes them the rest of the way through check in and explains how meals work. "You guys are in room 212." He passes Toure the cardkey.

Their fingers just barely touch, but it's enough to see a

faint **07:11** flicker before his eyes.

"Thank you," Toure says, eyes on Des' face. "We'll get settled right away then." He looks down at his watch. "It's too late for supper, of course, but I think it's safe to say we'll be interested in breakfast."

"Of course. Have a good night."

The men take their suitcases and head for the stairs. As soon as they're out of view, Des hears the employee door open. A pair of hands land on his shoulders and two thumbs slip under his shirt collar.

Des pauses, staring at the stairs and ignoring the **50:200** buzzing in the foreground. "Yeah. I don't like them either."

Florence washes her hands in the downstairs bathroom. She has a nail file in one hand and uses it to dig under her nails, picking out the dirt. Her curls are limp and damp, but her clothes are dry — she must have changed her outfit.

"Are they dangerous?" she asks, squinting at her nails.

"Dunno," Des shrugs, leaning against the counter. "I didn't see any weapons." He makes a face. "'Course, that don't mean much."

Her eyes cut his way. "No, I don't suppose it does." She ducks her hands back under the flowing tap water. "I'll be careful until they leave."

"Remind Vincent too," Des says, pushing off the counter. "We don't need another reason to have a story about us."

He's opening the door when she says, "I wonder if that's why they're here. That story."

He pauses. The reservation was only made last night. "Shit." He stands there for another couple of seconds before heading towards the dining room. There are still a couple and three girls to serve.

If you inhabit Port Haven long enough, you learn that this world holds a lot of secrets.

If you carry a secret (as most persons of Port Haven do), you start to recognize others carrying secrets. You learn that the further down they bury that secret, the more power it holds over them.

If you live long enough, carrying a deep secret and collecting others' secrets, you start to realize that Earth is a very dangerous place.

If you live long enough to come to terms with that, you'll understand that every time you look in a mirror, a desperate, dangerous person is looking back.

For some reason, when Des goes to bed that night, the other three are in his room.

The Port 13 Motel is not a big motel. It can't be: there are only four employees. Instead, The Port 13 Motel has exactly thirteen rooms. Four of them belong to the four owners on the attachment to the actual motel — connected by the employee entrance. Four of the remaining rooms are on the ground floor (110, 111, 112, and 114 -- because there is only so many thirteens they can take). Four of the other rooms are on the upper floor (210, 212, 214 and 215).

The last room is actually a suite and takes up the whole attic (300).

Last summer, they had three weeks where every room was always full. They hired two university students to help clean the rooms with Quinn. Vincent found an old student to help him in the kitchen. Florence was either in the courtyard or in their minivan running errands, and Des only left the front desk to catch a few naps or dish up a meal.

Let the record state: Des *hated* the motel being that full.

But, yes, Des walks into his room at ten o'clock because that's when the front desk closes. Des keeps a phone on in his room in case of emergencies, but those rarely happen. It's part of his spiel when guests check in.

But the three of them are waiting for him: Florence on his bed, brushing Quinn's short, dark hair, and Vincent leaning against the headboard, thumbs tapping at his phone. Quinn blinks sleepy eyes at him, then closes them again and hums from her place on the floor.

Des blinks, sighs, and then says, "I'm gonna have a shower."

"Bliss and Toure, huh?" Vincent remarks as Des crosses his room to grab a clean pair of sleeping pants. "They *sound* harmless."

"Hm." Des crosses back, pants in hand, and brushes his hand over Quinn's shoulder as he goes. **50:200.**

Are they here to kill us?

"Wolf in sheep's clothing," Florence is saying, waving the hairbrush slightly. "We must be very wary."

"Same numbers," Des murmurs. "No change." A sense

of relief sweeps through him, like a wave he can't control. He steps away and moves into the bathroom.

When he comes back, freshly washed, only Vincent is there. He's staring at the wall with a blank expression on his face.

"Man, get out of my bed."

Vincent holds out a hand, palm up, otherwise not moving. "How're my digits, Des?"

Des sighs. He drops his dirty clothes into the laundry basket, then walks over to the bed. He reaches with one hand and grabs Vincent's wrist.

30:300.

He frowns. "Well, they've changed, but nothing's happening this year." He gives a sharp tug. "Get outta here, man. I'm wiped."

Vincent goes with the tug until he's sitting on the edge of the bed, feet planted on the ground. "It changed?" he asks, eyes locked on Des' face.

"They change a lot," Des says. "They changed that Thanksgiving. They changed when we got this place. They changed last month when you finally bought yourself that new knife set. Don't worry, Vincent."

Vincent waits for a moment, then nods. "Yeah. Okay. Night, Des."

Let the record state: it wasn't murder. They didn't kill anyone. They saw an opportunity and took it. There was no way for Vincent Benoit to be charged with the death of Amelia Glawson, even if it was slightly suspicious.

So the forty-seven year old had a whirlwind romance

with a devilishly handsome man who married her just four months after they met, and inherited a good eighty percent of her sizable wealth, including the deed to a partially renovated motel off of Highway 60, when she passed away after a vicious six month battle with cancer? It wasn't like he had given her the cancer. That would be ridiculous.

So it was slightly suspicious. It was also incredibly romantic; and after all, the mysterious Mr. Benoit hadn't caused any fuss. He had just taken what was allotted to him and quietly left. Like some mythical creature, he had walked out into the fog…

And moved into that partially renovated motel a short drive outside Astico, Wisconsin.

"We heard a rumor that this motel has one of the nicest courtyards in the state — is that true?"

Des glances between the charming smile of Toure and the slightly bored expression of Bliss. He looks back at Toure's face and says, "We've put a lot of time and energy into our courtyard, yes."

"Must have quite the staff."

"We're very dedicated, yes."

Toure's dark eyes narrow. Des narrows his right back. They hold each other's gazes for several long moments.

Bliss grunts a kind of amused sound — Toure's lips curl and he blinks.

Des isn't sure he's won that contest; he feels like he's given something away instead.

"Maybe we'll spend the day there then," Toure says.

"We should get a fair bit of work done — and who knows? The foliage may inspire us."

Bliss rolls his eyes. 'Foliage,' he mouths behind Toure's back.

"If you want to, you're welcome to," Des says. "The entrance is down the hall to the right of the stairs. Just be careful."

Bliss' eyes shoot to Des'. "Careful of what?" His voice is very precise, each word distinct and determined.

Des cocks his head to the side. "Of the wind. It's only April; still pretty cool out there." He smiles. "You might find yourself getting chilled if you're out there too long."

The two guests glance at each other, then look back at Des. "Thank you for the warning," Toure says.

"Of course." Des' smile holds. "If you need anything else, please don't hesitate to ask."

The two men nod and then go up the stairs, seemingly to their room. Des turns back to his computer and starts clicking the mouse. When two arms curl around his shoulders and neck, he doesn't even blink.

"Why do I remember you being so much better at chess?" Florence muses, resting her cheek on his head.

31:12 is buzzing red on the screen in front of him. It holds and then fades as he relaxes into her touch. "I'm rusty," he agrees. "It's what we get for two years of peace."

She sighs — her breath rustles his hair. "I suppose we can't complain about that now, can we?"

He lifts a hand and rests it on one of her arms. **31:12.** "No. We really can't.

"...Unless it gets us killed."

Vincent peers out the window that opens towards the backyard — or the courtyard as marketing insists they call it. "I could poison their food."

"That's murder, man." Des reaches for another handful of candied walnuts, curls his fingers around them, then leans back against the kitchen counter. Quinn taps his fist with one gentle finger. **50:199.**

He opens his fist, and she fishes out a walnut.

"Only if we get caught," Vincent is saying.

"I'm pretty sure it's still murder whether we're caught or not. The difference is the consequences."

"Wouldn't take much. They wouldn't even taste it."

Quinn fishes another walnut out. Des pops one into his mouth. He chews and swallows before reminding Vincent, "They haven't even done anything yet."

Quinn looks at him with sharp, icy eyes. Vincent says, "*Yet*," with a great deal of certainty. "I'd rather get them before they get us," he adds. "That's how people survive— oh, shit, they saw me."

Des looks sharply at him — Vincent hasn't moved. "Is it the black man or the white?"

"Black," Vincent says. "My, what a lovely vest."

Quinn is very tense beside Des. He offers her the palm of walnuts. "He's the tricky one: Toure."

"Don't you hate it when dubious characters have such excellent taste in clothes?" Vincent muses, his body as tense as his voice is casual.

Quinn reaches out and takes another walnut. Her fingers brush his palm as they curl around the small nut.

00:02.

Des feels his heart stop, his brain stop, everything stop as that single digit comes into focus. Everything goes tight and bright for a long second... and then releases like rubber band.

The walnuts hit the floor with a series of sharp *rat-a-tat-tats.*

Vincent spins around; whatever he sees on Des' face makes him blanch. "Des. Deston, what is it?"

Quinn has both hands curled around Des' sticky palm. He feels her worry and concern pulse through him to the same rhythm of that bright red **2, 2, 2.**

"It changed," Des croaks finally. "Her numbers, they—" and he can't say any more because a single digit-!

Quinn makes a shushing sound, breath pushed out between her teeth, and brings his hand to her chest. Her heart thumps steadily against his palm and **2, 2, 2** beats before his eyes.

It's okay, it's okay, it's okay, she tells him. *Deston, it's okay.*

Vincent looks at them and then looks back over his shoulder, out the window. "Are you still sure I can't poison them?"

Florence tucks her hand into Des' curled arm and leads him around the courtyard like a stunned dog. He goes because he doesn't like fighting with Florence and because it's better than being inside.

The sun is beginning to set, and the sky is a mix of red

and orange. The atmosphere is still and soft like the first note of a lullaby, and it is so beautiful against the green of the trees and leaves and grass, and the flowers are sprouting, pushing up towards the sky. In a month, the garden will be a masterpiece.

Des hates it. He thinks if it weren't for Florence's hand, he'd sit right down and let his body be used for fertilizer.

"Well, they did not harm the plants. That's something," Florence hums. **31:12** is faded but still present. Normally he can ignore it, the same way you learn to ignore the common signs of your workplace, but not today. If someone else's number changes, he wants to know. He *needs* to know.

"Toure seemed impressed by the foliage."

"Foliage?" she repeats. "Is that what he called my garden?"

He hums.

"Bastard."

The laugh bursts out like an unexpected burp. He bumps his hip into hers and she leans her head on his shoulder. "Ah, Des," she sighs. "Don't be afraid. If there is one thing being your friend has taught me, it's that our fate is not set in stone."

Des swallows. "I think that might be worse, actually. The not-knowing. The wondering." The what-ifs that leave him staring at the ceiling for hours.

Florence is quiet as they walk, their steps soft on the pathway that curves around the backyard. Des glances behind them and sees that the plants are a little thicker, the leaves a little greener, and the petals a little brighter.

"Careful," he whispers.

She sighs a low sound. "Careful. All we ever are is careful."

Quinn curls up in her own bed that night. That isn't the strange thing: Quinn mostly keeps to herself, only invading the others' personal space when she requires something. No, the oddity is Des sitting on the edge of her bed.

Years ago, that was common. There were a handful of years between the car accident that stole their family and Quinn and Des arriving at Port Haven where it was just them. In those years, Des watched Quinn constantly — almost every other night. It's a habit easily picked up again.

Whether it was for his own sake or hers, it doesn't matter. They both had nightmares, they both appreciated the company. That hadn't changed through the years.

Tonight, however, Quinn is sleeping soundly. At least one of them is getting some rest — Des knows he'll be up all night watching her breathe. He's too afraid to touch her — her numbers might change right before his eyes, and he just... He just can't.

The problem with being a big brother is that it's impossible to be one without a younger sibling. Losing a sibling is more than losing a friend — it's losing a part of your identity.

Des has spent his whole life trying to figure out who he is, and maybe that's true of all people. But he loses and gains pieces of himself all the time, and this piece? This piece is so fundamental, if he loses it, he won't recognise himself. And then what?

Quinn's chest rises and falls, rises and falls, and her face stays serene. What is she dreaming of? Will she dream tomorrow too?

Vincent takes one look at Des in the morning and says, "Did you sleep at all?"

Des clicks on the mouse and shrugs a shoulder. "Nah."

"Deston."

"Vincent." He frowns at the screen. "Sleep is for the weak." It's something his youngest sister used to say before she died in that terrible accident. His chest pangs at the thought of her, but it's been long enough healing that it doesn't show on his face.

Vincent reaches out and grabs the back of Des' chair. "Don't be stupid. We need you to be alert and ready."

Des looks over at him and says, "I couldn't sleep. How could I?" The seconds pass — tick-tock, tick-tock — and there is nothing he can do. He doesn't know what he could possibly do.

"Des. It can still change."

"I know." Of course he knows. He sees it every week. He's seen in the three of them, seen it in other friends and family members. He knows things can change. But those people weren't Quinn. Quinn is his.

There's a heavy sigh above him, and then the sound of Vincent slumping into the chair beside him. "If only we had a clue of what they wanted."

Des stares at the computer screen and thinks of Toure

with his smirking mouth and velvet vests, and Bliss with that tattoo crawling out of his collar and that dammed chipped tooth. He says, "That newspaper article. It must've been that."

"So they're after us." This is now a statement of fact: there are too many coincidences for it not to be. "I guess the next question is, what for?"

Des closes his eyes and breathes for a few long seconds. "We'll know soon enough."

At the breakfast table, Toure is on the phone. His dark eyes are narrowed, and his lips are set in a firm frown. Across the table, Bliss taps his fork against his plate as he chews his toast, his eyes glancing around the room. There's a small family at a table across the room, and his eyes keep flickering in that direction every time one of the kids open their mouth.

"Yes," Toure is saying. "Yes, I know."

Des is trying not to look like he's listening, but he's tired and worried. He's fiddling with the coffeemaker and actually struggling with the filter because his fingers aren't working and because he's got more important things to focus on.

"Whatever happened to patience, Doctor? We still have— Yes, we are working. Yes, we—"

There is a touch on his arm, just above his elbow, and then **00:01** flashes before his eyes. He tenses — he can't help it — and the touch becomes a full hand pressing against him. *Shh...* whispers across his mind, and Toure gives a tremendous scowl and presses his thumb firmly against the touch screen of his smart phone.

Bliss grins. "Don't you miss the days of flip phones?" He stabs a piece of sausage and holds it up between them. "Hard to slam down a touch screen."

Toure inhales slowly and then exhales. "There's a conference at the end of the week," he says, voice perfectly controlled.

Bliss pops the sausage in his mouth and chews. Toure reaches for his mug and Des reaches for the milk to check and see if he needs to fill it again. Bliss swallows and says, "That shouldn't matter."

Toure takes a long drink, and Des determines that it wouldn't hurt to top off the milk. "No. We're still on schedule. He's just neglected to take his medication again; makes him anxious."

Bliss nods and stabs another piece of sausage. "Alright."

Des steps back, the half-empty milk jug in his hands. He glances at Quinn who looks back at him with wide, worried eyes. "Wanna check on the waffle mix?" Des asks her.

Bliss and Toure's reservation is only for another night. Des stares at the date on the computer screen, thinks of that terrible, red **00:01**, and for some reason remembers when he got the call from the hospital nine years ago. He doesn't understand why people seem to think he can remember that call with perfect recall, but it doesn't work like that. He remembers picking up the phone, remembers listening to a voice — but not what the voice sounded like or what they said — and then that dreadful sinking feeling in his gut, the numbness spreading through his body like poisonous gas. He remembers thinking, *I'll have to pick up Quinn at school.*

Now, staring at tomorrow's check-out date for the party of Bliss-Toure, he can feel that same numbness buzzing at his fingers. It's sinking into his brain, and making his heartbeat loud, and then: *Should we even bother buying groceries?*

"Deston?"

Des blinks once. The computer screen shudders back into focus. "I think I need to take a nap."

He can feel Vincent's eyes on him. "I agree. Should I have Florence man the desk for you or Quinn?"

"Flo. Are you still going grocery shopping?"

"I was planning on it. Did you want me to take Quinn?"

Des sighs, pushes away from the desk, and rubs his face. "I want you to, but I don't want Flo here alone. It only takes a moment for the place to get overrun, especially with just one person, so—"

"No, of course. I understand." Vincent lays a hand on Des' shoulder and **30:298** flashes and steadies itself in Des' vision. "I'll just grab the essentials and be back within the hour. You go lie down."

"Yeah. Okay. Okay."

In his dream, Florence is a tree. And not a beautiful tree, but one of those gnarled up weeping willows, and her hair is the branches that hang low and sweep the grass, and on the bed of grass at the base of Florence the tree's trunk, is Quinn. She is pale and still, and Des knows with the kind of certainty that only dreams create, that she is dead.

He walks over to her and he doesn't make a sound, and when he reaches down to touch her cheek, his hand passes through her.

"It's because you're a ghost, darling," Florence whispers, like the wind through her branches of hair.

I thought she was the ghost, Des says, or thinks — he's not sure because it's a dream.

"I am he is, you are we is, you are me and we are both together," Vincent says. "Or something like that; those Beatles must've been on the good drugs, don't you think?"

Des looks over, and Vincent is hiding in Florence's branches, high, high up, and every time the sun peeks through and touches his skin, it breaks out in bubbles, like an angry pot of water. Then shadows fall over it again, and the skin goes cool and smooth to the touch. Des watches this happen over, and over, and over again until finally Vincent reaches out for him and says, "Watch, Deston."

Des looks down at Quinn again, and she is sinking into the ground, falling deeper and deeper into the dirt. Des reaches for her, and his fingers scrape the ground, and nothing happens. It's like scratching your nails into the concrete — nothing happens. And still Quinn sinks, and sinks, and there is only her face, still and smooth like a porcelain doll's.

Then she is gone, and there is only disturbed dirt where she lay. And the wind blows through Florence's branches, and Vincent says, "Damn the sun," and Des is invisible.

Bliss and Toure are not at supper that night.

Quinn keeps brushing Des' hands and arms; it's supposed to be comforting, he knows, because she keeps sending words of affection and care with every brush, but every touch sends **00:01** flashing across his vision. He wants to tell her to stop, because every red **00:01** is like a punch in the gut, but every sound of her 'voice' is like a hug.

It's an awful kind of purgatory.

"What do you mean, they're not here?" Vincent snaps as he stirs a pot of spaghetti sauce with more violence that Des feels is warranted.

"I mean they're not here. They didn't come for supper."

"Bastards," Vincent hisses — and Des suddenly wants to laugh, because if him and Quinn are mirror images, then so are Vincent and Florence, and they are all doomed. "How are we supposed to know what they're up to if they're not here for us to watch?"

"We're not supposed to know what they're up to," Des reminds him. "This isn't a movie. There's no narrator telling us what's going to happen next."

Vincent's stirring slows as he thinks. Des could practically read Vincent's mind from the way he cooked. "What are we doing? Why am I even cooking this meal? What does it even matter?"

"It matters," Florence says, coming out from the pantry with a bottle of wine in her hands. "It matters because all we have are our lives and this motel, and we cannot afford to lose both." She stands at Vincent's side and says, "I thought this would pair nicely with dessert."

Vincent looks at the wine bottle, and then at Florence, and says, "You lush," with a ridiculous amount of affection. Quinn comes up behind Des, slinks her arms around his neck (**00:01** echoes over his vision), and thinks, *Family*.

Des reaches up with one hand and covers Quinn's small wrist. He says, "Quinn wants to know if the dessert is chocolate," and smiles at the pleasure/gratitude Quinn sends his way.

After supper, when everything is cleaned up, Des is at the front desk. He looks at the computer screen and notices — again — that Bliss and Toure are supposed to check out in the morning. He knows that he's not going to be able to sleep until they leave, and so he sits there, balancing bills, checking receipts, reading and responding to emails, and keeping his ears open. He does this for a very long time, and doesn't really respond when Vincent checks up on him—

(Deston? Hey, Deston, are you…? Okay. Okay. Good night, man.)

—when Florence pecks his cheek—

(Don't be afraid, darling. We're all in the same boat.)

—or when Quinn wishes him a good night.

(*Good night. Love you.*)

Which means that he hears a door open at 1:17 am,

and then the soft sound of footsteps. He stops, minimizes what he was doing on the computer, and waits.

Less than a minute later, Toure steps off the bottom step of the stairs, and looks over. He makes a face like he's repressing a smile, and then says, "Isn't the front desk normally closed at this hour?"

Des doesn't even know why he's still bothering. "Extenuating circumstances."

Toure lets the smile spread. "You think you know what's about to happen, don't you?"

"I don't have a clue what you're about to do," Des replies honestly. "I just know a plausible result."

Toure turns to face him fully. "Is that what you do? Predict plausible results?"

Des says, "I see numbers."

Toure's face splits, and his teeth are white in the dim fluorescents of the lobby, and his smile is beautiful. "You know, sometimes I wonder what the point of this even is. Why are they so obsessed with us? What do they think it will all accomplish?"

Des hates him. "You mean you don't even know why you're doing what you're doing?"

Toure chuckles. It's a soft, melodious thing. "Oh, I know why I'm doing it. I just don't know why *they're* doing it."

"You mean Bliss?"

Another laugh: "Oh, he does it for the same reason as me." And Des feels a presence behind him, huge and looming. Before he can do anything — move, scream, shout — there is an arm around his throat, a bright **06:94** flashing across his eyes, and sudden pressure against his trachea. He cannot inhale, he cannot exhale: he pushes out, reaches up with his arms to grab the arm around his throat, when suddenly there is a snake staring at him. The snake's eyes are small, black, and beady, and the pattern of its scales shift and shimmer, and there is no air. His vision, echoing with red pulsing numbers goes blurry and dim, just as Toure's voice states: "Because it's the only thing we can do."

There are shadows everywhere.

Des wakes up slowly, watching the shadows shift and move until they stabilize into form. It is the trees of the courtyard, their branches waving against the barely visible yellow light of the moon. There is a strong breeze, and it whistles through the leaves and the bushes around him, fluttering through his hair like a worried mother's fingers.

He lies there in the courtyard, staring up at the sky as the clouds slink across, casting their own shadows around him. He thinks, *I'm not dead. Oh God. Quinn.*

He sits up: he takes his time because he's not stupid, he knows how easy it would be to pass out again, but within seconds he is sitting upright and staring across the courtyard. He's just about to try to get his legs under him when he hears a low *hiss*. He glances over at his feet and stops breathing.

He had thought that he had imagined that snake before — a hallucination brought about by lack of air. But no: there is a snake with its head resting against his right ankle like a pet, its dark eyes focused on Des. It hisses with every soft exhale, and although Des cannot explain how he knows, he knows that it is a warning.

"Where the hell did you come from?" he croaks.

The snake does not move. If not for its breathing, Des would have thought it a statue.

"Finally," comes a voice; and Des recognizes it as Bliss' even if he cannot see the man. "I didn't think I choked you that hard."

Des frowns into the shadows — he thinks the voice came from the right of him. "You suffocated me," he says flatly.

"Whatever." There is the soft sound of footsteps, a crunch of shoes on the gravel path that meanders through the courtyard, and then finally: Bliss himself. He runs a hand through his hair, looks down at Des' feet and whistles once.

The snake raises its head, staring straight at Des.

"I take it this is yours then?" Des asks, eyes darting between the snake and the man.

Bliss grins, and his teeth are pale in the moonlight. "Yeah. She's mine." He makes a gesture with his hand and the snake moves, slithering up and settling between Des' legs, curling its long body underneath it so it sits like a sultan on a throne. The entire time, its eyes never leave Des' face. Although, to be fair, Des' eyes never leave the snake either.

"You might as well get comfy," Bliss says. "You may be sitting there a while."

"How long is a while?"

Bliss shrugs. "As long as it takes for the others to wake up."

Around them, the bushes rustle and the tree branches shudder. Des takes his eyes off the snake long enough to glance at the treetops. "What; I'm not enough for you?"

"Can't ignore The Prime Directive." Bliss peers around, a frown on his face. The frown deepens like he's seen something, and he whistles again. The snake turns its head towards Bliss, pauses for a few seconds, and then swirls out of his throne, slithers along the inside of Des' right leg, and away, disappearing into the bushes.

Des waits a moment, but Bliss is staring into the shadows, seemingly ignoring him. Des curls his fingers into the dirt, bends a knee up to push his foot into the ground, and then something circular and solid pushes steadily into the back of his skull.

"Don't," Toure's voice says from behind him. "I'd rather not waste the bullet if we can help it."

That sends a mixture of fear and insult swirling in Des' chest, and he scowls even as he straightens his knee back to the ground. The three of them stay there for a long minute with only their breathing, the wind, and the rustling plants to mark time passing.

Suddenly, several yards before them, the lights outside the motel turn on, their yellow outshining the moon far above them.

Bliss exhales a growly, "Finally. Let's get a move on."

The barrel of the gun pushes once into Des' skull. "Do yourself a favor and stay there, would you?" Toure doesn't wait for an answer before the pressure on Des' skull pulls away. "Don't let your guard down," he continues, aiming his voice in a different direction.

Bliss glances at their direction very briefly. "I'm not an

amateur." His eyes flick back to the lights and the motel, and he shifts his feet slightly.

Des eyes the trees around them, and then blinks as the bushes beside his left elbow shudder and begin to spread out, growing out fast enough for him to watch it happen.

A door creaks open in the quiet, and then slams a couple seconds later — Des snaps his head around to the motel to see the outline of a man standing right in front of the closed door. Vincent.

"Alright, bastards," he calls, his voice carrying like a professional orator. "You've got our attention. What do you want?"

"We wanted to extend an invitation to the four of you. Our employer would like to speak with you; he has a job offer for you," Toure says, his voice smooth and casual.

Des, although he cannot see anything distinct between the shadows and the distance, can still see Vincent shrugging with both palms up to the sky in that way he does. "Well, you've seen the shape of this place; we all have our hands full."

There is a rustling sound from somewhere above their heads; Des glances up to see that the trees look taller, with their branches stretching down further than they were before. He swallows and flexes his fingers in the dirt, shifting slightly.

"Yes, we're both aware of how short-staffed you are. Honestly, how do you stay in business?"

"Hard work and determination," Vincent calls back. He pauses for a moment, and Des can swear he feels Vincent lock eyes with him, but there is too much darkness to be sure. "Let me guess: Deston has a special invitation?"

"We wanted to ensure your full attention," Toure replies, voice cool. "You're all extremely busy; drastic measures were needed."

"Of course." There is another pause, as if Vincent is waiting for some kind of sign. Des thinks, *Oh no. Please don't*— and then Vincent continues, "It helps that we're extremely dramatic as well."

Des is suddenly very aware of how still everything around him is. The wind has ceased to blow. The trees are frozen, as if they are waiting just as Vincent is.

"We don't mean you any harm," Toure calls, and the back of Des' head throbs where the barrel of the gun had prodded. "We just have to be certain. You understand."

"Certain of what?" Des hears the words leave his mouth, even as he is sure he isn't supposed to speak and he has just made a critical error.

He can almost *feel* Toure's eyes on him. "Certain that you're who we think you are."

"And who do you think we are?" Vincent calls.

"Well..." Des can hear the smile in his words. "Certainly not a vampire. Nor are you ghosts. A witch on the other hand..."

And then, as if those were the words she'd been waiting for, Florence makes the world explode into greenery. Des gasps as the bushes that have been creeping ever-closer in growth envelop him in short, scratchy, twiggy leaves — his skin burns as dozens of cuts open as the bushes surround him. He feels Toure's surprise as his legs buckle behind Des, his knees stumbling into Des' back, and his body falling almost on top of Des. In the distance — for the world now ends inches away from his face — he can hear Bliss shout—

"Ha! So you *can* do something-!"

—and then there are hands grasping at his upper arms. **07:08** flashes bright red before him, a bright, blinding light that disorients him almost as much as the bushes have. "All right," he can hear Toure say, his voice low. "That was unexpected."

The anger surges in Des suddenly and fiercely, and he snaps, "Expect this!" and drives his elbow as hard as he can into what he thinks is Toure's chest. Toure exhales a rush of breath into Des' ear, and his hands falter where they grip his arms. He shrugs them off and then surges up onto his hands and knees. The bushes shudder and shake, and the twigs are surprisingly sharp, but he ducks his head low and pushes through them anyways. He keeps his eyes closed, but the leaves are so twisted and overgrown that he can't see very much at all. It is better to just crawl forward, push forward, move toward the voices in the distance—

Which, of course, is when a hand grips his ankle and pulls his leg down, sharp and sudden. Des gasps, grits his teeth, and then kicks backwards. He hits branches, and so he kicks again, and again, and again, until he manages to hit something solid and the grip slips off his ankle. He moves as quickly as he can, forces himself forward through the bush until the branches thin out; and when he reaches one hand out, stretching forward for some kind of space, a hand catches hold of his own.

00:01 flashes bright and bold, and then, *Don't let go* echoes through his mind. He thinks fiercely, *No, no I won't,* and lets his sister guide him out of the bushes. He falls into a ball at her feet when he escapes the branches and just breathes for several seconds. "Okay," he finally gasps. "Okay. What's the plan?"

From the corner of his eye, he can see something shift, and he looks up to see Quinn glaring at the bushes behind him, her hand curled around the handle of a frying pan. Des blinks at it, wondering if he's hallucinating again; but no. Quinn is still standing in the middle of the courtyard in an extra-large sleeping shirt decorated with a famous cartoon animal, gripping a frying pan in a fierce grip.

The words fall out of him without permission: "What are you, some modern Disney princess?"

Her lips quirk up, and then fall into a straight line as the bushes behind him rustle violently. Des shuffles forward, and by the time he has managed to get behind his sister and up on his knees, Toure surges out of the bushes like water out of a hydrant.

He collapses onto his hands and knees, out of breath just like Des was, and is in the process of saying, "What kind of hellish plant—" when Quinn readjusts her grip once more, raises her arm, and then slams the frying pan into the side of his head. He falls, like a tree felled.

Des gasps, stunned into silence. "Oh my God, you killed him."

She glances down at him, her face stoic and calm. She gestures at Toure's hand with her foot, and then looks back at Des. He inhales slowly, and then reaches out for the smooth, still hand. **07:08** flashes in his vision, and he exhales in a rush. "He's alive."

She doesn't say anything, but she grabs his shirt with her free hand and tugs him up. He lets her, stumbling up onto his feet, and as she turns him around, he lets the rest of the world start spinning for him again.

A few yards away is a large weeping willow that Florence has always loved; she is currently wrapped around it, her forehead pressed into the bark and her hands clawing the bark. She is on her knees, pushing her whole body into the trunk as if she can *become* the tree, and if not for her fierce grip that Des can recognize even from this distance, he would think she was unconscious.

A noise from his northeast pulls his attention, and he sees Vincent on his hands and knees, one hand at the base of his throat, head bowed low. Quinn surges forward, moving towards him with single intent, her grip still tight on the frying pan handle. Des thinks, *Choking. He looks like he was choking—* and Vincent raises his head, widens his eyes, opens his mouth—

And then, like Des is caught in a repeat of earlier, there is an arm around his throat, a bright **06:94** flashing across his eyes, and sudden pressure against his trachea. He cannot inhale, he cannot exhale: he pushes out, reaches up with his arms to grab the arm around his throat, when suddenly a voice hisses in his ear, "Why does it always end in a fight?"

"Des!" he hears Vincent call. His vision is blurry, the red digits focusing and blurring as he tugs at the arm pressed tight against his throat. He wheezes a breath, and the arm loosens ever so slightly; just enough for him to inhale in.

"Not that I mind fighting," Bliss continues, his voice more conversational than Des was expecting. "Adrenaline rushes are damn addicting. But, y'know, just once..." and the arm tightens sharp and sudden, cutting off all of Des' airflow again. "I'd actually like to have a peaceful conversation."

"Quinn!" Vincent barks — and Des' focus tightens and clarifies. Quinn is kneeling at Vincent's side, hands reaching up for her throat and eyes wide in her pale face. Des thinks he sees, but he can't be sure, he can't *breathe*, he thinks he sees something wrapped around her neck like a scarf or an arm or a—

"Forget this," Bliss grunts, and suddenly something connects with Des' left temple and pain explodes along with fuzzy digits and yellow lights. The arm around his throat releases, but his head is spinning, and so he falls forward, hands barely catching him before he faceplants into the ground.

Des gasps for breath and pain, and with blurry vision, sees Quinn teeter back and forth, and then collapse like a house of cards. He tries to say her name, but his throat is tight and aching and his lungs are burning. He can't get enough air in his chest to say anything.

"Enough."

It is not said loudly, but it echoes through the courtyard as if the trees and plants are speaking for her. In the blurry distance, Des can see Florence still hugging that willow; he watches as she shudders and tightens her grip, and then gasp.

Behind him, he hears movement, and then the low, alarmed curse of Bliss. He turns his head to see vines from the southern gate stretched out and wrapped around Bliss' ankles and wrists.

"Get off!" he hears from his other side. "Get off her,

you damn *snake*." He turns his head and sees Vincent at Quinn's side, hands yanking at something still attached to her. And there, between her body and Des', is the frying pan she had brought out from the kitchen.

Des slowly gets to his feet and grabs the frying pan. He stands and sways for a moment, feeling the blood pool in his head, the world spin, and his lungs protest. On his left, he can hear Bliss struggling and swearing, and on his right is Vincent demanding and begging.

He turns towards Bliss, raises the frying pan high, and then slams it into the man's face. He does it again, and then a third time, and would have done it a fourth time except the man falls forward, eyes closed and blood pouring out of his nose and mouth.

"Thank God," he hears behind him, and he turns to see Vincent pulling a limp snake off of Quinn's neck. Immediately, he bows his head to her mouth, waits a second, swears viciously, and then starts measuring hand spans down her chest.

Des' heart stops in his chest. *No.* He stumbles over barely noticing how the plants have finally stopped growing, and how the wind is rustling their leaves like it normally does. He collapses at Quinn's side and watches as Vincent starts CPR, thrusting down on Quinn's chest, lips mouthing a count. At twelve, though, he sways as if he can't quite move, and then starts to cough.

Des moves — he has to move, he has to *do* something — and forces Quinn's mouth open with his fingers and puts his open mouth over hers and blows whatever air in his depleted lungs he can. Red digits flicker in his vision -- **00:00** alternating with **67:111. 00:00-51:234; 00:111; 31:00;**

00:00; 00:00—

He lifts his head and gasps, "Don't stop!"

Vincent swears a low breathy word, but starts pumping again, gasping out his count. At thirteen, Des brings his face down to his sister's, and at fifteen, forces air into her mouth and ignores the pulsing **00:00, 00:00, 00:00, 54:116, 00:00**.

He lifts his head and Vincent starts thrusting again, and in the distance a light comes on. He isn't paying attention; he can't take his eyes off Quinn's pale face and red neck, and the flickering digits in his foreground.

"Oh my God!" he hears from somewhere above. "What on earth-? Jared! Jared, wake up! The police; we need the police—"

He lowers his head and breathes for his sister again, and the digits flicker **00:00, 00:00, 00:00**, dimming with every weakening pulse.

They say that The Port 13 Motel is haunted. But it can't be, it just can't—

TIMELINE V

"It was at that moment, kneeling in the street and trying to gather my wife's remains as Celena and The Womb stalked away, that I realized there was no *one* event that caused my wife's death," Mikhail said, cradling his beer in front of him. He had peeled the label mostly off, and it clung to the cool glass bottle by a thin strand of glue. "It is a convergence. A lähentymien. You are familar with the term?"

Dr. Zimmerman shook his head slightly, his eyes wide with shock and his face pale.

Mikhail smirked with melancoly. "It's a term my people use to describe a confluence of events coming together to form one effect — typically a bad one. Fog and ice and poor planning conspiring to sink a ship thought to be unsinkable. Static electricity causing zepplins to burn. Libraries sinking under the weight of their own books. Events not caused by one single action or one single person, but by the grouping of circumstance. As though the events themselves conspired to kill my wife."

Zimmerman adjusted his glasses. He was encased in the shadow left in the wake of the glow behind him, the engines of his generators running.

"I realized going back one day wouldn't do it. That there was no way to prevent decades upon decades worth of confluence in a single day... that string had to be unwound from its inception point."

Zimmerman nodded, cleared his throat, then nodded again. "That's... that's quite a story," he said finally, stammering. He paused. "I suppose I've said that before?"

Mikhail nodded. He brought the bottle to his lips and drank the last of it. "I have had this conversation before and drank this same beer before, the last one you had in your fridge. It tastes the same each and every time." He put the glass down. Zimmerman stared at it.

"I can't imagine... to watch your wife die once, let alone four times..."

Mikhail snorted.

"What?"

His face grew dark. He stared through the glass bottle and into the void beyond it, his voice becoming hollow. "I have watched my wife die eight-hundred and seventy-two times."

Zimmerman grew paler still.

"I went back to Signet a dozen or more times... each time driving a little faster, pushing a little harder. But there's nothing that can be done. It's been almost three years of my life on this one day... there's nothing that can be done with a day."

Zimmerman nodded. "You're giving up then, it's important. It's not your fault, but moving on will be --"

Mikhail's expression grew so dark it stopped him mid-sentence. "I am not, nor will I, give up."

Zimmerman stopped. "But you just said—"

"That nothing can be done with a single day. Which means I will have to go back farther than a single day. To the start of the thread."

"The Kincaid Engine can't send people back more than a day. The power needs of it would be—"

Mikhail reached into the bag at his side and produced a long, glowing cylider with blood swirled over its illuminated blue tubing.

Zimmerman stared at it for a long, tense moment that drew out like a blade. "That's a Remer power cell."

Mikhail did not respond and did not make eye contact.

"How did you get a Remer power cell?"

Mikahil squinted. "If it works it won't matter, it won't have happened."

Zimmerman swallowed.

"To the start of the thread."

"That's not how the Kincaid Engine works, I must have told you that some time before. *You* don't go back. Your *consciousness* goes back. Your consciousness is sent back into your past body, memories intact. You can't go back to before you were born no matter how much power you --"

"You're sure of that?"

"I'm sure of that."

"Has anyone tried?"

Zimmerman's face grew flush. "It's a natural consequence of the procedure. The Engine sends you back into your own body, ergo with no body you cannot be sent back."

"But it's never been tried."

Zimmerman huffed.

Mikhail nodded.

"Have we had this conversation before?" Zimmerman asked suddenly, squinting. "This... this talk of going back. Has this happened before?"

Mikhail said nothing, lowering his gaze so that the shadows under his eyes became deeper and sullen.

Zimmerman flicked his fingers back and forth. "There's no telling what would happen. You could arrive broken, unable to even know why you're there. You could just be a consciousness. There's no data on this, only theory. It's not like I could even perform an animal trial... what message could an animal send me from the past that I would understand to know if it had worked?"

Mikhail did not move or speak.

"...But at worst, it will end this. This loop will be over."

Mikhail nodded, pushing the Remer power cell forward on the table.

"I can recall with perfect clarity the day my wife died... and I'll have no more of it."

ENGEN TIMELINE

With over twenty novels spread over three different series by many different authors, the Engen Universe of titles is growing every day and into genres we couldn't have imagined! From the original ten book *Black Womb* thriller series, its crime novel sequel series *Xander Drew*, our flagship adventure title *Infinity*, or single-novels like *Jacobi Street* or *light|dark*, there's something in the Engen Universe for everyone with more books by more authors on the way soon!

...But how do the events relate to one another, chronologically? While some astute readers have guessed at the potential timeline (some accurately, some not), we're going to finally set the question of the Engen Timeline to rest.

Turn the page for an up-to-date guide of the ever-widening world of Engen, featuring the works of Ali House, Ellen Curtis, Erin Vance, Paul Carberry, Matthew Daniels, Andrea Hackett, Sarah Thompson, Jay Paulin, Sam Bauer, Kelly Rose, and Matthew LeDrew!

In the 10 Years Prior Black September

"Reptilia" by Matthew LeDrew published in *light | dark*.
"Reptilian" by Paul Carberry published in *Undead Rebirth.*
Danger descends on a small secluded town in the form of a deadly virus with fantastic and terrible side-effects. Can a small group of doctors escape alive?

Compendium by Ellen Curtis
Three short stories forming the basis for the Engen Universe's ties to suspense, genetic engeneering, and the supernatural. Features the stories "The Tourniquet Revival," "Falling into Fire" and "At Midnight, the Dawn."

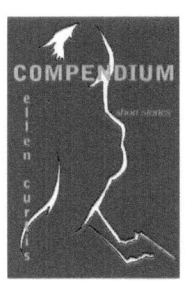

"The Theogony" by Matthew LeDrew published in *light | dark*.
A tale of young Theo Flaherty of the *Infinity* series and his time admitted against his will to the Black Springs hospital, where he learns to paint, and seeks out his father.

Black September

"Revving Engen" by Matthew LeDrew published in *light | dark*.
A direct lead-in to both *Infinity* and *Black Womb*, Tasha travels to Coral Beach, Maine on a hot tip about a recently discovered young man with incredible abilities.

Infinity by Ellen Curtis & Matthew LeDrew
Faced with a destiny he's uncertain of, the enigmatic Victor must bring together four unique people with very special abilities… or face the tasks ahead alone. Guaranteed to excite!

Black Womb by Matthew LeDrew
Fifteen years ago, something happened in Coral Beach, Maine that resulted in the present death of a seventeen-year-old boy. Now four high-school students must try to solve the mystery… before the killer picks them off.

Jacobi Street by Matthew LeDrew
When a mysterious painting shows up at an art gallery he works at, Bob must work with Eddie and Sloan to track down its sinister origins and convince the people living on Jacobi Street of them, before its too late!

Transformations in Pain by Matthew LeDrew
When two girls are assaulted and one is hospitalized, the residents of Coral Beach must put their shared tragedies behind them and stop the man responsible, as well as unlock the secrets behind the true nature of the Womb…

Year One: October

Variety Show by Ali House
Local performer Wendy is introduced to the drama and mystique of The Quaint Little Theatre of Jacobi Street. But backstabbing aren't the only dangers at play in this venue...

Smoke and Mirrors by Matthew LeDrew
The approaching trial of Genblade brings closure to the people of Coral Beach, until people start showing up dead in the same manner they did when he was at large.

"The Inevitable" by Ali House
published in *The Lightbulb Forest*
A young woman must contend with the emergence of a frightening new power alongside the emotional high of a first date.

The Tourniquet Reprisal by Curtis & LeDrew
A man lives in Atlanta, Georgia that people don't talk about, but everyone knows he's there. He arrived a year ago and turned a gaggle of uneducated youth into something new, something to fear.

Roulette by Matthew LeDrew
As the teen suicide rate in Coral Beach starts to climb astronomically fast, Xander travels to Los Angeles to fight his most terrifying adversary yet… and learns that the only thing worse than looking for release… is finding it.

Year One: November

Exodus of Angels by Curtis & LeDrew
Victor's enigmatic past is illuminated when Jaycee accompanies him to visit a new friend in the paliative care ward of the Black Springs hospital, where Theo also happens to be searching for a cure for Leigh.

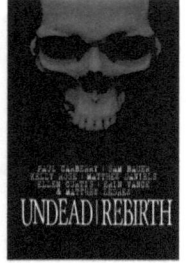

The Irony of Glass by Matthew Daniels published in *Undead Rebirth.*
Abby and Chad track down a man with the ability to project his emotional state to a remote town, and struggle to escape.

Ghosts of the Past by Matthew LeDrew
Coral Beach faces its most awesome threat when one of Engen's past mistakes is unleashed upon the unsuspecting populous. Friends and enemies unite to fight a common enemy… but will even that be enough?

Touch Your Nose by Matthew LeDrew
Simon Monk must infiltrate the San Fransico branch of Shane Industries, a massive company with deep ties to the Engen Universe. Where do his true loyalties lie? And can he get out without causing harm?

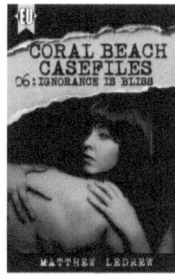

Ignorance is Bliss by Matthew LeDrew
After being set through the ringer one too many times, Xander decides that his life with Julie needs a little more attention… which is bad news because a new villain has come to town with his sights set on Adam Genblade.

"Gristle While You Work" by Jay Paulin &
"Scarlett" by Andrea Hackett
published in *light | dark*.

"A Night to Forget" by Kelly Rose &
"New Employment" by Sam Bauer
published in *Undead Rebirth*.

Becoming by Matthew LeDrew
For months Xander Drew has been doing his level best to keep the streets of Coral Beach clean, which means it's time for the forces of darkness to strike back… all at once.

Inner Child by Matthew LeDrew
Julie is hospitalized with life-threatening
wounds to both body and soul. But the
real threat comes from the hospital walls
themselves, as a demonic presence makes itself
known to Xander and his friends.

"Comfortably Numb" by Ellen Curtis
published in *Undead Rebirth.*
Xander and Cathy spend an evening hunting
the remnants of Coral Beach's gangs when
Xander begins to lose control of the Black
Womb, threatening their secret.

End of Year One

Gang War by Matthew LeDrew
The Tees, a homicidal gang of evil men, has
finally been taken down by Xander Drew. But
his victory is short lived, as retired Tees are
mysteriously killed. With a town of suspects,
anyone can be the culprit… including one of
their own.

Chains by Matthew LeDrew
Sociopath Derek Smith has been freed from
prison and is praying on the weak; and none
are weaker than August Styles: a pregnant girl
with Down Syndrome who has run away from
home.

"Omega" by Ellen Curtis
published in *light l dark*.
A sinister division of Engen begins a series of experiments on pregnant women in a fashion eerily similar to those that created the original Black Womb project.

The Long Road by Matthew LeDrew
Xander meets the American people — and realizes that the world is harsh and wicked, but can also be soft and gentle, even loving. Xander Drew comes of age on the road, and sets his new direction.

Year Two

Cinders by Matthew LeDrew
Detective Horton enters a violent and dangerous world he didn't know existed beneath the veneer of order and structure that he has based his entire deductive method around.

Sinister Intent by Matthew LeDrew
One of the killers Detective Horton could not catch has resurfaced: a serial killer who flaunts his sinister intent in front of the Los Angeles Police Department, making it so that no one is safe.

Faith by Matthew LeDrew
Xander's mysterious and troublesome past
returns to haunt him on the streets of Los
Angeles; a place where even more people can
get caught in the crossfire of the games of
death and deceit that makes up his life.

Flickers in the Night by Matthew LeDrew
Lisa Rowdan is hunted by her haunting --
and powerful -- ex-boyfriend Ryan through a
lonely city street. Can she escape him?
One of over twenty great sprine-tingling short
stories!

Garden of the 8th Circle by Curtis & LeDrew
Victor brings Chad, Abby, and Alice into a
dangerous conflict a decade in the making,
fighting an out of control cult for the fate of a
young soul. Meanwhile, Theo investigates a
mysterious event in Los Angeles.

Family Values by Matthew LeDrew
Xander and his new friends Crowley, Lisa, and
Tim investigate a series of kidnappings and
murders that stretch back decades, all of which
have the same similar twist: victims being
found after years of being missing.

The Rats of Refraction by Curtis & LeDrew
When Abby and Alice's secret lives are discovered, they must defend their home and way of life with everything they have against the forces of Circe, a shadow agency that will stop at nothing to abduct people with supernatural abilities.

Fate's Shadow by Matthew LeDrew
When one of Xander's old cases comes up for trial, Megan Greene returns with it. The former friends are led into conflict regarding her client's innocence. However, they put their difference aside when they both become targets of the vigilante known as Shiro Gilbert.

First Aid by Matthew LeDrew
Xander takes his feud with mob boss Stephen Fields to the streets, and his attracts the attention of the *Infinity* team. Before the arrive, he'll have pushed the mob boss into an all out gang war, the likes of which the city will never recover from.

Exposure by Erin Vance
Joshua Deering just wanted was to pass his final photography project. But that's not what happened. But hindsight is 20/20, and now creepy cemetery guy Adrian, Josh, and Josh's two friends are being stalked by nameless, violent strangers.

"The Port 13 Motel" by Erin Vance &
"Living Light" by Sam Bauer
published in *Undead Rebirth*.
The unlikely return of both Kemp and
a cannibalistic serial killer to the Engen
Universe.

The Future

"Remers" by Sarah Thompson
published in *light | dark*.
In the not-too-distant future of the Engen
Universe, young athletes are the targets of a
scouting program to create the next stage of
super soldier with cybernetic enhancements.

Timeline I - V by Matthew LeDrew
published in *Undead Rebirth*.
Faced with the death of his wife, Mikhail
breaks the laws of time and space to find a
way to save her, only to discover that her fate
was sealed in the distant past...

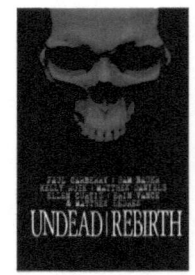

DARK STORIES FROM ENGEN BOOKS

THE HOWL BECONS

Growing up without his father, Tyler had no way of knowing the horrible secret that has plagued his family for generations. To free himself and find the cure, he will have to look beyond himself and into his dark history.

"A very ambitious novel… the horrors of everyday life can be worse than anything in fiction. The idea of using werewolves as a metaphor – to me this pushes the book a bit above much of what is out there… Brad [Dunne] is a very good writer and obviously has a deep background."
— Andrew Peacock

WESTON'S WAR

Something evil grows in the heart of Colorado. Bill Weston was a man of the West. He knew it – its land, its people, its stories. It was where he plied his trade, hunting men for money. His life wasn't easy, but it was predictable. That all changed when he captured Faraway Sue and he was led on a trip through the Colorado forests

"Take a little Zane Grey. Add a little Penny Dreadful. Read with Sam Elliot's voice. Discover Jon Dobbin's masterful The Starving."
— Darrell Power,
Great Big Sea